WIZARDS AND DRUIDS

by
Eric Carlton Neperud

For Clive, who made reading fun, and reminded us that life should be an adventure.

By Eric Carlton Neperud

THE LIMBO CHRONICLES
    Trees And Weeds
    Limbo
    The Octagonal Knight
    Dragons And Golems
    The Brotherhood Of Giants
    Wizards And Druids

THE YELLOWSONE TRILOGY
    Wonders Of The Wilderness
    Fleas Upon Snow
    The Periphery Of Sorrow

Copyright © 2018 by Eric Carlton Neperud
All rights reserved.
ISBN: 0998383856
ISBN-13: 978-0-9983838-5-9
Published by Valhalla Books

Cover Illustration by Eric Carlton Neperud
Map on back cover by Eric Carlton Neperud
Map on page 220 by Eric Carlton Neperud

I was summoned.

The Three sat on their mobile thrones in the center of the White Room. Symbolically, the combination of all colors, boldly offsetting the primary tones. Peace was precariously balanced. The sovereign of Min sat in the blue chair. Of Cor, in the red. Of Fas, in yellow. Microcomputers and cup holders provided for their needs. Their tactile manipulations surprised me. The reports of thoughts controlling electronics were premature. The Three were notorious for flaunting new technology.

The breach was instantly sealed after I entered the White Room. As a precaution, the room was enveloped in ten-meter thick lead. When someone was required to enter or leave, the shell was enticed, creating a corridor. When the enticement was terminated, the gap filled in.

The Three rarely left the White Room. When they did it was individually. Only one member of the Triad was permitted to leave the White Room at a time, to retain governmental continuity. There was a risk of mental contamination outside the protective cocoon, but with comparisons of brain scans before and after, such tampering would be recognized. These excursions were rare, taken more for a lark than for physiological necessity. Any setting, any environment, could be uploaded. If the Three wished to be on a snowy mountain or on a sandy beach it was just a finger movement away. I had hypothesized to distraction where I would appear to be when I spoke to them. I preferred rolling green plains in the spring with wild flowers, simultaneously exhilarating and relaxing---a palette of visual and olfactory stimuli. I saw nothing---just white. And the red, blue, and yellow of the three thrones.

I looked around as I waited for the Three to notice me. Where was the bathroom? The chairs probably took care of that too. All I saw of the Three were their heads, all bald. Their bodies

3

were sealed in the chairs, in a sack of fluid that precisely regulated body temperature. How many rash decisions were made by rulers who were too cold or too hot, too wet or too dry?

"Lynn Louise Cornelius?" The woman in the blue throne in the center finally became aware of me. The thrones maneuvered incessantly. Modifying orientations. Exchanging positions. None of them came closer to me than two meters. I preferred it to be due to a safeguard than hierarchal positioning.

"Yes. I'm Agent Cornelius." It had become commonplace for those in authority to no longer be called Sir or Ma'am. Those situated in a higher position knew it, as did those beneath them, so why make a spectacle announcing the distinction. Sometimes people were still addressed in that manner, but only when being mocked, or when someone insecure in their leadership required it.

"You have been chosen to go to Dartmoor." The pale-skinned woman was facing me. I couldn't ascertain if she *saw* me. No emotion registered. No focus. Being constantly stimulated, emotions were blunted. If they still existed, they were restrained, externally.

"Have I been accused of committing some crime?" Dartmoor was a prison. Not just any prison, a penitentiary world, a penal colony spanning an entire planet.

"You have been assigned to monitor Dartmoor. Unpredicted events are occurring."

"What do the probes and scanners suggest?"

"None function. Terraforming has created atypical electromagnetic properties that have disabled electronics."

"What's the duration of my mission?"

"Unknown."

The yellow throne bumped the blue, supplanting it in front of me. It didn't physically touch the other. The same safety precautions that prevented me from being struck prevented the thrones from making contact with one another. The blue moved to the left a couple of meters to permit the yellow to displace it.

"Min's proclivity to be succinct is derived from her obligation to be precise. The less one says, the less likely they are to stray from the truth. Your mission is indefinite because we don't know if we can retrieve you. If nothing with a circuit works on Dartmoor, we may not be able to transport you back." The man who spoke had a round face and flat eyes.

"Can't you just fly me out?"

"We put an energy seal over the part of the planet we chose to become the penal colony. We cannot remove the seal without damaging what the terraforming created."

"So, you modified just a portion of the planet?"

"It was necessary, to safeguard indigenous artifacts. You may decline the assignment."

"An agent does not decline an assignment. Difficult and dangerous are parameters, not limitations."

The blue throne nudged the yellow to maneuver itself back in front of me. "Fas believes an agent who is psychologically detached won't succeed."

The yellow throne returned. "A person insecure in intention may not be able to counter every unpredicted obstacle placed before her."

It was finally time for the red throne to make an appearance. The dark-skinned woman said, "We need someone to physically interface with Dartmoor. Your records indicate a series of successful immersions. We don't need a voyeur. We need someone who is capable of interacting."

"Communication?"

The blue throne displaced the red. "The deactivation of electronics isn't instantaneous. We believe a portable transport portal will function long enough to release you."

Red again. "We believe, because we haven't yet tested it. We have sent probes. They were programmed to return immediately. They were successful. You will be the first human trial."

Yellow. "You see. With so much uncertainty we can't add emotional doubt. The person we send to Dartmoor must be prepared for anything, and must be committed to do whatever is necessary for her mission to succeed."

A became an agent for the excitement, as most people did, but also for the variety, for the lack of predictability. Neither would be lacking in this mission. Would I be able to do everything that was required to complete the mission? I killed many people, some that were innocent, to get to those who weren't, sacrificing the few for the benefit of the many. I'm willing to die for the Republic, for the order it creates. I've been so close to death on so many occasions that I no longer fear death. I've done many things while in service I wouldn't have done in my personal life, including permitting men who I despised take pleasure in my body. Provisional toleration accommodated by restrained duration. Could I live on a penal colony permanently? Could I live with people I despised for the remainder of my life? Thousands have been sentenced to Dartmoor. Initially, only the worst of the worst were sent there. It didn't take long for it to become a dumping ground. Qualifications became less severe. Local jurisdictions wanted in on the action---they also had malcontents. There would be felons there, but also serial offenders, white-collar criminals, and vendors of illegal stimulants.

The thrones returned to the positions they were in when I arrived, with blue in front of me. "What is your decision?"

"I will go to Dartmoor."

An egress appeared. What backdrop had they put behind me? I preferred it wasn't jungle. I didn't like humidity. It was likely each member of the Triad surrounded themselves with a different landscape. Would it be wonderful to be wherever you wished to be at a touch of a button, or a curse to be enclosed within a protective bubble? Likely, some of each.

Instead of being portalled directly to Dartmoor, I was sent to a station on the fringes of a system, then shuttled to an artificial satellite orbiting a planet I assumed to be the location of Dartmoor. Instantaneous travel would have been more efficient, but substantially less secure.

Unaccustomed to so much unscheduled time, my mind began to wander. The hours it took the shuttle to travel from the fringes to the satellite might be my last as a free woman. I permitted myself the luxury of not fretting about the mission. What planning could I do without specific knowledge? I believe one of the reasons I was chosen for the mission was for my ability to *think on my feet*, to instantaneously adept to an environment.

Cognizant that I might lose myself to become the person that I needed to become to survive on Dartmoor, I contemplated how I fit into the universe, in my present state. In the line of work I was in, it was in flux, but there was a consistency in my core. A person no longer was classified by race, but by what percent of their genetic material was from a particular attribute. I was Cor 52, Min 35, and Fas 13. With my primary being Cor I was more in-tune with my physicality. I liked to be on the move. I enjoyed seeing different places. When I was in school I was that kid who always got into trouble for not sitting down, or for not paying attention, because I was easily distracted. If a secondary consisted of more than third of one's genetic material it also made a significant contribution. Min were in tune with their intellect. They enjoyed learning, and were likely to be well-organized, often to the extreme. My sense of right and wrong was also determined by my Min. I was able to do what I had to do as an agent, because I believed the universe was better for it. A low Fas meant I wasn't very emotional. An agent couldn't be. It was rare for an agent to have a Fas over 20.

Russet clouds concealed the planet. As the shuttle came closer to the satellite, a convex energy field covering a small part of the world---about a 10th of its visible circumference---was revealed. It was difficult to distinguish features within the shield. If it wasn't for the artificial sun hovering near the top of the shield, it wouldn't be visible at all.

Energy---and light---were desired in remote regions, at the fringes of solar systems, and sometimes beyond. The risk of transferring a large amount of hydrogen by portal was severe, but the rewards, equally astronomical. After many explosions, and many lives lost, the bugs were fixed. The sun, many kays below me, was evidence of that.

Most entrances into prisons were noisy. It was deadly quiet during my walk to the portal that would transport me to the planet. The satellite wasn't large enough to house many prisoners. Most had to be sent down to the planet the day they arrived. Every walk to the portal must have felt like a death march. The freedom from execution barely compensated for the impossibility of escape.

I was escorted to a stainless-steel room. The wall closed behind the two burly men who hurriedly discarded me---perhaps concerned they too might be forced to abandon their freedom. While on the shuttle I changed into an orange prisoner jumpsuit, to blend in with the other inmates I might come into contact. Why hadn't someone been able to create something original? Actually, they had, briefly. It was deemed inhumane for prisoners to not wear stylish attire, so they were given the option of wearing designer clothing. Everything goes in cycles. Most of the privileges granted to prisoners in that era were discontinued. Orange did make the prisoners more visible, and a one-piece was easier to maintain.

"Undress." I've heard of prison guards taking advantage of female prisoners. I assumed I wouldn't have to deal with any of that. This was a state of the art federal penal facility, the crown jewel of prisons. I've been through worse, so I did what I was told. I was able to survive certain uncomfortable situations by separating myself from my body, and at times, even my mind. The ability to displace myself is what makes me a good agent.

"Raise your arms, spread your legs, and open your mouth." After I did so a fine mist filled the room. My skin felt a mild tingling sensation, like very nimble ants were walking over me. I tasted antiseptic, then ozone. The mist evaporated a couple minutes later.

"Step through the portal." It was circular, slightly larger in diameter than the tallest man. The portal's destination was opaque. I hesitated before stepping through the oil on water swirling plasma. My subconscious told me I was walking into hell. A star. Possibly, an alternate universe.

My last thought as I stepped off the ledge: Where was that portable transport portal?

Chapter 1

GULAG

As expected, there wasn't a portal behind me. Even if the portal was programmed to be one way there was always the possibility---slim---that a particularly bright inmate may be able to reverse the direction.

Without an anchor there was some randomness where a person materialized---with safety constraints implemented, of course. We wouldn't want civil rights attorneys bogging down the correctional bureau with litigations. I believed I would be sent to a processing center, but in many ways, this was better. The major drawback: finding the dismantled transport portal. How far away might it be? And would someone find it before I? If I knew how far away I was from the intended drop site I could narrow my search radius.

I looked around, scanning the area for both people and the portal. I was in a meadow, within foothills of a mountain range.

The wildflowers I loved were beneath my feet, scattered over the hillside. Trees obscured the view below me. Above me, was a rocky ridge. From there I should be able to see what was beyond the vegetation.

Agents were required to be in impeccable shape. Flexibility, endurance, and strength were not only demanded for retention, but often, to stay alive. By the time I reached the ridge I was barely out of breath. I scanned the horizon. My mind being as agile as my body, I permitted the periphery of my focus to appreciate the aesthetic aspects of the view. Beyond the trees, a plain stretched for a far as I could see. At their boundary---about ten kays away from where I stood---a city began. I wasn't able to discern anyone from this distance, but there appeared to be over one-hundred buildings. A thousand residents, perhaps. Ten-thousand? There were ten times that many sentenced to Dartmoor this year. Two-hundred-fifty thousand since the penal colony opened. How many survived, without clothing and tools, food and water?

Seeing signs of civilization reminded me of my nudity. Modesty didn't concern me, but I was apprehensive how a planet populated by criminals might react. A woman walking through a prison created a charged atmosphere. What might the men do if there weren't any bars between them and me? There were some women here too, but fewer than one in five. Would having some women present change the attitudes of the men who liked to take what they wanted? My lack of attire likely wouldn't modify their reaction to me. With hundreds of arrivals every day the locals would be desensitized to nudity.

There was still no sign of the dismantled transport portal. It looked like I wasn't going to find it on my own. With thousands of inmates remaining in the area, and new arrivals every day, someone would eventually see it. Would they know what it was? Probably not. To them it would look like a handful of decorative spheres. Valuable? Perhaps. But not the most desirable thing on Dartmoor.

It was time to become a member of society. What might that society look like? There had never been a prison planet before. The closest thing were penal colonies established in remote areas of planets. Would a government, or governments, be established? Would chaos reign? Would Dartmoor create its own culture and art, or would it fall into being a self-pleasuring pirate outpost? It was my job to determine what that future might be. Moot if I wasn't able to find the one method of reporting it.

The city was named Gulag. Ironic. Gulags held political prisoners. Modern judiciaries strived to prevent such abuses, going so far as releasing convicts arrested under biased pretenses. Of course, those released were monitored, and often re-sentenced for supplemental crimes.

Being the nucleus for new arrivals, Gulag was the nexus for the penal colony. Five major roads diverged from it. I intersected the one heading into the mountains. The dirt path was wide enough to walk two abreast. The wagon wheel ruts and horse droppings boldly confirmed---odoriferously at times---that a transport system had been established. I was careful where I stepped. No one wished to step in excrement, more so when one's feet were bare.

The forest was lovely. The thirteen percent of me that was emotional recognized that. The trees were predominantly pine. The forest floor was covered with needles, including the road. The temperature was just warm enough to pleasure the vegetation into releasing its cologne. I felt neither hot nor cold. The intermittent breeze contrasted delightfully with the few strands of sunlight that were able to circumvent the lattice of limbs.

The enthralled stupor that had overcome me had nearly caused me to be run over by a horse and rider that had come up from behind. My agent reflexes took over an instant before the potentially fatal collision. The rider was nearly as startled as I. She stopped to examine my condition. "Sorry. I don't know where my head was." The woman wore a simple green dress that terminated at her knees. The only other thing she wore were a pair of poorly made leather boots. What was considered lacking off-planet was likely the norm in a society where industry had to be reinvented.

"It was my fault. I should have heard you coming. It's easier for pedestrians to move out of the way. I'm surprised horses were given to us."

"It wasn't intentional. The engineers who created this place wanted the terraforming to be as realistic as possible. If our wardens got their way we would probably be walking across an endless plain of concrete." The woman studied me. She had blond hair and green eyes. Her skin was mauve, the most common pigmentation in a modern, racially-mixed society. Many people modified themselves---not just their hair and eye color. Some chose to lighten or darken their skin, some extremely, dying it green or purple.

"You better put something on." The woman leapt off her horse and rummaged through a saddle bag. My profession drew me to the bow and two daggers strapped to it. She pulled out a green dress similar to her own. "Men are more likely to prey on infants. If you are dressed when you enter Gulag they won't think you just stepped through the portal."

"Thanks." I pulled the dress over my head. It fell loosely over me, like a night gown. It almost concealed my femininity. There was the slightest of protrusions were the material flowed over my breasts. It wasn't the most attractive dress, but it was practical, and I imagine, relatively easy to manufacture. "What now? What does a new arrival do their first day? Where do I stay?"

"There are plenty of men in Gulag that would put you up for the night, but you wouldn't get much sleep, especially the first night. After you establish a routine you'll have to take care of him. If you like him well enough, you'll stay for a while. If you don't, there are plenty of other men that want someone to keep them warm at night and well-fed during the day."

"That doesn't sound too modern."

"It's better than being a cave woman. Society could have reverted to that."

"Is that how you live your life? Alternating between a whore and maid?"

"Hardly. A group of independent women have formed a society in the mountains. We call ourselves Amazons, but we're not brutal, unless someone is brutal to us first. It's amazing what one-hundred women can accomplish together."

"No men at all?"

"There are times when men might come in handy, but women have this propensity to allow their emotions to influence them. It we could just become physical with a man and leave, that would work, but women can't make it that simple."

"Are there alternatives to whoring?"

"You could become an Amazon. We're always recruiting. Saving women is what we call it." I nearly accepted her offer. It would make my life easier---in some ways---but my mission was to study Dartmoor and I wouldn't be able to do so thoroughly if I lived in a fringe society.

"No thank you. At least not for now. I want to see if I can make a life for myself in Gulag first."

"To each her own. Some of the women we ask---usually the more frightened ones---immediately join up. The more aggressive ones also tend to join, particularly those who want to pay back the men in their lives for what they have done to them. They often become disillusioned after they learn we don't spend all our time attacking men. We defend ourselves, but we don't choose to initiate the violence. Violence breeds violence. We prefer to be left alone. Sometimes women who originally declined our invitation, or ones we haven't talked to yet, get tired of city life and make it to our village on their own."

"So, a woman here doesn't have many options?"

"Those who chose to live in Gulag, but wish to remain on their feet, find work in one of the pubs. Making alcoholic beverages

13

was one of the first things people did when they arrived. Men prefer a woman serving them if they're given a choice. Even if all you choose to do is serve, someone will hire you. Demand is much greater than the supply."

"Thank you. After I make some money I'll pay you back for the dress."

"It's a gift. Preventing another woman from being attacked prevents all from being attacked. I'll walk with you the rest of the way to Gulag. We're almost there. If you're with me people will think you're an Amazon, so they'll leave you alone."

As the woman climbed back onto her horse and strolled beside me I brought up the subject of the dismantled transport portal, giving her just enough information for her to know what it looked like without indicating its function. "No. I haven't seen anything like that around here. I'll keep a watch for it though, and mention it to my people."

Gulag was in the center of the portion of the planet that was shielded. The inmates were more efficiently dispersed if the drop site was centrally located. It wasn't a bad choice. Gulag was at the intersection of a prairie and forest. Crops could be grown, and lumber harvested. Mineral-rich mountains were nearby. The one drawback to the location was its lack of a large water source. The closest river, the Sparkling, was 20 kays away. There were creeks in the area, but their volume was insufficient to support a large settlement that would continue to grow as long as new inmates were released on Dartmoor. Wells were dug, a temporary measure until a canal was built.

Being a city of necessity, Gulag's streets were not well thought out. Right angles were almost non-existent. Someone believed the capital of Dartmoor deserved some dignity, resulting in the central streets beginning to be paved with stones found in the Southern Spine, the mountain range to the east.

My escort stopped in front of the *Mounds and Trunks Tavern*. The name denoted the local scenery. Likely, not all of it mountains and forest. "This is one of the more respectable drinking and dining establishments." Great. "My name is Michelle. If you need anything, leave the city the way we came. If you go far enough, you'll find Amazonia."

"Thank you. I appreciate the help. All of it. The advice. The clothes. My name is Lynn."

Michelle waved, then resumed her journey, her destination too personal or mundane to share with me.

There was a difference in the way men stared at Michelle and me compared to how they stared at other women. Some of the men may have *contemplated* the challenge of forming a temporary relationship with an Amazon. Most of them appeared more wary of us than lustful. I expected with Michelle's departure the men might view me differently. They didn't. Still hesitant, but with a hint of curiosity.

I walked into the Mounds and Trunks. All the buildings I had seen so far were one story, including this one. It was rudely constructed of wood timbers. They were chinked with a mixture of mud and grass. It wasn't done very well. There were still a few gaps between the logs. The communication in the building ceased when I walked through the open entry.

"Who might I ask for a job?"

"That would be me." A man dropped two clay mugs onto a table, then headed behind a half wall. "We don't hire no Amazons. They tend to scare away the customers. In fact, I think you better leave right now. It's never a good sign when the clientele is this quiet. Even when they're passed out they at least snore."

"Aren't you afraid you might offend me?"

"I'm more concerned about making some money today. It's not easy running a business in Gulag, when half the people don't have no vouchers."

"What's a voucher?"

"Don't the Amazons still use them? You've become self-sufficient?"

"I'm not really an Amazon. Someone just gave me this dress."

"So, you're an infant." The pubtender examined me with his eyes as he circled me. "Quit turning around. You said you wanted a job. I'm trying to interview you."

"But you're not asking any questions."

"I'm not checking out your speaking ability, filly. You'll do. You're much more fit than most new arrivals. That's not always a good thing. Most men like to see a little jiggle. You're too much of a hard body for that."

"How much do I get paid?"

"That depends on how many men you bring to the Mounds and Trunks. After a week I'll evaluate your pay. I usually work the day shift alone, but I'm willing to try pulling in some more revenue. Most people work during the day---those with jobs. Most, but not all."

"Will I get some type of advance on my wages? I need a place to stay and something to eat until payday."

"All my employees have cells in the back. They are free of charge, but any additional money you make back there you'll have to split with me."

"I don't think...."

"You're not required to go into self-employment. Some of the men like the innocent ones." I smiled. It's been awhile since I was called that. "It makes them think they are sharing a drink with their sister or mother. If you chose to eat here it will be deducted from your pay. Your uniform will also be deducted." The pubtender/proprietor pulled a white dress from a shelf behind the half wall. He threw it at me.

I stretched it out, then dangled it in front of me. "I don't think it's the right size."

"It is if you're working here."

"Isn't it a bit thread bare?"

"The men you serve won't care. Let's get you situated in

that cell."

A hallway was adjacent to the bar, that area behind the half wall. There were six doors, three on each side. They looked like they were constructed from branches, and about as tight as the exterior logs. "You never get complete privacy here, do you?"

"Relative to most of the planet, this is a four-star hotel." That wasn't too encouraging. "The first room on the right is my room. If you ever want to work off some of your food deduction you know where I am. If I'm busy, try another night. I'm not as young as I used to be. I don't think I can take on two fillies at once anymore."

"That won't be happening."

"To each his own. I wouldn't mind having a little sister here instead, or a daughter." I would. "You not really being an Amazon, you might need some protection."

"I think I can take care of myself."

"If anyone bothers you say you work for Pubtender Bill. Most men will leave you alone. The regulars of the Mounds and Trunks will become protective of you. They'll be consequences if someone roughs you up or molests you. The last room on the right is unoccupied. Take a few minutes to settle in, then we'll put you to work. The sooner the men see you and spread the word the sooner my daily business picks up. Don't forget to change into that white dress."

Pubtender Bill waited a moment to see if I was going to change in front him. He walked back down the hallway. I pulled the door towards me, until obstructed by the frame. There wasn't a lock---or even a latch---but it didn't look like the door was going to reopen on its own. I changed dresses quickly. There wasn't a window in the room, but there were enough cracks in the wall to allow plenty of sunlight in. The tube dress wasn't tailored at all. It was snug against my breasts, hips, and buttocks. It was shorter than the green Amazon dress, stopping about mid-thigh. I had to be careful bending over. The dress was more opaque than transparent. If I didn't get it wet I might retain some modesty.

There was a burlap mattress lying on the dirt floor. It crunched when I sat on it. Leaves or some other dried vegetation in it. There were two log rounds. One had a small clay basin on it, half full of water. The residue above the water line indicating it may have been full when the previous occupant left. The only other thing in the room was a wooden dowel. A branch, straight and uniform, that stretched from wall to wall. The Dartmoor equivalent of a wardrobe?

I yanked at the dress where it bound, attempting to facilitate better movement and more efficient breathing. The fabric was clearly cotton. This region didn't have the climate to grow it. How far have the inmates spread already? Did they do so to improve their condition or to circumvent the perpetual influx?

Working at the Mounds and Trunks wasn't as dreadful as I believed it would be. For the two rude men I might encounter in a day there were twenty who were kind. Sex wasn't the only thing men wanted from a woman. Her gentle demeanor and ability to communicate were also appreciated. Men often didn't talk about their problems to each other, but they were thrilled to talk about them to me. They didn't view it as losing face if they revealed their weaknesses to a woman.

I learned many things in the months I worked in the Mounds and Trunks. A society was indeed forming on Dartmoor. Most criminals were too independent to want to form a single government. City-states began to form. Gulag may have been the center of the world, but it never became the nexus of a centralized government. There were half-a-dozen other city-states now, and another forming every year.

The second largest was Coolatta. It was 350 kays west-southwest of the pseudo-capital. Those new arrivals who wanted to flee from where they were deposited often chose to live in that city. It was a flat, straight journey, typically completed in a week. Food production fed its economy. It supplied most of Dartmoor with meat, grain, vegetables, and fish. The largest river on Dartmoor---which most residents just called *The River*---passed through it. The Sparkling was one of its tributaries, but it took a more north-south route, so few used it to travel between the two cities. Boats were still nearly non-existent on Dartmoor. The ones the colonists built looked more like rafts, and weren't very efficient. Someone once commented in the Mounds and Trunks about establishing a city-state at the mouth of the river. Serpent Glade was between here and there though, named for its many resident snakes, most of them poisonous or constricting. No one had successfully circumvented the river, yet. The closer the river got to the sea the more wet the terrain became. After a while it became impossible to travel by land. No one trusted their boats to successfully navigate the water, not with crocodiles infesting the delta.

Many of the plants and animals on Dartmoor were familiar. Some weren't. Did the scientists and engineers create them to torment us, or were the mutations created during terraforming? To populate the planet quickly, growth cycles were accelerated. Uncontrolled growth often led to mutations in tissues, including cancers. Some of the creatures that had been created, intentionally, or accidentally, were definitely cancerous to our new society. The more exotic ones tended to be the most dangerous.

The grasslands between the Spring Woods---that forest between Gulag and the foothills---and the River was called the Insect Prairie. The insects living in the prairie weren't particularly numerous, but many were much larger than what one was accustomed to. The largest was the size of a small horse, but with tentacles instead of legs, and suction cups, like an octopus's, instead of hooves. The tentacles, four meters long when fully extended, were inundated with barbs.

I saw my first death on Dartmoor at the hands of one of those creatures. Once a week I got a day off. I often used that day to search for the dismantled transport portal. I was fortunate

19

someone else was in the area. I couldn't believe how foolish I was to get that close to that thing. My curiosity had gotten the better of me. The man was ripped to shreds by those tentacles. Afterwards, the insect ate the man. Bite by bite the tentacles brought the five sim long chunks to its mouth. If I hadn't seen so many gruesome deaths in my life already I might have gotten sick. I felt mildly embarrassed experiencing fascination.

My second encounter with a mutant occurred on one of my trips to Amazonia. I kept in touch with Michelle and the other Amazons. I saw them at least once a month. The trip up to their village on foot took more than an hour. If I wanted to spend more than a couple of hours with them I had to leave early in the morning. Before the sun was up I tripped over a vine.

The sun didn't really rise. The artificial sun had an intense and non-intense cycle. When the sun was less intense it appeared as a full moon. It wasn't that dark, but it was significantly dimmer than during the day.

My contact with the vine was a triggering mechanism. The vine wrapped around me as did dozens of others that were connected through a central stalk. I had a dagger with me. Who didn't in a place where both people and animals might attack under little, or no, provocation. The dagger, a gift from the Amazons, was constructed from a sharpened antler. Not metal, but it got the job done. But not this time. I've had ample experience escaping from ropes, but the techniques that normally worked were ineffective against the vines. I couldn't breathe. Not only was my throat being choked, my lungs had collapsed.

Chapter 2

AFTERLIFE

When I woke I was more surprised than relieved. How could I have survived? After passing out from not being able to breathe my brain should have died a few minutes later. Did my lack of struggling after I passed out cause the vines to stop squeezing me? Where were they now? Where was I? I was no longer in the forest. It looked like the sloped meadow I was transported to two years ago. The location wasn't the only thing the same. I was naked again. Were my clothes torn from my body when I escaped from the vines? I don't remember escaping. Did the trauma give me amnesia? I attempted to stand, to examine myself. Where were the scratches and bruises? Before I could become completely erect, I got light-headed and was forced to sit down. Why was I so fatigued? I felt my chest for cracked ribs. I'm confident I heard a few crack. They appeared to be intact. What was going on?

"Lynn." Someone called out to me from the base of the meadow. It looked like John, one of the regulars at Mounds and Trunks. He ran up the slope towards me. When he became aware of my attire---my lack of attire---he adverted his eyes.

"Did you free me from that plant? I was unconscious...."

"We've been looking for you for two days. When you didn't show up yesterday Bill thought you may have run off to live with the Amazons. We assured him you wouldn't do that, not without saying goodbye. We formed a search party." I was just a waitress. Why would those guys hanging out at the pub bother with trying to find me? The agency was never that concerned with my safety.

Now that I felt safe again---not only had I been freed from that plant, I was returned to a familiarity that had eventually given me comfort---I became concerned with the ramifications of my attire. Once an agent, always an agent. Cause and effect didn't cease during a sabbatical. I backed away after achieving a defensive stance. "Did you take advantage of me, after you freed me?"

John's face reddened. "Miss Lynn. We at the Mounds and Trunks don't think of you like that. I would rather kill myself than force myself on you."

"I'm sorry. I believe you." And I did. I asked the question for the reaction more than for the answer. Agents developed the ability to determine if someone was telling the truth. John was. "I don't understand any of this."

John removed his backpack, pulling a cloth tarp from it. They were common on the penal colony. They had multiple uses, but primarily as a rain poncho or shelter. He handed it to me, being careful not to look directly at me. I wrapped myself in it. It made me feel more secure, more emotionally than physically. Being an agent for so long had desensitized me. Interacting with a *normal* person---someone I wasn't investigating, who was unlikely to harm me, in particular, someone I had contact with on a daily basis--- triggered a contrary reaction. I had felt embarrassed--- EMBARRASSED---when John had seen me naked. "I thought I had died, then I woke...like this."

"I'll walk you back to Gulag. Everyone has been worried sick about you." John wrapped his arm around me, escorting me like I was elderly or a child. Before my arrival on Dartmoor I would have been offended by the gesture. Now, I welcomed it. I actually enjoyed someone taking care of me.

As we walked, John attempted to entertain me. "There have been stories of people dying then showing up somewhere else. Sometimes they don't look the same." I thought I had seen the man who had been killed by the insect. I rationalized. The man I saw must have just looked like him. Did Dartmoor really have people coming back from the dead? Was I a walking zombie? If I ever found the transport portal I would have at least one substantial thing to report. Or did I? Would my superiors think I was mad?

When I returned to Gulag I was greeted with cheers. Even Pubtender Bill was affected by my safe arrival. He gave out free mugs of his most stale beer. "I'll have to dock you for your extra day off. Unless you want to work it off in the back." That was our running joke. He would probably have a heart attack if I ever took him up on his offer.

Things settled back to normal after a couple of days. I was gradually building up my savings. Vouchers were Gulag's equivalent of currency. The I.O.U.s were written on very primitive paper. Much care was taken to prevent their deterioration. The I.O.U.s were transferable, and could be exchanged for goods in the central market or any of Gulag's other business districts. Bartering was used the first year. Its limitations demanded its replacement, resulting in the voucher system being rapidly enacted. There have been a few instances of people and businesses promising more than they had, but with the threat of violent government-induced foreclosure they were rare. To pay for Gulag's small constable force, and various civic improvements, taxes were collected. The constables spent a majority of their time collecting the taxes, a tenth of what a business collected. Many businesses balked. Their proprietors modified their opinion after tending to their wounds. Raising the price of shoes or a loaf of bread by ten percent to compensate barely diminished sales when everyone followed the practice.

I intended the money I was saving to be used to buy a horse. The problem was the price of horses kept going up. There was supposedly an infertility issue. I believed it more due to price gouging. An economist would call it *supply versus demand*. Whatever label you give it, the bottom line was too many people arriving wanting to ease their burden as much as I. What worried me was not seeing a foal in more than a year. The consequences for survival could become dire.

With better transportation I would be able to expand my search radius. The more I saw of Dartmoor the better my report, and the more likely I was to find the transport portal, to turn in that report. No one had seen any sign of it. I was becoming discouraged. No, I hadn't yet come to the conclusion that the portal may not have actually been sent. Internally, perhaps, but my external psyche was still optimistic.

I spent three more years in Gulag before I made my break. I had now been on Dartmoor as long as the penal colony has been in operation before my arrival. Rarely has an agent been in the field, on the same assignment, for so long. I was approaching the end of my most productive years as a field agent. Getting old was distressing for the average person. It was devastating for an agent. The will was still there, but the body didn't always respond. And when it did, recovering from the strain took longer. An agent unable to adequately respond to subsequent assignments was given a desk job. Most agents weren't able to readjust, abandoning the agency many years before retirement.

The thing about getting older was...I didn't. No one did on Dartmoor, not noticeably. No gray hair. No additional wrinkles. I remained fit, but not the same. The reflexes used to wait tables weren't the same as those needed by an agent. Muscle memory atrophied, even with doing my daily exercises. Terraforming was done rapidly, so Dartmoor could be occupied within years instead of decades. Residual radiation from the process must have given us extreme regenerative powers. Having a paramilitary background, the implications were both exhilarating and frightening.

Chapter 3

Third Time

Many improvements were made to the city. The canal had finally reached Gulag. Wooden pipes carried running water into all businesses and houses within a kay of the city center. Plumbing was promised to the rest of the city within a year. A sewer system was the next major project. The top priority was preventing the waste water from contaminating the canal. Twenty-thousand people now lived in Gulag. That was a lot of waste. It had to go somewhere.

Religion finally reached Dartmoor. For many, being sent to the penal colony was a new lease on life, an opportunity to reinvent, to live the life they should have lived. They viewed their arrival as divine intention. The *Second Time Church* was built at the crossroads of Gulag's two thoroughfares. Businesses had to be relocated, but that was an acceptable inconvenience for progress. It was the first building in Gulag over ten meters high, and the first to use stone as its primary building material. They had to be hauled by wagons from the mountains. It took half a year to build, but worth the wait. It was stunning: stained-glass mosaics, two steeples, one slightly higher than the other. The taller was over 30 meters high. The resources required to build the church---materials and manpower---was a significant boost to the economy. Miners, stone masons, carpenters, artisans and engineers had to be paid. The money trickled down to the businesses supporting them, most prominently, the housing industry. The scarcity of children meant few families, resulting in few individual structures. The lack of automobiles permitted apartment complexes to be built closely together. In some of the denser areas of Gulag, a person leaning out their window could shake hands with their neighbor. The church became a spectacle. People who hadn't been to Gulag since their arrival returned to see the church. A tourist industry began to flourish. Craving communal ownership in such a magnificent structure, people who hadn't been to church since their incarceration made it a priority to make an appearance. Daily services had become so popular an afternoon session had to be scheduled.

The comprehensiveness of my report required I attend one of the services. The Second Time Church was the one place in Dartmoor where there were nearly as many women as men. Why were women more religious? Were we more morally sound than men? I think it had more to do with the socialization. Prior to the service commencing, there were more conversations occurring than I would hear in a week in the Mounds and Trunks. The women weren't just talking to each other, but also to the men. Church becoming a dating service and a pick-up joint? With the type of people sentenced to Dartmoor, and the in-equitability in the number of men to women, the relationship between the two genders had become strained. Women had difficulty becoming peers with men. They were either treated as sex objects or goddesses. Being in a religious setting, and having similar numbers, the women no longer felt like outcasts, so they were able to function as they would in a conventional society.

The minister was dressed in a white robe. Attached to it was a gold broach: two vertical bars capped and footed by two horizontal bars. Veins of precious minerals were discovered over a year ago in a mountain range 900 kays to the northwest, near the boundary shield. That was something I eventually needed to see. Not just the shield, but the people who lived near it. What kind of society would be created by the most anti-social criminals on the fringe of civilization?

A port, Bronze Glade, had finally been established in the delta. A road was being constructed from Gulag, but it would be years before it was completed. The most difficult part would be constructing the bridges and causeways. Bronze Glade is currently water locked. It sits on an island at the tip of the tidal flats, a staging area for the harrowing journey across the sea.

Dartmoor had four seas. They intersected in an area called the Crosshairs. The straits connecting them were much narrower---averaging 40 kays. The journey across the Western Straight to the Berry Peninsula was relatively short, but often dangerous. The waters closest to the Crosshairs were the roughest. The oversized rafts often rocked, sometimes enough to tip over. One trip in fifty didn't make it to Markusmo, the terminal port.

Woodworking had greatly improved since my arrival. The pews were magnificent: skillfully carved, lacquered, and polished. The minister stood on a platform, constructed with similar care, in front of the thousand people primed to devour every syllable and punctuation he uttered. He studied his paper note cards. Paper may have been re-invented to facilitate currency, but it was perfected to publish Church literature. The Second Time Bible was perpetually *nearly complete*. An adolescent religion's greatest detriment was the flux in its tenets.

"Ladies and gentlemen. Please stand in appreciation of creation and second opportunities." Everyone stood at the minister's beckoning. They had become as quiet as they were noisy seconds before. "May we rejoice in the construction of this fine structure. And may we rejoice in your attendance. God has deemed us worthy of a second chance---a do-over. May we not abuse such gratitude. You may be seated."

We did as were told. I noticed many of the people spent as much time looking at the architecture as they did the preacher. "It has come to my knowledge that there are demons amongst us." There were gasps in the audience. "Some of us haven't used our second chance for salvation. Some of our people have transformed into grotesquely deformed wildmen. They have chosen to attack God-loving citizens. So far, these attacks have only occurred in isolated areas, outside the city, to those who have chosen to wander alone. As their numbers grow these wildmen will become bolder, attacking groups, possibly even entering the city. Brother Michael has seen them. Brother Michael, tell everyone what you saw."

A man I didn't recognize joined Father William on the platform. "It was after sundim. I knew it wasn't safe in the Springwoods after dark, but I needed firewood. There were three of them. From a distance they looked like you and me, but they were more hunched over, ape-like. They were tearing apart something and placing pieces of it in their mouths. I knew I should have run back to the city then, but my curiosity got the best of me. I had to see what they were eating. Is curiosity a sin, Father William?"

"It can be son, if you are curious about something you know is evil."

"I believed what they were doing might be evil, but I was uncertain."

"Morality sometimes is gray. I think informing us what you saw makes up for any sin you may have committed in your zest for knowledge."

"As I slowly came closer, I began to see abnormalities. The men were dressed, but not in clothes. They were covered in hair. Not as thick as a dog. More like on a pig. Their faces were malformed. It wasn't just the shapes of their faces that appeared feral. It was their expressions. Their humanity had departed." More gasps in the audience. "Viciously, they tore at meat with their unnaturally long, sharp teeth. I couldn't tolerate being there any longer. Before I could tear myself away I saw a boot, then a leg." More gasps. "Not much more remained of whoever that was. I backpedaled first, my fear of not becoming aware of their potential brutal approach outweighing a hastier retreat. After I felt it was safe to turn around, I did so. Then I ran back to Gulag as fast as I could. I don't think they noticed me. They were so fixated on their devilish feast. I pulled up lame once I returned home. God had given me an extra boost of speed, but my mortal legs couldn't take the strain."

"PRAISE GOD!" someone shouted. Other comments were made, but not as loudly or as profound.

Father William raised his hand. The congregation instantly calmed down. "Praise God, indeed. And damn Satan who has also chosen to make Dartmoor his home. I have also heard of people returning from the dead looking no different than they did before they died. The love of God in their hearts didn't diminish, and in some cases, greatly improved. Who here has returned from the dead? Do not be afraid to announce this admission. There once was a greater man than any of us who rose from the dead."

Hands began to rise. One here, then one there, then small clusters. One of the tenets of being an agent was not making yourself stick out. After a significant number of hands were placed in the air, I felt it safe to do so myself.

"Thank you for being so honest about what had to be an uncomfortable admission. You may put your hands down now." There had been over a hundred of them, more than ten percent of those in attendance. "As you see around you, Satan isn't the only one to protect his dominion. God has also given his followers eternal life. In essence, we have been given a third opportunity to do God's will. From today onward this church will be called the *Third Time Church*."

Father William removed his four-bar emblem and replaced it with a five-bar one, three vertical with one above and one below. The audience erupted into applause. They stood up and shouted, and embraced one another. Some parishioners openly wept.

Father William raised his hand again. "To counter the demon insurgence, we must form a pact, a *human pact*, to fight together Satan's soldiers. Man must no longer fight man. If we are to survive we must work as one. We aren't just striving to save our homes, our businesses, and our lives, but our souls. Those who aren't members of the church must become aware of the demons. They must also join the pact. Together we will be triumphant. Separate we will fall."

There was another emotional celebration. Father William chose to allow his congregation to enjoy the moment. Nearly a quarter later he announced informally that the session was over. Many parishioners stayed until it was time for the next group to enter. Politely, Father William asked those lingering to leave.

I felt better about myself after learning so many other people had died and returned from the dead. It was one of those things about myself I was ashamed of because I believed I was a freak, that I was the only person like that. There were probably thousands of people on Dartmoor who have been reborn. What would a society transform into if no one died, not permanently? Would population run amok? There weren't many people on Dartmoor yet, but if thousands were sentenced here every year, that meant tens of thousands in a decade? A hundred-thousand? More if the number of people sent to Dartmoor continued to increase, which was likely. But what about natural population gains? Children grow up to have children who have more children. Where were the children on Dartmoor? I never considered myself mother material, especially since becoming an agent. Thoughts of children didn't come naturally to me. Have my observational skills become so weak that I didn't notice any of the women carrying babies? I knew for a fact some of the women here weren't as chaste as I. We must be sterile. Did that mist that was sprayed on us do it? Or was it the biochemistry of terraforming? Other modified planets didn't make women sterile. This planet was unique though. People didn't return from the dead on those other planets. So Dartmoor gives, and Dartmoor takes away.

A month later a military order was created to counter the demons. The *Knights*, as they were called, erected a building to rival the Church. It was built at the fork of the two eastern roads. *The Castle*, as it was referred to, had a central courtyard for arms practicing, and four tall towers, one on each corner, to watch for suspicious activity. The towers were 100 meters tall. The structure was constructed of stone, like the church, but without the ornamentation. The church had its own construction. A third spire was added. Not wanting to be outdone by the Knights, it was 101 meters tall.

With ore becoming more readily available, smithing was becoming profitable. The iron age was upon us. There were nearly as many weapons and armor manufactured as horseshoes, buckets and utensils. The Knights looked their part after they were provisioned with breast plates, shin guards, and helmets.

Chapter 4

AMAZONIA

With it became increasingly chaotic in Gulag, I spent more time in Amazonia. I convinced Pubtender Bill that having worked over five years for him I deserved a second day off every week. He grudgingly agreed, not wanting to lose me.

It was peaceful in the foothills where the Amazons lived, but it was becoming less so. As Gulag's population blossomed more people began to live on its fringes, even with the increased threat of goblin---what we now referred to the deformed, violent mutants--- attacks. Amazonia now had neighbors. They weren't bad neighbors. The lack of privacy is what bothered the women. They

31

didn't like hearing male voices in the distance. Some of them could be peeping at them from behind a tree or a boulder.

Internal dissention had also developed---a power struggle. One contingent just wanted to be left alone, to be able to participate in their activities privately. Another, preferred the Amazons to be more aggressive, to become a force to be reckoned with.

I made a suggestion. "Maybe you could do both." Women continued to join the Amazons, but not in as great of numbers as the first few years. With Gulag---and the rest of Dartmoor--- becoming more civilized, women felt safer and more a part of conventional society.

"I don't believe it's possible for a private, peaceful society to co-exist with a public, violent one." Michelle had become the leader of the doves.

"We don't need an army to become powerful," countered Anna, the leader of the hawks.

"By selling bread and garments?"

"We have the herbs."

"You want us to become pushers?"

"The mind weed isn't the only thing we cultivate. Some of the herbs alleviate pain. Others start fires or heal bones."

"We may become wealthy if we market the herbs. But do we care about such things? Will becoming rich make us happier?"

"It will make us more powerful. The more power we possess the easier it will be to change society in the way we feel fit."

"We chose to live here to flee society. Why would we want to become part of it?"

"We didn't want to be a part of *their* society."

"That's your perspective. I enjoy *our* society. I don't want things to change."

"You'd rather sit in your hammock smoking the mind weed all day."

"You'd be happier if you relaxed a bit, instead of doing all that ranting."

The discussion continued with many more women having their say. Heated arguments became shouting matches. Decorum disintegrated. Paradise lost.

Michelle talked to me about it as we lay beside one another. No, we didn't have a physical relationship. I didn't have a place to sleep, because I wasn't a permanent member of the village. Friends sometimes shared beds. Woman could distinguish between sex and companionship. "I think there's going to be a nasty divorce. We're already separated, but still living together. If some of us leave, will you join us? You mentioned wanting to see the rest of Dartmoor. I want to go far from here."

I had enough money for a horse now, and traveling provisions. "Yes. I'll travel with you. When do you think you might be leaving?"

"Soon."

Chapter 5

SOUTH

Pubtender Bill and the regulars at the Mounds and Trunks--- most of them my friends----were sad to see me go, but understanding. They knew it was coming. Criminals had more wanderlust in them than society as a whole. If they were content with their condition they would have settled into a less exotic profession.

The horse I bought was a paint I named Stewart, after my father. If I had children I would have named my first son after him. I never knew him, so naming my horse after him wasn't so much honoring the person, but the person he may have been.

There were fifty of us. The Doves that stayed did so not for their lessened desire for peace, but for their aversion to change. We hadn't intended to parade through Gulag, but the only road in the direction we wished to travel passed through the city. There were many negative comments. A few positive ones. Most of the spectators simply gawked.

Our goal was to travel south, as far as we could, then establish a community. We chose south because there wasn't a sea in that direction to delay us. The southern road, paralleling the Southern Spine Mountains, meandered through the Springwoods. Most of the women didn't have horses, dictating a crawling pace. We provisioned ourselves minimally, not wanting to be perceived as stealing from Amazonia.

We intersected the Sparkling River at noon. It wasn't deep this close to its headwaters. We easily crossed it at the ford the road directed us to. "Let's set up camp here," suggested Michelle. Without anyone present to oppose her she became the legitimate leader, instead of just one voice of many. "We don't have much food. Let's accept the generosity of Gaea's bounty." It wasn't too surprising that a group of women living in the wild began to believe in the Earth Mother. More shocking were those thousands of people living in more traditional societies that did so.

The women with me may have appeared passive, but when they madly thrust their spears into the water they looked more hawk than dove. A feast was had, albeit a homogeneous one. What wasn't eaten was returned to the perimeter of the fire to preserve it.

Half-an-hour of sunlight remained after eating. We relaxed beside the river, beneath the trees. Some of the women pitched hammocks and turned in early. It felt like I was on vacation. The mood changed when someone screamed.

We rushed towards the voice. One of the Amazons was squished between two leaves. The calamity? They were larger than she and squeezed her as tightly as those vines that killed me. She had stopped making sounds before we could cut her out. The task was surprisingly difficult. The leaves were thick, and as tough as rubber. The antler knives couldn't take the strain, many of them breaking. Fortunately, we also had a few metal ones. We almost wished we hadn't. What remained of the Amazon was a husk, all her juices squeezed out of her like a grape.

After re-creation was discovered, pyres replaced burials. It was believed the obliteration of a body hastened its host's return. It was dusk by the time we lit the fire. The dancing flames in the darkness reflected off Michele as she spoke to us. "May Rose return from the dead a better person. May demons not possess her soul." We bowed our heads in respect. As was the custom, those who knew her well spoke of her, so others would remember her.

The evening was somber. Volunteers were requested for watch shifts. And easily found, the glowing embers reminding us of the consequences of careless vigilance.

I lay beside Michelle. "Do you think Rose will find her way back to us?"

"If Gaea wills it. I didn't think leadership would be this difficult. I believed I was as qualified as anyone to lead us to our new home. Maybe if someone else led, Rose wouldn't have wandered off and been so careless. I should have suggested people pair up before they left camp. Leading isn't a power trip for me. Someone had to do it, so I stepped up." I put my arms around Michelle from behind and hugged her. She clutched them tightly and began to sob, silently. She wouldn't allow anyone else to be aware of her lack of control. Women may have been able to allow their emotions to control them, but leaders couldn't.

The next night was also spent in the Springwoods, but 40

kays further down the road. We were resolute in being more vigilant, to prevent additional deaths. It would be foolhardy for something to attack a group our size. As long as someone didn't wander off alone---like Rose---it was likely all of us will make it to our intended destination.

The one atypical thing we saw the second day was an intertwining of silk thread in the trees above us. "Should we collect it?" someone suggested. I marveled at the Amazons ability to weave. I took a moment to picture myself wearing a beautiful dress made from those translucent strands.

"I believe it belongs to someone already. Look at those patterns. How large must the creature be that made thread that thick? I don't want to make it mad. All I can think about are spiders dropping down from the trees on top of me."

"All I can think about are the beautiful clothes we could make with the silk. Honey is taken from bees."

"And beekeepers often get stung. I don't wish to get stung by something as large as I." Michelle kicked her heals into her horse. She rode bareback, as did all Amazons.

The next day the trail climbed out of the forest, entering the foothills. There was no logic in it. The person who made the trail must have just felt like it was time for a better view. The Springwoods remained below us, but they began to thin out. It wouldn't be long before they left us completely. The third night we set up camp beside a creek. The Cool River was south of the Sparkling, so it was likely one of its tributaries. We fished again. More fish was consumed and more stored away.

The fourth night was also spent in the foothills, but without a flowing creek to serenade us. A dusty plain replaced the Springwoods. Far off, there appeared to be a forest. From our height that might have meant 50 kays or more from us.

Midday the following day we passed through the hamlet of Jumping Rapids. Glacier Creek meandered through the peaceful mountain settlement. The sentiments of its residents were similar to the Amazons'---they simply wanted to be left alone. After sharing with them we were just passing through, they obliged by directing us to our intended destination. "Just follow the trail. It becomes rougher after a few kays, but it will guide you to the tip of the Spine. From there continue due south, where the shadows point. The Honey Mountains snug up to the barrier. You'll know you're close when you enter the Alloy Desert. You'll probably see the mountains before, but sometimes sandstorms obscure the area. If you want to go as far from civilization as you can, that's the place to go."

"How much further is it?"

"500 kays." Two-thirds of our journey remained.

The trail was becoming difficult to follow, but it soon fell towards the plains. At the base of the foothills we spent our fifth night.

The next day we walked through more dirt than grass. We were becoming worried we might not find water again until we reached the Honey Mountains. We were relieved when we crossed a creek at the end of the sixth day. We set up camp, then washed ourselves and our clothes. As our clothes dried we filled our canteens and fished. We were unsuccessful with the latter. We still had some of the smoked fish, and most of our original rations. We weren't concerned about having enough to eat the remainder of our journey, but what would we do after that?

The trail ended. Sporadically, we saw something that might have been footprints. Just as likely, they were weathered hoof or paw prints. But if animals could survive in this dusty environment, so could we.

Before leaving the creek, we refilled our canteens and encouraged the horses to have their fill.

By midday of the seventh day the mountains began to diminish. By the end of the day they were completed gone. We had reached the tip of the Southern Spine. What lay on the other side? Was the land more exotic, or just more pristine without humans contaminating it?---so far. One day I hoped to see for myself. I planned to see all of Dartmoor eventually. The way it was looking, with me not being able to find that transport portal, I had plenty of time to do it.

A creature greeted us in camp that evening. We believed it to be a bird at first, possibly a scarlet or a cardinal. It was bright red. Then we believed it to be a bat, due to the similarity of its wings. But its body was all wrong. It looked more like an iguana, but the size of an eagle.

"Come here," coaxed one of the Amazons. She held out a piece of smoked fish. It snatched it from her hands then flew off. It landed a short distance away. It dropped the piece of fish, then tore at it with its mouth as one of its clawed feet held it in place. It flew back for more. It took the small pieces one at a time, always flying away, but slightly less distant each time. Eventually it became secure enough in its environment that it didn't fly away at all. Believing it was tame, one of the women attempted to pet it---a bad decision. Instead of pecking at her, the bird blew out flame. She was badly burned, but her injuries weren't life threatening. The bird no longer got a free hand out, but it didn't leave. In what was a cross between a chirp and a growl it begged for more food. It either hadn't realized the severity of what it had done, or didn't care.

In the morning it was still within sight of the camp. Michelle had a suggestion. "If we don't feed it, it will go away." A good idea, but it didn't work. It followed us through the dusty plain.

"We should call it Rose." The Amazon who suggested it was one of the Rose's closest friends, so it wasn't intended to be insulting. "It's red like Rose's hair, and likes to eat. Rose never turned down a meal. It also has a bit of an attitude. She would feel honored."

Rose continued to follow us. It continued to call out to us periodically. I couldn't take it anymore. I placed a piece of dried fish on the ground and walked away. I must have been getting sentimental being around the dove Amazons. Rose snatched the fish. In seconds it was consumed.

We hit water two days later. The earth just suddenly dropped, and at the bottom was a river. The gorge varied in width from one-hundred meters to three-hundred, and in depth from fifty to over one-hundred. It was a sheer drop in most places. We had to travel three kays upstream before an intersecting gully provided access to the water. The horses drank heartily as we filled our canteens. There was an intermittent shore, ten- to twenty-meter strips of sand and rock covered with minimal vegetation, but more than what was at the top of the canyon. The water was surprisingly cool, a welcomed break from the stale tepid liquid we endured the past three days.

"Let's set up camp down here." Most of Michelle's suggestions have been good ones, but this was one of those rare occasions I had to disagree.

"I don't think it will be safe. Arid canyons are prone to flash floods. Even if it doesn't rain here, it might upstream. Sometimes mountain ranges create their own weather. If the canyon fills up tonight we may not be aware of it until it's too late."

"I can't argue with that. After bathing we'll make the trek back up. I would love to spend the night at this oasis, but I don't want to get washed away. We'll have to bring the horses down again tomorrow morning before we leave."

The water felt cold relative to what we were used to, and to the air temperature, but once we got used to it, it was quite nice. It had to be about 15 degrees, cooler than one wished to bathe in, but acceptable if one was active. And we were extremely active. The water was flowing gently enough that it felt like we were in a lake. We swam and splashed, like we were young children.

"Tell me that was your leg."

"I'm over here."

There was a shriek, then both of the Amazons headed towards shore as quickly as their thrashing allowed. They were so intent on escaping that they stubbed their toes and scraped their feet on the rocky riverbed. Something that looked like a snake snapped at them. Rose darted towards the distress. She blew out a burst of flame. It incinerated the creature, charring its head. Rose wasn't done with it. She flew to where the current had taken away its limp form. Her talons snatched it from the water. She dropped it in front of the two women. They backed away from it, huddling together, shivering. Not getting the reaction she expected, Rose landed beside the eel and began tearing pieces of flesh from it.

Michelle snatched a blanket from a saddle bag and wrapped the two women in it. "It might be for the best to skip a day of fishing," she suggested.

I watched Rose gorge herself. She cooed between bites. "The eels appear to be tasty. Aren't they supposed to be high in protein?"

"Help yourself. The river is apparently laden with them."

Always being up for a challenge, I tried to catch one, but failed, badly. Skewering a fish was one thing, but attempting to do the same to a narrow swirling, rubbery mass was nearly impossible. I say nearly, because I was relatively confident a small explosive might get the job done.

The women who were chased by the eel had recovered enough from their ordeal by the time they reached the top of the gorge that they could joke about it. They were the center of attention the remainder of the evening.

We followed the canyon the next two days. If possible, the

terrain became even more desolate. Camping was less pleasant. We had the view, but not easy access to the bottom of the canyon. Our lone opportunity occurred late morning the third day. The horses were watered, and canteens filled, but no one chose to swim. The eels may have been isolated in that part of the river we first camped, but we had no way of knowing unless we examined the river more thoroughly, and no one wished to do that. Without argument we named the body of water that flowed beneath us the Eel River. I added it to the map I was making of Dartmoor. Most of it was blank. Did all explorers feel this overwhelmed?

The terrain became more extreme. The earth was cracked in many places. Cacti began to appear. Most were prickly, to ward off animals that wished to reach their internal water reserves. The Eel River Gorge began to widen. As it did, the canyon walls lowered. As the water spread to fill the wider space, multiple channels were created, squirming their way around sand bars and islands. The shallower water brought more animals, predominantly birds. The largest mammals were hippos. They spent most of their time below water, with just their nostrils poking through the surface. Infrequently, they surfaced long enough to nibble on the reeds on the islands.

Michelle was moved by the sight. "They look like they have a peaceful life."

"Eating and bathing all day, what could be better?" My statement had equal doses of sarcasm and sincerity. I understood Michelle's romantic inclinations, but I was predominantly Cor, so I couldn't live that lifestyle.

The Honey Mountains became visible. The base of them looked as desolate as our surroundings, but it was darker near their peaks, indicating vegetation. It would take a few more days before we hiked that far up.

Our collective mood improved drastically once an end to our journey was within sight. Partying ensued that first night after spotting the mountains. Much dancing and consumption of intoxicating substances occurred. Wishing to never lose my sense of control I declined the alcoholic beverages and the mind weed. Inebriation exaggerated emotions, bringing to the surface hidden desires. Michelle became more touchy-feely---not like she wanted to make out with someone---more clingy. She loved everyone, and she wanted everyone to know it. Women having less testosterone than men, weren't aggressive drunks, for the most part, not physically, but there was a proliferation of verbal altercations. I lost respect for some of the Amazons that night, including Michelle. I wouldn't be able to stay in their company indefinitely. Wanderlust, and desire to complete my mission, would eventually force me to leave. My reaction to the way they were acting confirmed it.

Our camp wasn't as festive the next morning. I and a couple of other women who chose to take it easy that night remained awake to...man?...the watch shifts. It wouldn't have been very productive for the others to do so. Watching for wildlife and demons was nothing compared to preventing women from wandering away from camp. None completely got away. The only injuries were a few scratches and bruises.

When I had an opportunity to be alone with Michelle I brought up a subject that had been bothering me. "I say this to be helpful, not hurtful. Acting the way you did last night diminishes your leadership. Those you lead must always see you in control. Loosening up might make you their friend, but they won't respect you for it."

"I was just having a little fun. I don't want to be that type of leader who can't interact with her people. I never wanted to be in charge. I stepped up because someone had to." Michelle moped off. She wouldn't look at me the remainder of the day. Our relationship was never the same. I was not the only one she distanced herself from. I never saw her completely out of control again. She became a better leader---I could tell that from how the Amazons reacted to her---but she also became less happy, more glum. Should I have spoken to her? If she really didn't want to lead, she could have resigned. She wanted to lead *and* be everyone's buddy. Was the future survival of the Amazons important enough to lose your best friend and make her, if not miserable, at least closer to being so?

Chapter 6

HONEY

We lost the Eel River the following day. The shallows were brief. New canyons enclosed it, this time in a shattered extension of the mountains. The only way we could continue to follow it was by walking in the water. Even if the water was shallow enough---it wasn't---the eels were still fresh in our memory.

To bypass the irregular, broken land we turned southwest. We were still heading to the Honey Mountains, but at a diagonal. At worst, a day delay.

A salt flat opened in front of us. Typically formed from a dry sea bed. Extremely unlikely on a planet transformed a decade earlier. How detailed was the terraforming? Was the salt flat created instantaneously, or was the natural shifting of land masses and erosion accelerated, to a near biblical magnitude?

The salt flats were crossed in two hours. Beyond, were sand dunes. We attempted to bypass them. Negotiating them was going to take more out of us then we believed we had left. It had been an arduous week. We abandoned the detour after a quarter, believing the extra energy expended would be wasted if the crossing was inevitable. The dunes appeared endless.

Our second casualty occurred less than a kay from the salt flats. One of the Amazons was snatched, being dragged into, then under the sand. We assumed she had fallen into a hole, but a hole doesn't keep pulling. The woman beside her tried to drag her back up, but the force on the other end was stronger. The last that we saw of her were her fingertips as they slid through her potential liberator's mortified hands.

The more forceful Michelle took over. "Everyone huddle together, so we may protect one another. Weapons out. Only move if you're attacked. If we're lucky, whatever snatched Connie will think we've moved on." Either the ploy worked, or one meal had satisfied the creature. After waiting ten minutes we resumed the crossing.

"What was that thing that snatched Connie?" someone asked.

"I think I saw jaws," the woman who had tried to save her responded. "It had a long snout, like an alligator. I thought they only lived in the water."

"Poets have compared dunes to the sea. It must *swim* in the sand, as easily as fish in water, likely all the way down to the aquifer."

"How far is that?"

"Considering the lack of water in the area, at least twenty-five meters, possibly fifty."

It wasn't as easy travelling so bunched together, but it was safer. Connie was the only casualty. The end of the dunes was reached an hour before sundim. We wanted to put as much distance between us and them before dark. We spread out, to accelerate our pace. What attacked us may have just lived in the dunes, but we weren't willing to tempt fate.

Five kays of relatively flat terrain abruptly transitioned into sporadic hoodoos. Hoodoos were weathered rock formations, often in the shape of columns. There was room between the stone spires. Navigating them wasn't what bothered us. They seemed out of place. Suddenly the ground went from being flat to having these monoliths impeding us. They were so randomly placed it was impossible to travel a straight path through them. We were forced to make detours, heading east or west as often as south.

It was insane to make our way through them this late in the day. After a few minutes of attempting to do so we turned around and set up camp on their perimeter. The red sandstone was extraordinarily beautiful, enhanced by the dim sunlight shining on it. Being so far from the center of Dartmoor, the rays from the artificial sun were closer to being horizontal than vertical, giving the area a wintery glow.

Instead of the splendor causing contentment I began to feel discombobulated. "Is there something strange about this place or is it just me?"

"I think we're just impatient to reach the Honey Mountains." The hesitant tone in Michelle's voice betrayed the confidence the statement intended.

Camp was quiet that evening. Thoughts weren't shared. No one wished to appear *that* irrational. If Rose hadn't incessantly squawked there may have been no sounds at all. She had been troubled since our arrival at the hoodoos. And she wasn't shy about expressing that displeasure. She hadn't followed us as we took our short excursion into and back out of them.

She didn't follow us the next day, either. We had become attached to her, so we were saddened by her departure. Technically, our departure. We continued to hear her squawk many minutes after re-penetrating the hoodoos. Why were pets sometimes harder to leave than people?

Other than retaining the uneasiness, the trip through the oddly shaped stone pillars went well. By noon we were completely out of them.

The foothills began almost immediately after that. They began as moguls, gradually growing into hills many times taller than us. For the most part we kept to the troughs between them. When it looked like a particular trough wasn't going to break in the direction we wished to go, we climbed the mound beside it. For every two meters we gained in altitude we lost one a moment later.

This was the most tiring day of our journey---so far. Even more draining than the crossing of the dunes. Michelle determined it was best we erect camp early. We needed plenty of rest to prepare for an even more arduous hike the following day. The mood in camp was better than the night before. I don't believe we felt any more at ease with our surroundings, but we were beginning to become accustomed to them. It was like having a chronic ache or a missing tooth. Once the novel event became familiar you no longer noticed it as much. Sometimes, not all.

The climb up the mountains the following day wasn't enjoyable. Not only were we drenched in sweat and our muscles ached, flies began to attack us. Couldn't the engineers who designed the composition of fauna left out the insects, the pesky ones? Welts covered our bodies by the time we reached the tree line. Michelle suggested, in her new forceful manner, those of us with horses should volunteer to carry the packs of those less fortunate. It was a fair decree, so there was little grumbling. It was excruciating. I had become too accustomed to not traveling under my own power. I was embarrassed. I was determined not to allow myself to get into that bad of shape again. If it took walking half the day beside my horse, then that's what I had to do.

We hiked into a forest as far as we could before decreased illumination forced us to set up camp. We hadn't come to any water yet, but we were confident there had to be some nearby for the forest to flourish.

The next day it was decided, instead of climbing further into the mountains we would parallel our elevation, as we explored. Eventually we had to come to a creek. Once we did we could establish a base camp, and from there scout the range to find the most appropriate area to construct a settlement.

An hour into our morning stroll we heard flowing water. Ten minutes later we saw it. It was a torrent of white-water. Like a skier, it swooshed down the mountainside in wide switchbacks. We followed it upstream, stopping when its course began to mellow. It was nearly flat as it meandered through a lush meadow. The water widened, forming a small lake. It was the perfect setting to end this leg of our journey. All that remained was finding the perfect track of land, large enough to build a settlement, within range of resources.

In the morning we were eager to explore. We set out after a token breakfast. It was wonderful not being burdened with packs and taking care of animals. We divided into six groups of eight. One group went due east, another due west, both paralleling our current elevation. The third group went east, but slightly upward. As did the fourth group, but west. The fifth group went straight up. Only the hardiest, most rugged Amazons volunteered for that assignment. Their mission was more terrain reconnaissance than locating a suitable area to build a city. The sixth group was to care for the horses and defend the camp---if necessary. Reactive was more fun, but proactive saved more lives

I was in the reconnaissance group. I wanted to prove to myself I still had the ability if I pushed myself. It was easier than I thought it would be. Whatever had been stiff the day before loosened up. I was a bit sore when I started, but after I stretched my muscles they began to feel better. It took us two hours to reach the crest of the range. There was snow in the saddles between the numerous peaks. The terrain sloped steeply down the backside of the range. A kay back, it abruptly ended. I was close enough to the energy shield that I could see the shimmering. I was tempted to climb down, to touch the shield, but didn't have the time if I wished to return to camp before it got dark. That was assuming I didn't kill myself on the way down, or back up. I wasn't too concerned with the pain of making contact with the rocks below---it would be brief. I feared returning from the dead near Gulag and having to take the trek south again. If that happened, it was unlikely I would return. There were many areas closer to Gulag that I hadn't yet explored.

From what I could see from the ridge, I was about in the middle of the range. I could see a large body of water far off into the distance, towards the northwest. It must be the Western Sea. Just south of it was a forest. To the northeast, the horn of the Southern Spine was barely visible. The Eel River could clearly be seen, and two others, one due north, the other to the west. I tried to spot our camp, but the trees were too dense below me.

"I see someone," spoke one of my companions, pointing to the northwest.

I spotted him---her. "It must be someone from the group that headed southwest. I see someone else." I couldn't yet tell if they were our women, or even human. They did move, and look, like they were human, in a very rudimentary manner. If they were part of that group there should have been more of them. The others may have been concealed. We were above the tree line, but they just below it.

"Whoever they are they don't appear to be wearing any clothes," spoke a second companion.

"Goblins?" asked a third.

"Wherever people die there's likely to be goblins."

"Connie died too far away to make it up here."

"Shouldn't she have returned closer to Gulag?"

"We don't know if it works like that. It makes more sense for her to return closer to her body."

"Connie couldn't, wouldn't, return as a goblin. She was...is...too nice."

"If that matters. Maybe we start with a clean slate. Instead of just returning to Dartmoor, we are re-created."

I felt obligated to interrupt. "I was one of those people who returned from the dead. I didn't change, not significantly. If we are re-created from scratch why do I look and feel the same?"

"I don't see them anymore."

That was a surprise. We were more involved with discussing the people we saw than meeting them. Woman may be more nurturing than men, but sometimes that's all they focus on. Socializing sometimes superseded accomplishing goals. "Let's just head in the direction we last saw them. It's likely we'll spot them again unless they become evasive."

It was more fun descending than ascending. The jarring on our feet, legs, and knees was more severe, but our hearts and lungs welcomed the aerobic reprieve.

I began to feel happy. It may have been the endorphins kicking in, or the thrill of skipping downhill, but it felt more encompassing than that. It was like spending a spring day in a meadow full of wildflowers. The sun shining. The breeze blowing. The scent of those flowers, and grass, and cedar in the air. It reminded me of the uneasiness I felt entering the hoodoos. But instead of feeling uneasy I felt blissful, sated with contentment.

Chapter 7

GODDESS

"There they are." In the distance was a wide-mouthed cave. Water seeped out of it, filling a pool below. The overflow dribbled behind it, creating a creek. Evergreens enveloped the water, but not as densely as those defining the lush meadow we had set up camp in. The setting may not have been as lovely, but it was more protected from the elements, which were unpredictable in the mountains, sometimes severely.

They looked human enough, and definitely female. They hadn't yet seen us. One of them appeared to be crying in the arms of the other.

"Connie?"

The two women turned. We had quietly made our approach. When we finally made contact with them we were within fifty meters. "Rose?"

They looked like our slain sisters, but not exactly. Their bodies and faces looked younger: more fit, healthier. Sag and cellulite become more prominent as one ages. Both women had been over ten, but now looked like they were seven or eight---too old to be children, but too young to begin decaying. Their most drastic modification was their height. The previously average height women were now both over 250 sims.

Upon recognizing us, they unabashedly ran towards us. After many embraces, and tears, we exchanged tales.

"So, you just woke up near this cave?" asked one of the shorter Amazons.

Rose answered. "I knew I was dead when that thing *captured* me. I wasn't in any pain. As it squeezed the air out of me I became sleepy."

"It probably injected you with a sedative," I conjectured. "I wouldn't want my food moving."

"I woke up here. I found Connie...days later. I'm not sure how many. I haven't been completely coherent."

"How long has it been since....?"

"Two days," I answered.

"I woke-up here yesterday. I guess that means it takes a full day for a body to be...*reincarnated*? I don't think I want to be this tall." Connie began to cry again. "Large men are brawny. Women, big-boned or fat."

"I don't think anyone will call you fat. You're tall, but thin. Toned, not scrawny. Athletic looking."

"Butch?"

"Hardly. More grace and beauty than brawn."

"You look like a goddess," one of the shorter Amazons concluded. Rose and Connie did look like goddesses: powerful, but retaining the most admired physical attributes of their gender.

We returned to camp, with our previously displaced friends in tow. The embracing and crying began all over again. I couldn't stand so much sentiment. My 13 percent tolerance for such things was overflowing and about to rupture. I had to walk away. When I returned, the women were discussing how to clothe Rose and Connie. They were too large now to fit into any of their clothes. Togas were made from the bolt of cloth we had with us, reinforcing their transformation into goddesses.

It was decided our permanent settlement be near the cave. There was immediate shelter, and water. A natural observation promontory was just five-hundred meters upslope from there. And it was the location of probable future re-creations. The site by the lake wouldn't be wasted. A lodge would be built. Hunting and fishing activities would originate from there, and any excursions into the Alloy Desert, and beyond.

Most of the following year was spent constructing. Trees were cut to build the lodge and the settlement beside the cave. A garden was planted in the cleared land. Obtaining seeds for that first crop was an issue. The only things edible in the Honey Mountains were deer, fish, and berries. We had to return to civilization to buy seeds for fruit trees and vegetables. The South was sparsely populated. The closest settlement was 400 kays away: Rhinopolis, a small village on the fringe of those trees we had seen from atop the ridge. Its population was barely a hundred. It was likely to grow in prominence, it being the only settlement in the area.

We discovered why the range was called the Honey Mountains. There weren't any bees in the hills and cliffs, but they were within sight of them. Along, what I had christened the Honey River---the river to the west---were endless fields of prairie flowers. Something had to pollinate them. There was also a scattering of cottonwoods. The trees were full of hives, and the hives full of honey. Someone traveling through the area must have seen the bees and their sweet crop, with the mountains as their backdrop. After our first crop sprouted we relocated some of the bees. Initially we grew vegetables, but in time the fruit trees matured, and we were able to harvest apples and pears and plums and peaches.

The years passed serenely. The Amazons, who just wanted to be left alone in peace and solitude, got their wish. Periodically, they died. Accidents did happen, like falling off cliffs, and there continued to be deadly encounters with animals. Most of the women who died returned a day or so later, taller, more beautiful, and more fit. We discussed, ad nauseam, what happened to the others. Were they re-created somewhere else? Where they re-created into something other than a goddess? Did they just die, ceasing to exist? Was re-creation an absolute? Or was it a possible post-death occurrence? Could some of the demons we began seeing in the eastern half of the Alloy Desert be death gone wrong?

To distinguish the taller from the shorter variety of Amazons, we began to call the re-creations Titans. What else could we call them---giants? That was too negative a connotation for women. Weren't the Titans gods and goddesses? The conventional-sized Amazons continued to be called Amazons. Jealousy ensued, and envy. One particularly unhappy Amazon attempted to expedite the process of transforming into a Titan by throwing herself off a cliff. She didn't return. Cognizant that suicide wasn't compatible with becoming a Titan, further expeditions didn't occur.

Many years later I finally got around to investigating the

energy shield at the base of that near sheer cliff. I arrived sooner than I wished. I lost my footing. After breaking my back. And cracking my skull. I rolled against the electrified wall. It pushed me away with nearly as much force as I hit it with.

Chapter 8

LYNX

I assumed I would wake as a Titan in Aerie---the name we attached to the cave city high in the Honey Mountains. I got the mountain part right, but it was a different range. I was in the foothills of the Southern Spine. Spending my initial, impressionable years there, the memories of my youth flooded back to me. I found myself in rockier terrain than my first re-creation. The land's exposure provided an ample view of the forest below. There was no sign of Gulag, implying I was significantly south of the metropolis.

I itched, a frequent complication of re-creation, nearly as common as being sore or fatigued. It was my back leg, not my hand, that reacted, making a raking motion as it alleviated the irritation. Something wasn't right. I looked down at my body. I stood upon four legs, the pads at their termination defiantly planted in the scree. My tail flicked instinctively.

I was devastated. I wasn't worthy of becoming a Titan. It was assumed those not returning to Aerie after dying had done something in their lives, something dreadful, to prevent them from obtaining the lofty re-creation. Occasionally, someone kind didn't return. Our only explanation, she had hidden dark secrets she never expressed. What did I hide? Was being an agent considered evil? I stole and killed, but did so for the wellbeing of humanity. I wasn't altered after my first death. What had happened since then to force such a drastic physical change? The only thing I could think of was how I treated Michelle when I informed her she wasn't being a good leader. I didn't do so to be mean, and it was well intentioned. There was one upside. I didn't need to procure clothing.

What was I going to do now? I was too embarrassed to return to the Honey Mountains. And I couldn't just walk into a town looking like this. It felt hopeless.

After regaining my strength, I began to wander. I wasn't seeking anything in particular. I just felt like I had to move, to stretch my legs. Being primarily Cor, I had difficulty remaining motionless. Reclining for more than a couple of minutes felt like I was wearing a straightjacket. Becoming feline apparently exasperated those feelings. But didn't cats sleep all the time? How would that fit in with my hyperactivity?

I began to get hungry. Assuming no one was going to open a can of cat food for me, I would have to supply the nourishment. Being an agent, there had been occasions when I had to live off the land. I also did some hunting and fishing while I lived with the Amazons. I did all this food procurement with tools though. An animal's tools were innate, primarily its claws and teeth. I raised a front paw and flexed it. Four sim long claws extended from the tips of the pad. I could do some damage with these.

My first potential victim was a pica, a small rodent common in rocky terrain. I pounced on it. When I got up I expected to find it squished beneath me. Nothing. Somehow, it escaped. Most animals had some type of protection. Picas had their agility. I wasn't going to catch one of those guys, not with my inexperience in hunting, in this form. I had to stalk something slower. Bigger usually meant slower.

My senses were more acute than they had been before my re-creation. There was more activity in the Spring Woods, below, than in the highlands. At the fringe of the forest was a hare. It nibbled on lush meadow grass. I leapt. The hare was significantly larger than the pica. It couldn't squirm away without me knowing about it. After I neutralized its mobility I thrust my claws into it. I felt its heart beating hundreds of times a minute. It was terrified. It pushed off with its back legs, first against the ground, then against me. It scratched me. I wasn't used to having my food fight back. I lost concentration, which caused me to lose my grip. The hare leapt away. I followed it into the forest. I caught up to it numerous times. Every time I made that final lunge, it abruptly changed course. I was more agile as a cat than I was as a human, but not nearly as agile as the hare. Like most predators, my advantage was greatest initially. I tired rapidly. If I hadn't been re-created so recently I may have caught the creature. Instead, I lay on my side, panting profusely.

After I recovered, I attempted to leap back up, but something deep within me told me that sleeping on the soft leaves and pine needles might be the perfect thing to do right now. I stretched my front legs in front of me, then set my head down on them. I would sleep for a few minutes, then my senses would respond to something moving in the forest and I would wake. Usually, I could scan the perimeter with one eye or ear, but occasionally I would be coerced into lifting my entire head. I was conflicted. I didn't want to be disturbed while I napped, but I was very curious. Annoyance. Excitement. Comforting drowsiness.

The emptiness in my stomach became too much. My nap was over, temporarily. I stood up on all fours, then pushed my front paws forward in order to arc my back into a stretch. That felt good. My third attempt at self-serve was a successful one. Understanding that my prey might resent being attacked, I was prepared for its rejection of me. Another hare nibbled on tender new shoots. Moments later I nibbled on it. It was said that having

55

many small meals throughout the day was better than gorging. The person who said that wasn't a predator. I tore into that juicy, warm meat until my stomach was extended. I walked a few meters away from what was left of the carcass and resumed my perpetual nap. Scavengers noisily picked clean the few scraps I left on the bones. Why couldn't the forest have separate rooms for sleeping and eating?

Once the scavengers left, and digestion took over, I was able to enjoy a full sleep. When I woke it was dark. For humans, being in the dark, especially in the woods, was often frightening. For a predator, it was time to play. If I hadn't so recently eaten it would have been a perfect time to hunt. Thoughts of eating never-the-less had entered my mind. Aware of the detriments of a fat cat in the wild, I encouraged those thoughts to dissipate.

I was thirsty. It was amazing how sudden a thought would enter my mind in this form. Once entered it became imperative that thought become reality. Humans prefer drinking water from a clear, cool, fast-moving stream. Animals prefer quieter water. It was also tastier if it had been sitting around for a while, particularly with a lot of algae and vegetation in it.

Yes. This pond will do nicely. I raised my nose high in the air. To assist the flow of fragrant air into my nostrils. I opened my mouth. I smiled in bliss. I leaned my head towards the water, then curled my tongue to cup the water. My stomach was full again. Nap, part three, commenced.

I was content with my new life---for the most part. It was still new enough to me that I hadn't yet got bored with it. Exploring as a cat was different than exploring as a human. I remembered going to certain places, but the memories of those places weren't as chiseled into my brain as they would have been if I was still human. Another day heading to a pond, or into the mountains, or up a tree---I particularly liked climbing trees---felt like doing it for the first time. All it took was a branch falling, or a frog hopping, to make it a new experience for me.

The one thing I was having trouble with was loneliness. If there was one other cat in the Spring Woods, it would have drastically improved my mood. There were other cats---mountain lions and bobcats---but they were animals, not re-creations. I was almost getting to the point of traveling to Gulag or one of the other settlements in the area. I would make a good pet, as long as I was fed often enough. I would be able to protect my master from danger and keep him or her warm at night. No, I don't think I could do that. I needed my solitude, and becoming someone's pet would be like selling myself into slavery. Sometimes I would go to the edge of a village to watch people. On top of a hill or in a tree, I had a good view, yet felt safe.

Predators sometimes have predators. I don't know if those wolves really wanted to eat me. My prescience alone may have triggered the attack. The pack chased me for more than a kay. They were better equipped for long distances than I. They were almost upon me when I suddenly found myself someplace else---fifty meters or so in the direction I was travelling. Did the stress of the chase induce the blackout? The unexpected displacement must have disturbed the wolves nearly as much as it did me, because they broke off the chase, turning around abruptly, yelping as they fled.

I forgot about the event until it happened again. This time I was leaping from one ledge to another in the foothills. I miscalculated the distance. I wasn't going to make it. Suddenly I found myself many meters beyond my intended landing.

It took many days to connect the pieces. Transporting myself instantaneously a short distance was a mutation, an ability gained instead of a physical transformation---like becoming furry. It took me many frustrating hours, with many naps between attempts to soothe me, to duplicate the feat that I was able to do twice instinctively. A person can try too hard. My ability worked best when I didn't think too much about it, allowing instinct to take over. Another thing I learned: I couldn't transport myself whenever I wished to. There were limitations. The ability had to recharge. I had to wait more than an hour between transports. As I became more practiced in the ability, the delay lessened, but not significantly.

In time I discovered additional abilities. I could double my size, or reduce it by half. I could communicate mentally---perplexing, and frightening, for the receiving party. I could move small objects a short distance. I also had a chameleon like ability, being able to blend into the environment. While cloaked I could perform phenomenal surveillance. If I had such abilities as a human I would have become the preeminent agent in the history of the agency.

Chapter 9

GAEA

My abilities provided hours of frolicking every day. Between that and sleeping---and eating---I had a good life. I forgot about the Amazons and being an agent. Until I met a bear.

The black bear wasn't particularly large. It didn't have any unusual markings. It wasn't remarkably ferocious. Bears were usually more frightened of people than people afraid of them. What made this bear extraordinary was its ability to speak. No, not through growls and grunts, or rudimentary body language. The bear spoke fluent Esperanto. Thought it, actually. Its mouth moved as if it was constructing those words, but no sounds were emitted. The words formed in my mind. If it had begun talking to me like that my first day on Dartmoor I would have reacted differently. So many odds things have happened since then that I was able to have a conversation without believing I was becoming insane.

"It's a fine day, isn't?" The bear sat on its enormous behind. It apparently wasn't used to having its forelimbs sticking up. It didn't know what to do with them, so they just dangled.

"A bit chilly for me. Cats like to be warm. After we get done making introductions may I sleep on you?"

"If the bear allows."

"Do you always refer to yourself in the third person?"

"The bear is an avatar. I am borrowing its body for a few minutes. It won't hurt the animal. It won't even remember we had this conversation."

"You're a pilot?"

"You're thinking of an aviator. An avatar is the physical embodiment of a god."

"So, you're a god?"

"As much as those deformed creatures that prey on the unchanged are goblins, or those women in the Honey Mountains are Titans."

"You know quite a bit about what's going on in the world."

"I must, for I am the world."

"You look kind of small to be a world."

"An avatar is a sensory outlet, not a personification. I'm not really the world, just that part of it you call Dartmoor."

"Are you a computer intelligence? Something the wardens control?"

"I am neither digital or associated with those who have imprisoned you. I was created as all are created, from the combining of genes through physical intercourse."

"So, two planets...ah...mingled...and you were the result?"

"The genes I speak of are the collective biological matter of terraforming and the species deposited."

"So, you are saying, in essence, we, meaning all of us who

were sent to Dartmoor, are your parents? We had this huge biological orgy and you were what formed."

"Precisely, with bits of animal, plant, even mineral matter, thrown in."

"Why chose to share this information, now? Are you suddenly feeling underappreciated? Wishing the inhabitants of this world would become aware of you so they might worship you?"

"I fear this worship has already begun---under their terms, not mine. No, I have no great need to be *appreciated*. I am neutral when it comes to emotions: completely void of Fas. Void of Cor too, or saturated, depending on your perspective. So that makes me Min, unadulterated, within the bounds of current parameters."

"So why burden us with your existence now? Isn't Dartmoor chaotic enough without you?"

"Dartmoor is---nearly---as orderly as it is chaotic. You just notice the chaos more. No, this contact isn't an attempt to relieve your boredom. You are the first person I have ever spoken to. Your decision to consider it an honor or a curse."

"Why choose me? I'm not the most important person on Dartmoor. Or the best conversationalist."

"You are a Galactic Agent. That's rare."

"How...?"

"Gods are all-knowing. Once a person dies I become connected to them, you and all the others who have died and been reborn from the primordial soup."

"Are bears the only thing you can control?"

"Can I control the unchanged? Humans?"

"If you could, we wouldn't be having this conversation."

"Very perceptive. Because this bear is an animal, with only animal intelligence, it doesn't have the capacity for craving sovereignty, to the degree humans do. I can't tamper with free will."

"If you are all-knowing, why recruit an agent?"

"I know *most* of what's going on, not everything."

"Why should I help you, other than preserving my life? No one wants to get struck by lightning or have a boulder fall on their head."

"Not all that the planet re-creates has been beneficial. Goblins aren't the most dangerous creatures to terrorize Dartmoor. As the years pass the negative biological influences will become more extreme. To counter them, the positive ones must also prosper. But Dartmoor is populated by criminals. Which type of demon is most likely to be created?"

"Are you able to see into the future, or are you just making predictions?"

"No one is clairvoyant. The future I predict is derived from near infinite parameters. Freewill limits reliability. If everything continues to occur in the fashion it has occurred, I am 99 percent confident what I predict will come to fruition."

"But if I or someone else chooses to do something unpredictable---something chaotic---like killing this bear---the outcome may be altered? You could be wrong."

"It's extremely unlikely you will do so, but the calculation is a component of my predictions. Chaos by the way, although troublesome, can be circumvented. One chaotic event can't be predicted, but a cluster of them can. If one looks at such events in a grander scale---those involving many individuals, or over an extended period---reasonably accurate predictions can be made. You will eventually be able to make such predictions, if you choose to assist me. As my conduit, many of my powers will become available to you." Who wouldn't want that much power? But doesn't absolute power corrupt absolutely? I wouldn't have absolute power though, just more than anyone else has ever had.

"If I allow myself to be your conduit would you be able to control me like this bear?"

"You will have free will. Our relationship will primarily consist of you providing a sensory conduit."

"Can't you do that already? See and hear through the re-created?"

"Surface awareness: a consensus of occurrence. If you allow yourself to be my conduit, I will have complete monitoring access to you. I will not only see what you see, and hear what you hear, I will also think what you think. The only thing I can't touch, even with your permission, is your soul."

"So, we really have souls? Mankind's greatest mystery has been solved."

"Acknowledging their existence doesn't mean one understands them. When a person dies their soul is the only thing that is transferred to the biological matter you become."

"Doesn't part of our minds also have to be transferred, so we can retain our memories? I remember everything that has happened prior to my two deaths."

"Do you? How would you know? The soul is the individual, not the matter that forms skin, heart and mind. Because one's memories are much of what a person is, they imprint on the soul."

"There is too much to process."

"We will speak again. It is time I returned control. The longer I possess the bear the longer the side-effects will linger."

"So, there are dangers becoming an avatar."

"The side effects I speak of are feelings of uneasiness, that there are things occurring it isn't aware of. Enjoy the rest of this lovely day. It's been sunny for too long. If I don't add a bit of rain here or there people will no longer appreciate the pleasant days. Goodbye."

When the bear reclaimed its body it nearly fell over. It appeared to be dazed. It dropped to all fours then waddled away, veering awkwardly this way, then that way.

Would having all that power compensate for someone perceiving every thought? It wasn't possible for even a saint to have completely pure thoughts. Would I feel like I always had to be on? That someone was not just in the same room as me---but in my mind? Being an agent, I had become accustomed to having little or no time for myself. But even in the most intense of situations I could still hide, still relax, in my own thoughts.

Dartmoor's *god* returned to me the following week, as a marmot. A marmot is like a pica, but with ten times the bulk. "Let me share a few predictions before you make your decision. I know you haven't made up your mind yet. Your actions these past ten days proclaim your confusion. Fifty years from now a power will emerge in Dartmoor that will be powerful enough to enslave the inhabitants of the colony."

"Fifty years?"

"It sounds like an eternity. For mortals, perhaps, but no one is mortal on Dartmoor. Everyone living here today will be alive in 50 years, as will millions of new arrivals, in one form or another."

"It sounds like you want someone just out of school to begin planning for their retirement."

"If the timestream persists. If you assist me the control of Dartmoor will be delayed for an additional half-century."

"So, there isn't any hope that this world-wide enslavement won't occur at all?"

"Twelve percent, assuming you will help. For certain groups of people the ultimate goal is ultimate power."

"So, I must humble myself, to you, for a hundred years, and my reward will be enslavement?"

"Once this power has conquered this planet it will pursue more universal goals."

"It will have enough power to escape the energy shield?"

"It won't have to. Also, in approximately a century, the penal colony will cease to be. A movement will occur off world that will view harassing Dartmoor with additional inhabitants as inhumane. Particularly burdensome for a burgeoning new member world."

"You think that's likely?"

"The certainty is greater than the *great power* conquering

Dartmoor. By exploiting the unique resources of this planet, this power has the potential of ultimately ruling the galaxy, in as cruel a manner as they will rule Dartmoor."

"You aren't making it easy for me to refuse."

"The likelihood of you accepting is great."

"That almost makes me not want to do it. What if I choose, one day, to no longer be your conduit? May I have my life back?"

"One's life changes daily. It isn't possible for it to persist in its present state. Freewill will permit you to terminate your service with me whenever you wish, but it is unlikely to happen. Once someone sees a holograph they don't want to return to just reading a book."

I agreed. It *was* highly likely. "I don't feel any different."

"The changes will be subtle. When you wish to communicate with me I will be able to read your thoughts. I won't intrude unless it's necessary. Consider my observations as someone viewing a sporting event and you being one of the athletes. Once the game begins you won't even notice I'm there. Any outcomes you wish to predict will come to you as if you were setting the parameters and making the calculations. Saying goodbye is a contradiction, isn't it?"

The marmot became as dazed as the bear. After shaking its head, then its entire body, it crawled into its hole.

Chapter 10

CONDUIT

I became very busy, talking to this group of people, then that group, delaying Dartmoor's demise by weeks to years, depending on how much influence a particular group had. Sometimes I had to alter events clandestinely, increasing their likelihood for success, or preventing them from coming to fruition. As Dartmoor became more populated, and its citizens more mutated, its dynamics became more complex. In some communities I could walk through the center of town and no one would notice me. In others, I would be killed on the spot.

As the arrival of the power came closer, its characteristics became more defined. It was likely to be human. Mutants had better things to do than rule the world. Survival, for most of them, was their agenda. Isolation and debilitating metamorphoses took their toll. Two major human factions developed. On most worlds empires originated as regional powers. On Dartmoor, it was the expansion of professions.

The Hawk Amazons became very proficient in selling their herbs. To retain their market share, they improved their product and diversified. Herbs became potions and medications. It was discovered that elem---sub-atomic energy particles, a byproduct of terraforming---imparted powerful properties to the herbs. The Amazons were able to isolate the elem. When five of them bonded, the properties manifested. To create a mystique, the Amazons began calling themselves *Wizards*. To better relate to Dartmoor's predominantly male population---or to at least be perceived as relating---membership was extended to males, initially as salesmen. As the science of elem gathering and binding improved, more product was distributed. In addition to capsules, multiple-charge rods were developed, and infinitely-charged rings---saturated clusters of elem were found to be self-sustaining.

The other faction gaining power was the Third Time Church. Father William retained his principles, but he was just one man of dozens in the theological hierarchy. Churches were built in most settlements, the largest supporting numerous structures. The Church became as much an industry as a spiritual institution. Father William became disgruntled with the direction the Church was heading, so he left it. Without his moderation, the Church doctrine mutated grotesquely.

Everyone on Dartmoor wasn't just given a second chance, but a third. Who gave us this opportunity? God. Who, or what, is God? The creator. Who, or what, creates and re-creates? The planet: terraforming was still active. The Third Timers determined the planet itself to be their god. They called it Gaea, after the earth mother. It was, in essence, the same entity I worked with, but the Third Timers worshipped her, while I just thought of her as a powerful personification of the planet. The Third Timers weren't content with praising Gaea spiritually. They wanted to make physical contact with her, to make love to her. The Church became very creative in its methods to do so. Many of the Church practices consisted of expressing that love. The Church wasn't a significant threat at the moment, but its copious congregation of fanatics provided ample opportunity for it to become so in the future.

One of my greatest successes was helping create the Brotherhood of Giants. The Titans wished to be left alone, in peace. The same couldn't be said for their cousins. The Titans retained their homogeneity: 250 to 300 sims in height, porcelain features. The smallest Gent---what their cousins preferred to be called---was 250 sims tall, but some of them grew to two, or even three times that height. The Titans were a quaint anomaly. Some of the Gents were monsters. Gaea believed their collective had the potential for countering future powers. The Gents bickered more than made group decisions, but that *potential* persisted. It alone delayed the Wizards rise by more than a decade.

The other great re-creative power were the dragons, draks as they referred to themselves. They were less of a pack animal than the Gents, so it was more difficult to cluster them. The best I could do was encourage a *Draconian Census*. Every four years the draks would gather. No group plans were discussed but information was exchanged. Again, the appearance of unity was nearly as important as any actual action.

The years passed. More inmates entered Dartmoor. More mutations. As the population expanded, to nearly 10 million---the success of abandoning the undesirable, forever, increased sentencing substantially---human and mutant populations dispersed. Every prairie, mountain, desert, forest, mountain, swamp, and sea of Dartmoor became occupied. There were ten major city-states now, with Gulag still being the largest, with over 200,000 souls. There would have been more people in Gulag---and the other city-state---if so many hadn't lost their humanity. Ninety percent of those deposited on Dartmoor had been noticeably mutated, some more severely than others, many beyond recognition. Gaea determined order had to be established to blunt the clashing mutational ideologies. Chaos would reign as one kind of demon attempted to destroy another it deemed inferior. The extremes had to become isolated, pushed to the fringes of Dartmoor. Those with neutral morals and ideologies would remain in the center of the colony. Mutants with conflicting views were encouraged to move to opposite fringes. Gaea didn't create the mutations, but she was able to tamper with them. She wasn't able to choose which mutant received what mutation, but she could choose where someone, or thing, was re-created. She also was able to create a moral environment on the fringes that would attract individuals with like ideals.

One-hundred forty-one years after the creation of Dartmoor, DC 141, I received a communication from Gaea that I had been dreading. "Within a year the Wizards will initiate their domination."

"So, there is nothing we can do? We linger until the inevitable?"

"There are always opportunities to modify outcomes."

"So, you have a plan?"

"You are to finally leave Dartmoor."

"Can you transport me off this planet?"

"Indirectly. You will use the portable transport portal that followed you to the planet."

"I had forgotten about that. You have it?"

"In essence. I am the embodiment of the colony and the portal is in it. Its components were separated and scattered."

"So, you were aware of it for a hundred and thirty-six years, and kept it from me?"

"It wouldn't have served my purpose, or your own."

"That was for me to decide."

"The calculations indicated you would have been less content if you left Dartmoor a century ago. Even if they hadn't, the benefit to all outweighed the benefit to the individual."

"And the calculations now indicate its best---for all---that I now leave? Very gracious of the variables and parameters."

"Once all the pieces of the portal are collected. It is time those off-world become aware of what is happening here. Knowledge is power. If this happens, the probability that the Wizards will conquer the galaxy will be reduced."

"Reduced? So, no matter what I do we're doomed?"

"Predictions aren't absolute. If the Wizards fall it's likely they will not only be prevented from ruling the galaxy, but also Dartmoor. The greatest descent is from the highest perch."

"I perceive the location of the scattered pieces. Some of the demons who possess them will not easily relinquish them. If they only knew how truly valuable those jeweled orbs are. I'll immediately begin collecting them."

"You haven't been the one chosen to do so."

"But you said...."

"I said you will use the portal to leave Dartmoor. Once this other individual has collected the pieces and connects them you will pass through the portal."

"Wouldn't it be best if I did the commandeering? Is it wise for another to become involved? Is she also to become a conduit?"

"The man I have chosen to collect the spheres has abilities you do not possess. Do not be concerned, you will remain my sole high priestess. This man is perfectly balanced: 1/3 Min, 1/3 Fas, 1/3 Cor. He is immune to elemental manipulations."

"Where is he?"

"He has just arrived. He is currently in Polygulch Prairie, heading towards the Bluewoods. You may need to direct him a bit here and there if he strays too far from his path."

"There are things you are not revealing."

"Even a god is allowed to keep some things to herself. Experiments must be tested, sacrifices made."

"I don't have a place that is entirely my own, not with you sharing my mind."

"There are some parts of yourself that remain a sanctuary."

"I wish I would have known that a hundred years ago."

"I wished to leave the option open for probing. The necessity hasn't yet occurred."

"So, you have the key to my diary, but you haven't yet used it?"

"There is so little time remaining relative to the time that has passed."

"So, the end is truly near?"

"The isolated need their gods. The universe, doesn't."

I first met Hornet Polygulch as he and his three companions

were on the precipice of being obliterated by insects, specifically, ants. A naming process had evolved. The first person who meets a new arrival names them. Their surname is in reference to where they entered Dartmoor. These *ants*, like many things in the colony, had been mutated. They were the size of small dogs. One or two might be easily defended, but not a hundred. After saving them from being brutally ripped apart, I joined their party. They were adventurers, infants and toddlers who wished to make a quick buck by reclaiming lost treasures. Most of these *treasures* had relocated, into the hands of demons. Not being able to retain their humanity, they didn't wish others to. Over time the possessions of their victims accumulated. They often didn't amount to much, but occasionally something valuable was added to the collection. The longer someone lives on Dartmoor the stronger their desire to *settle down*. As a person matures, their tolerance for flux weakens, particularly when it manifests as battling monsters and adjusting to physical and emotional metamorphoses. The four individuals I had companioned myself with hadn't yet gotten to that stage in their life.

After they were safely on their way to the first piece of the portal, I left them, temporarily. I shared minimally with them. They hadn't yet been made aware that the Emerald Pearl was a component of an instrument of egress. I intended for us to reunite along the Sun Coast, after they had retrieved the two spheres in the Positive moral fringes, what the humans called *frontiers*.

The Sun Coast was likely the location of the Wizards first assault, so I intended to also do some reconnaissance. To circumvent aversion to contrary moralities, and expedite travel, the Wizards constructed subterranean transportation.

The majority of my predictions---the vast majority---were successful---but there was the occasional blunder. I was as much in the dark as anyone without parameters. I believe Hornet being perfectly balanced had something to do with it. His ever-evolving band of friends and supporters was more successful than I had given them credit. They had completely bypassed the Gold Coast, by riding draks. Who could have forecast such an event? By the time I had realized how far off my failed prediction was, they had already found four spheres and were in the process of collecting a fifth. The portal was divided into six pieces. If I didn't act soon Hornet might leave me behind.

Hornet had met a woman and married her. His wife---Dinga---had become pregnant. How was that possible? It was one of those things Gaea had kept to herself. If children could now be born that meant new potentials for Dartmoor---or Limbo, as the humans began to refer to the penal colony. Having eternal life, but being stuck in a small corner of the universe, was limbo, wasn't it? Hornet would want to be with his wife when she gave birth. Gaea assisting in accelerating the gestation.

Chapter 11

REUNION

They were startled to see me, they being Hornet and his current menagerie of companions. A major component of my encouragement of Gent relations was establishing a rapid transit system. Assisted by subtle behind-the-scenes maneuvering, transport platforms---similar to portals, but with a much less limited range---were developed. The energy shield enveloping the penal colony deflected all transmissions. Maybe, not all. Gaea assured me when the portable portal was reconstructed and activated I would be able to depart. Necessity dictated I tap into the

Brotherhood's transit.

"Lynn?" Hornet had grown remarkably since I last saw him. He was no longer an infant, and barely a toddler. He appeared to want to hug me, but was unsure of the proper etiquette? I weaved through his legs, confidently asserting my friendship. He was less confident in his response, stroking my back, from my neck to my tail. If he had tipped me on my side I would have allowed him to rub my belly. Our relationship had been short, but strong enough to have faith in him not doing me any harm.

"Where's your boyfriend?" That was Centaur Beetlewoods. He also petted me, rougher than I liked. Being over 100 kilos, little of that fat, it was difficult for him not to do something roughly. He also had become married since I last saw him. His mate was a lycan named Twig. Centaur had become a pseudo-changeling himself, after his wife had infected him during a courting ritual. Being more familiar with caressing wolves than cats, the ferocious nature of his contact was understandable.

"I don't kiss and tell." The person Centaur was referring to was the origin of my departure. A very handsome wildcat, who I choose to remain nameless, lured me away. I became giddy in my admiration for him. Being so focused on assisting Gaea this past century, she believed I needed a break, a vacation from my routine. Being so close to the arrival of certain events, I needed to be at my peak, fully rejuvenated, ready to take on the world. I hadn't been this carefree, living in the moment, since I was a child. It wasn't some great romance that was going to change my life forever. Cats weren't like that. They are hot and cold. After a couple of days of intense stimulation, it was over. The beast actually hissed at me when I didn't leave his territory quick enough after ending our relationship. Gaea insisted I take additional time off, alone, to complete the revitalization.

The other two members of Hornet's original party were missing. One had mutated into a terran---a burrowing hominid. He lived in the Copper Forest. The other had recently died---to the extent he was capable of.   At the brink of death an Octagonal Knight's soul is transported to the Octagonal Prism, before terra-reforming is able to encase it in another shell. Knights must remain pure, to never be re-created. Octagonal Knights are a small elite corps established many years ago in Gulag to defend the unchanged from mutant invasion. Their mission has changed over time, becoming *Proponents of Neutrality*, only butting in to stabilize balance.

Others present at Ursa Major, Lord Bruin's ice castle: Lord Bruin, a five-meter tall gent. Pulp, a much shorter gent, and companion to Hornet since he left the Copper Forest. A trog named General Paint, from the Platinum Mountains. And Sumac, an ogra, a human-ogre half-breed, miner by trade, inebriate by lifestyle, who agreed to lead Hornet and friends into the Dreadful Mountains to appropriate the fifth piece of the portal. Lord Bruin's servants, the minken, appeared intermittently. Mutations weren't limited to humans. The bipedal minks were more intelligent than their genetic ancestors, but still significantly less intelligent than---most---humans. They were not only beautiful---their pristine white coats were precious---in both value and loveliness. They were also dedicated workers. They did a magnificent job of maintaining the castle.

"Your child will be born within a week," I announced.

After a minute---or two---of stunned silence, Hornet said, "We need to return to Dinga." Hornet had looked so together a moment ago. Now, so frazzled.

"You're not even a little curious how Dinga was able to skip two months of gestation?" asked Centaur.

"This isn't the strangest thing that has happened since we've been marooned on Limbo. All I'm concerned about right now is Dinga's health and finding the shortest route back to her."

"Short of riding a drak I don't think we're going to reach her in time," said Twig.

"There is a way." I looked over my shoulder. "If Lord Bruin permits."

"Feel free. You may be short a couple of charges. I use it so infrequently, there isn't a need to stockpile."

"This may be of some use then." I placed a metal rod on the floor in front of Lord Bruin. Yes, I had the ability to not only conceal something, but to transport it. Something small. I had a few limitations. Lord Bruin picked up the rod and inserted it into the port provided at the portal's base. He hit the trigger. The rod's contents flowed into the transport.

"You amaze me," said Hornet.

"If I was mundane would you listen to me?"

"There isn't a gent in the Raspberry Mountains is there?" asked Centaur.

Pulp shook his head. "Fir lives the closest. He's in the Platinum Mountains. From there six to seven days to Berry City. We might make it."

"We're transporting to Mist's island. It's near the Gold Coast."

"We'll have to cross the Northern Sea," stated Hornet. "Is it possible to reach Dinga in time if we have to make a sea voyage?"

"Dinga isn't in the Raspberry Mountains. Her studies have taken her to the Gold Coast."

"She didn't go alone?"

"The Druids accompany her. Their appetite for knowledge is nearly as great as hers."

We portalled the next day. Hornet wished to do so immediately, but Pulp needed one more day to recover from the injury he received collecting the fifth sphere.

The minken had two favorite spots to sleep: in front of the four-face fireplace in the castle's great room, or on one of the unoccupied beds. Lord Bruin's castle had many rooms. Even with the plethora of guests he currently had, some of the beds remained unoccupied. I choose one on the third story, the highest level of the keep. The minken apparently didn't perceive me as a guest. They huddled around me like I was their queen. I appreciated their warmth and affection---but a couple of them snored. I was so accustomed to sleeping alone, the sounds of others disturbed me. I remained awake most of the night, my affection for them preventing me abandoning them.

Chapter 12

BIRTH

Pulp went first---a precaution. A stranger surprised a gent...once. The gent was transported to Mist's platform on the other side of Limbo, travelling 1800 kays instantaneously. Hornet, Centaur, Twig, General Paint, and I followed a couple of minutes later.

Mist was as tall as Lord Bruin. The only gent noticeably taller was Toe, the leader of the Brotherhood, more facilitator than director. Mist looked like a beach bum. He was bare-chested, and footed. He wore colorful shorts. His bronze epidermis was well-chiseled. He looked more athletic than strong. His muscles were toned, but not bulging. His demeanor was laid back. He lived in Ornu, the Neutral-Order Frontier. His orderliness manifested as a steadfast daily routine: sleeping in, eating, swimming, fishing, eating, shell collecting, more eating, then falling sleep listening to the rolling surf. The island he lived on was small---barely 100 hectares. It was primarily sand, with a few palm trees and grass at its crest, a meter higher than the sea. His home was modest. The wooden-framed structure was on stilts, to preserve it from water damage during one of those infrequent major storms that pummel the islands. It consisted of a single large room open on all sides. Shutters blocked the wind and rain. They were rarely used. The only other object on the island was a sailboat. It was a dinghy relative to Mist, a schooner to those of us of shorter stature. I preferred spending some time on the island---it was a tropical paradise---but Hornet was eager to see his wife. Relationships were wonderful, but sometimes inconvenienced others.

"We all here?" Mist scanned the odd assortment in front of him, processing, analyzing. "Good. We'll head down to the ship now. It won't take long to reach the mainland." He headed towards his boat. He appeared eager to get rid of us. The time he spent with us had to be made up somewhere. He couldn't skip lunch, that meant he had to spend less time collecting shells. Acquiring shells wasn't his true objective. Walking on the sand, looking into the water, was what he looked forward to. Like fishing, the process was more important than the product. Finding the perfect shell was a goal, but that didn't always happen. The walking and the looking, did. Mist saw more than shells when he looked into the liquid. Plants and animals also inhabited the sea.

The water was calm. Ripples were uncommon enough that when one was made, attention was drawn to it. It was sunny and warm, but not too warm. The breeze was just enough to alleviate any discomfort the artificial sun might deliver. Mist let us off on a sand bar. "Bye now. Enjoy your reunion with your wife, Hornet. Sometimes I get the urge to have one myself, but then I remember how unpredictable they are and flee back to my island as fast as I can."

"THERE ARE BENEFITS TO HAVING A WOMAN AS A COMPANION THAT COMPENSATE FOR THE CHAOS SHE BRINGS!" Hornet yelled back to Mist, who was already a hundred meters into the sea. "Now, where's Dinga?"

"She's in a camp on the Nupo border. It's still seven kays away."

76

"She isn't in a city? How does she plan to deliver the baby if there's no hospital?"

"The healers in Newport don't have a clue how to deliver a baby. And announcing its arrival to the world, wouldn't be wise, until..."

"Until?"

"That's still to be determined. Don't worry, women have been having babies for thousands of years off world. Some of the druids with her are healers. The best is her second in command."

"Pistachio is with her? If he can't help her no one can. Maybe not the best choice of words. I'm not going to feel good about this until I see her."

After a few minutes of walking, we were on the beach. Turning left, we followed the coastline. "We could go inland," I suggested. "There's a road there, but it's more scenic beside the water."

"Hornet?" Centaur was a newlywed, so he empathized with someone being away from a loved one.

"This beach looks flat and straight enough to make good time. I don't think I'm *that* desperate to see her, to deprive my friends of this view. She may not be as conciliatory."

"She doesn't know you're coming."

The reunion was overdramatic, if you ask me. I'm all for a bit of physical contact between two individuals every decade or so, but after a while all those hugs and kisses became overkill.

This was the first time I *saw* Dinga. I was aware of her through Gaea, but until you are in the presence of someone you can't say you truly know them. She was of medium height and build, except for the lower abdomen pooch common to pregnant women. Her black hair and green dress created an earthiness. The other druids were all men. They wore smocks, also green, but of different hues. Did the hues symbolized rank, specialization, or personal style? I didn't care enough for further contemplation. Life was simpler if you wore the same coat every day. The dress and smocks were inundated with pockets. Some appeared empty. Others had porcelain vials sticking out of them.

"Maybe Hornet and Dinga would like some private time. I believe we can make introductions later." Twig was the only person, other than the couple, that reveled in the shared emotion. The others appeared disturbed. There was much nervous foot tapping and many furtive glances. Dinga led Hornet to her tent.

Centaur made introductions. After the initial novelty of new companions wore off, the druids returned to their work. Some placed plant specimens on platters and examined them. Others wrote in journals. A third group crushed plants with a pestle and mortar, emptying the powders created into vials.

"It looks complex," Centaur commented, looking over shoulders and between smocks.

"More physical than mental," Pistachio replied. "It becomes routine after a while. New discoveries are rare. Our ultimate goal is to catalogue the elem potential of all flora on Limbo."

Trogs, characteristically, had a substantial disinterest in elem. Herbalism was mundane enough to pique General Paint's curiosity. "Is it wise to have so many elem in such close proximity?"

"Most of the plants don't have any elem. The few that do we place into vials immediately after crushing them. Five elem create a penta. If we ever have that many elem exposed at one time we are vigilant to separate them, by many meters. The Wizards have wasted so much time extracting elem from the environment when they could have kept them in their natural form."

As the discussion of the druids' work became more involved, more of our band joined in. Twig and Pulp wandered over to the tables. Gaea's perpetual prescience provided more knowledge than I wished to know.

"Are you able to find all four varieties of elem?" asked Pulp.

"Yes, but in dissimilar quantities. Blue and green, as one might expect, are prevalent in the tropics. The heat and breeze also creates an environment for red and yellow, but in smaller quantities. I believe every environment will produce all four elem if one just knows where to look. It took centuries to harness the power of the atom. Apparently, it takes as long to harness elem. Why hasn't anyone studied it before in as much in detail as we have the past couple of weeks?"

I wasn't completely oblivious to the conversation. "If Wizards provide all elemental needs, why reinvent the wheel? It may appear they provide a wonderful service for Limbo, but the true reason for their pental shops may be to discourage others to create their own."

"They are geniuses," stated General Paint.

"Geniuses with too much power," stated Centaur. "What would happen if they used that power, instead of hoarding it?"

"There is a reason I have returned to you when I did," I declared. "The Wizards will use their power to control Limbo. Preparations are being made as we speak."

"How long do we have to prepare?" asked General Paint.

"Less than a year."

"There's no hope, then." Twig was new to this type of intrigue, but she recognized the ramifications.

"It may be possible for us to produce enough of our own penta by then to counter them," Pistachio hypothesized. "It will delay our research, but if the Wizards prevail there won't be any more research. They won't just discourage competition, they'll squash it."

"So, our mission has changed," Centaur commented. "Finding that last sphere isn't as important as saving Limbo."

"But it is," I insisted. "It is time the galaxy is made aware of what is happening on Limbo. Anything we attempt may fail. A last resort may be to harness off world support."

"If we contact the authorities won't they just return us to Limbo?"

"Unlikely. I cannot say why. Freedom will not be a

consideration a year from now."

"No one knows, with certainty, what will happen in the future," stated Twig

"Lynn does. When we first met her she accurately predicted many things. She even foretold us reuniting on the Gold Coast."

"But you reunited with her before we got here."

"We're still here, together. There is one thing about that prediction that didn't come true. You said you would reunite with three of us. There is only Hornet and I."

"You haven't yet left the Gold Coast."

Hornet and Dinga joined us, appearing disheveled. "Did we miss anything?"

Before we could resume our retrieval of the last piece of the portal, Dinga had to give birth. We waited seven days. I understood the concept of a baby having to eventually leave its mother's womb. I just didn't think it was possible. How could something that large pass through an opening that small? It did, somehow, after much coaxing, and piercing exclamations. Creating a child and expelling it was more miraculous than producing penta or bringing someone back to life as a re-creation. It was truly the most wondrous thing that has happened on Limbo.

We had to wait three more days for Dinga to recover. She wasn't going with us, but Hornet wouldn't leave until he was certain his wife and child were well. We spent most of that time watching the baby. It ate and slept most of the time, with occasional outbursts of wanting to let the world know it existed. For some reason it was particularly attached to me. I was never one of those girls who wanted children so much that I played with dolls. But with this miniature human nuzzling my fur my maternal instincts came out. I suddenly wanted a child of my own. I asked Gaea if she could do this one thing for me. I hadn't asked her for anything before. She ignored me. I hated her for a moment. As my emotional cloud gradually dissipated I realized her lack of a response was rooted in compassion, not cruelty. Not saying anything kept certain doors open. I repented.

The little girl was named Hope. Was the name wishful thinking? Was regaining the ability to reproduce that momentous? Would the opportunity for change be wasted? Could we circumvent our grim future?

Chapter 13

PAINTED-WOMEN

The day before we intended to leave, a woman entered our camp. She had green skin, and hair, and wore a tight-fitting top and shorts---or so we thought, from a distance.

"SHE'S NAKED!" Hornet blurted. What had looked like clothing was natural, a patterned coloration. Which we discovered later in the day, when the temperature dropped, could be modified, her summer clothes becoming long pants and a sweater.

If there had been a few people who hadn't noticed her when she arrived, they definitely did after Hornet's announcement, Dinga the most blatantly. "I bear your child three days ago and you're already looking at naked women."

"I...."

"I what? I'm returning to my tent. I refuse to witness you flaunting your indiscretions."

"My indiscretions? She came up to me. Turning around, or fleeing, would have been rude." He followed his wife.

"Maybe her hormones will be less intense after a couple

more days," Centaur suggested. His wife gave him a disapproving look.

The colorful woman either chose to ignore what had just happened or hadn't paid any attention to it. She began her oration as soon as she was within distance to talk to us instead of shout. "My name is Ash. I'm a painted-woman. My sisters and I live on the Right Eye." The *Countenance* was the collective name of the three islands in the Northern Sea shaped like two eyes and a mouth. The Right Eye was the northernmost island. "The mongrels, who live in the interior of the island, were attacked two days ago."

"Forgive my callousness, but how does that involve us?" asked Centaur.

"We believe the mongrel attack is the first of many transgressions. We are in danger, as are the octos, who live off the northern coast. After we're exterminated, the transgressors will likely move on to other locations."

"Conjecture," stated General Paint. "Why would something wish to kill multiple species? And then repeat the process in a different location? If their intent is to invade the Right Eye, it's a strategic miscalculation to spread their forces too thin by moving to additional locations. How can they possibly maintain control of the island? If what you hypothesize is true, what is their goal? Are they wreaking havoc for their amusement, or are they attempting to control more than just the island?"

"It's beginning." I spoke softly, more to myself than for the benefit of others.

"What did they look like?" asked Centaur.

"They wore red armor. It glistened like fresh blood. They carried curved blades, one in each hand, also constructed of the blood-red metal. Their flesh, what little of it was exposed, looked like rotting meat."

"Zombies?" Twig questioned. "But why wear elaborate armor? If they are already dead does it matter if additional damage is dealt to them?"

"If Stick was here he would be able to answer your questions, in detail," spoke Pulp. "They are Death Knights. Half-and-halfs. Neither dead nor alive. Something went wrong when they were re-created, like the mongrels, but more extremely. Instead of being re-created into a new body, they were re-created into their corpses. Having such a thing happen would put anyone in a bad mood. Their one goal is to make others as miserable as they are. Ash, were the mongrels actually killed?"

The question startled the painted-woman. "They weren't. They were tortured, then propped up against trees and boulders, held in place by some invisible force. They weren't given any food or water. Are they going to die from thirst first or from their wounds? Does anyone know? Anyone?" The painted woman became hysterical. Pistachio medicated her to calm her down.

"Aren't Death Knights supposed to reside in the Negative Frontier?" asked General Paint. "The only time we've seen groups of demons leaving their moral homelands was underground."

"Ash, where did these Death Knights come from?" asked Centaur. "From what direction?"

"I didn't see their arrival personally. There was a mound of earth, at least as tall as I am, near the village. It looked new, like someone had just tilled, in preparation for planting a crop."

"They couldn't have tunneled all the way from the Negative Frontier, could they?" asked Twig.

"Not all the way from the Frontier, but maybe to the surface," said Pulp. "Remember those sub-arbol rails under the Sabre Desert and the Dreadful Mountains?"

"Wasn't the Lich involved with that?" General Paint questioned. "He was also one of these half-and-halfs."

I kept my mouth shut. The more I spoke the more likely I might give something away. Also, it was difficult to hear others while you spoke. Many of the things mentioned caught me by surprise. Could the half-and-halfs be involved with the Wizards?

And if they were, were they partners or pawns? My prediction of three of the original members of Hornet's party coming to the Gold Coast was about to be realized. If Death Knights were creating trouble where they didn't belong, it wouldn't be long before Octagonal Knights arrived to balance the disruption.

Hornet and Dinga emerged from their tent and joined us. "What did we miss?"

Chapter 14

STRATEGY, TACTICS AND LOGISTICS

"A suicide mission," Centaur declared.

"Possibly, if it was just us," Twig countered. "The painted-women will help. And the octos. How many premature re-creations will there be if we don't do something?"

"How many of us will be prematurely re-created if we do?"

"If we attack, let's plan the wake, now," stated General Paint. "I have fought more demons than the lot of you---combined. I know what we're up against. Trogs don't frighten, but we're realists. We're not powerful enough to prevail. Strategy, tactics and logistics can only carry us so far."

"We have elem," Hornet reminded them. "From the stores I have seen, as much as we need."

"It could determine our success," Pistachio agreed, "if we could properly implement it. If you shoot a bolt of lightning through a man who needs his disease cured, you'll kill him quicker than if you did nothing."

"So, to be effective we must study the Death Knights' weaknesses and develop a counter," said Dinga. "That's sounds like a job for the druids. As you polish your armor and practice your intimidating stances we'll construct your weapons and plan your attack."

The painted-woman's contribution to the campaign was to provide transportation. Almost anything could be used as a steed, as long as it was large enough. Ash's people employed gigantic water beetles. Sluggish on land, but extremely swift in the water. Beetles varied in shape. The water variety was elongated, making it possible to straddle. "Grip it tightly with your legs." Ash demonstrated on one of the three-meter long beetles. It began moving in the direction it faced. After releasing the pressure, the beast stopped. "Sometimes they become anxious to return to the water. If you fall they won't stop, they'll continue in the same direction until something distracts them or until they tire."

"How do we turn them?" asked Centaur. "I don't see any reins."

"Leg pressure. Pressure on both means forward. More pressure on one side will turn it the opposite direction. It seems contradictory, but if something strikes you on the left, don't you automatically want to go to the right?"

"I guess it's time to mount." It was easier for some than for others. With his long legs, Pulp was able to stretch a leg over and across his beetle. He looked like a clown on a toddler's bicycle. The unchanged had more difficulty, but through trial and error they were able to eventually make a successful leap and twist. General Paint had the most trouble. He couldn't quite leap up to the top of his beetle. He would almost make it then slide down the slick shell.

Pulp dismounted. "I'll give you a boost." He did more than that. He actually picked up the trog and set him on the creature. Pulp returned to his mount.

I hopped behind Hornet. If someone wasn't going to fall or

sink it was him. Being perfectly balanced---in attribute---would prevent him from being involved in any catastrophic event.

Ash began moving. We followed---except General Paint. "THIS DAMN THING IS TOO TALL!"

"Hold up." Ash turned her beetle around in a maneuver seemingly impossible for the lumbering insect. She returned to the beach.

Some of the riders were more talented in controlling their mounts than others. Centaur wasn't able to stop. "Try not to apply any pressure," Ash advised. "If that doesn't work, disrupt contact with your legs. Sometimes heavy legs feel like you're squeezing."

"It's this damn armor. It prevents bashes and slashes, but it weighs a ton." Centaur finally got his beetle to stop. He looked like he was having a gynecological exam.

"Maybe you just have fat legs," Hornet suggested.

"I would come back there to show just how fat my legs are, except I don't think I can turn this thing. I'm too afraid to attempt it. Instead of going right or left, the thing might dive."

"You may have to share a beetle." Ash had hoped the trog had placed pressure incorrectly, but it was more than that. His legs *were* too short. "Who weighs the least?"

"That would be me." Twig turned her beetle around, then turned it around again, and again. "I keep forgetting that right means left." After a few more mis-directions Twig arrived at the beach. She attempted to pull General Paint up, but he was too heavy. Not only that, the counterpull was strong enough to dismount her. "That's going to leave a bruise."

Pulp had to help again. He was the most skilled in riding. He didn't make any wrong turns, and was able to stop when he wished to, this time a couple of meters in front of the fallen. After Twig re-mounted, he placed General Paint behind her. "Hold tight."

"I don't believe that would be proper."

"Is it any more proper to fall into the water?"

"She's a married woman."

"You have my permission," said Centaur.

"So kind of you," said Twig. "Drop your hands a little lower." The trog blushed.

"That leaves an extra beetle," said Hornet.

"It will return to its kind after it realizes it was left behind." Ash rushed back to the front of the caravan.

"Then that provides an opportunity for me to tag along." Pistachio climbed aboard the abandoned beetle.

With baby in her arms Dinga walked up to him. "What are you doing? You're no warrior. You'll get yourself killed."

"Battles need a healer. I can also provide technical support. A person can't just shallow a random elixir and hope it benefits his cause."

"You've already briefed them on the tactics they should use."

"Use elixir A if event B occurs? Things never work out the way you plan. If modifications are required, who is better qualified?"

"How about the research and the accelerated collecting we've agreed to do?"

"You're the boss. I'm just your chief lackey."

"But I have a baby now to look after."

"The druids' dedication is unrivaled. If you point them in the right direction they'll get the job done."

Dinga's loss was our gain. I was still not pleased with our delay in finding the last piece of the transport portal, but at least we now had a better than even probability of not mutating. It was likely the Death Knights had some connection to the Wizards. Destroying any of the Wizards' tools before the final confrontation improved our odds for success.

It took us ten minutes to reach the Right Eye. Once the beetles came up to cruising speed they sped across the surface of the Northern Sea. We landed beside a very frantic group of octopi. They paced back and forth in the shallows.

Ash dismounted. We followed her lead. She spoke to the creatures by waving her arms wildly. Words, sentences, entire paragraphs were written in the air. The octopi responded in kind. There was a brief pause in their hyperactive activity, then they resumed it, but with a more enthusiastic flair. "It would help if I had a couple of more arms. Confusion sometimes arises when I use too many abbreviations. The octos have agreed to help us. They have a lot of nervous energy. One or more of their tentacles is moving at all times. They would have preferred to attack the Death Knights immediately, but commonsense prevailed. Without assistance they wouldn't have stood a chance."

The octos swam out to sea, then submerged.

"You sure they aren't running away?" asked Centaur.

"They are preparing," Ash replied. A moment later the octos returned with seven of their arms holding some type of weapon or shield, their eighth arm remaining free for very succinct communication. "A ship sunk off the coast of the Right Eye many years ago. Do you approve of the octos method of recycling?" The octos paused a moment for the twelve of them to muster, then they headed towards the interior of the island. "They don't move well on land, so they're getting a head start. They'll appreciate you reaching the Death Knights the time they arrive." One might think the octos would push themselves along on their arms, but they moved like slugs. Their lower abdomen was somehow able to self-propel itself. Their single eye in the center of their bulbous heads diligently peered forward.

"Will the Death Knights still be there when the octos arrive?" asked Hornet.

"Octos are slow, but persistent. They won't stop, day or night, until they reach their destination. The surviving painted-women are in a cove on the eastern end of the island. We'll remount the beetles and ride around to them. It will be faster and safer." Ash's coloration now made her appear like she was wearing a bikini.

The cove must have been the natural habitat for the water beetles because it was full of them. There were 30 or 40. After we dismounted on the sandy beach at the crook of the cove, our mounts immediately left to play with their kind.

A narrow, sandy path cut through the sea grass, towards a cluster of palm huts. Seven of the painted-women greeted us. Their colorations looked like armor. I looked back at Ash. She was now similarly attired.

"We knew Ash would find someone to aid us. She is the most gregarious of us." The oldest of the women spoke. People did age on Limbo, but more slowly than they did off world. When someone was re-created their new form had a more youthful appearance, looking around eight, if they were at least that old when they died. Children were never sentenced to Dartmoor. Five was the minimum age, and no one was sentenced that young unless they were an extreme case. I've pondered how a child would look when he or she was re-created. Would they remain a child or suddenly become a young adult?

"I am sworn to protect the virtuous from the depraved," stated General Paint.

"I'm not certain we are that deserving. We just want to be left in peace."

"I endorse your attire." Only a military man would think armor on a woman was fetching.

"It doesn't provide any protection, but it does put us in the proper mood. The only weakness we have discovered so far in our adversaries is they don't function as well under a full sun. It must roast them in their metal coffins. The flesh underneath is already in pretty bad shape. Cooking might tenderize it too much. They recover once the sun dims, but for an hour or so in the middle of the day they aren't at full strength."

"Trogs aren't accustomed to the sun shining down on their armor either. On a particularly warm day it feels like I'm cooking myself for dinner." When had General Paint become such a conversationalist? If I wanted to match him up with someone after the war all I had to do was randomly choose a woman and cover her in armor.

"It isn't midday yet," said Centaur, "but there's no way the octos are going to reach the Death Knights today, not during the daylight hours. Can one of your painted-women contact the octos and have them attack about an hour before noon tomorrow?" Seconds later one of the women was off. She appeared to be wearing running shorts and a tee-shirt.

With so many painted-women dead or missing there were plenty of beds available in the cove community. How many women had the Death Knights already killed? And that had to be just a fraction of the number of mongrels that were killed.

We discussed strategy around the evening campfire. Under different circumstances the painted-women may have changed their appearance into something warmer, and cozier, but needing to retain their mood they retained their armor. "Our primary duty will be reconnaissance," spoke the oldest painted-woman. "Whatever firepower we would add would be minimal. We know this island much better than the Death Knights do."

"The octos will attack the Death Knights head on," stated General Paint. "They are poorly protected, but have many offensive options. I will protect you as you're firing a barrage of arrows."

"Don't apply the cold salve to the arrows until the last moment," Pistachio warned. "The longer it's on them the more likely it will come off. Normal arrows probably won't penetrate that armor. Remember, intense cold will burn as severely as intense heat. If any of that salve is rubbed off on you, wipe it away immediately."

"How about something defensive?" Twig suggested. "The best defense for a wolf is to run away, but I don't think that will be very effective if we wish to defeat the Death Knights."

It was time for my input. "If the Death Knights can't reach you they can't hurt you. I predict a high probability they don't have a ranged attack. For the arrows to be effective you must have the opportunity to use them. You won't be able to shoot an arrow accurately if you're defending yourself."

"Maybe we could soften the ground?" Hornet suggested. "Turn it to mud with one of Pistachio's elixirs."

Centaur replied, "That will slow them down, but it won't prevent them from reaching us."

"How about some form of barrier?" Ash suggested.

"Barriers work both ways," Pistachio responded. "If the Death Knights can't penetrate the barrier, we can't either. If our goal is to make a defensive stance that would work, but I thought we wished to destroy them."

"We need something more isolated then," said the eldest painted-woman.

"We are limited in the harm we can enact, because of them not being completely alive," said Pulp. "The only thing tangible we can harm is their armor. That's where the cold arrows come in. Red may indicate red elem. If it is countered with cold, it should weaken their armor enough to allow penetration."

"I THINK I GOT IT!" Ash squealed. Images of lightening flashed across her body that had become the evening sky. "Without beetles we move very slowly through the water. We are hobbled. What if we take away their beetles? If their armor can't move, they can't either. Is there some way we can restrain it?"

"If their armor is fused with red elem, won't the ropes and nets just burn away?" asked Centaur.

"Would it do any harm to air?" asked Pistachio.

"It would make the air warmer," Pulp answered. "Condensation may occur, possibly creating fog. We might be able to use air to push them back, but won't that also affect our missile attack?"

"We could create openings for our arrows. If air is concentrated enough, it can be shaped. It doesn't have to be randomly thrown about. If we can mold this concentrated air into chains, we'll be able to bind their armor to the ground. As the chains become more concentrated they will become both stronger and thinner. The thinner they become, the less likely they'll be deflected."

"Do you have enough experience to weave the air like that?" I asked. "Only the most gifted Wizards can. Using penta at that level becomes more of an art than a science."

"That's something else you may want to work on, Pistachio," said General Paint. "If the elixirs are to be effective, those using them will have to be able to hit their targets."

"Druids aren't a military order."

"Then you better find someone you can work with who doesn't mind fighting."

"Are trogs up for something different?"

"Trogs are very ordered. If they haven't done something for decades they probably won't care to do it. If they have only turned right, they would be hard pressed to turn left, even if it might save their life. Permit us to fight with our axes and hammers. Using that bow tomorrow will likely scar me for life."

"Who'll be more receptive to using penta?"

"Arbols might," Pulp suggested. "They'll do anything if it entertains them."

"I suggest, after we finish this business here, the druids move their operations, south."

"How about you, Lynn?" asked Centaur. "You appear to know everything. How accurately can you direct penta?"

"Very accurately, if I was permitted to do so. My gift of predicting the future prevents me from participating in the disagreements of others."

"You can't be on the fence about this." Ash's body was covered in a kaleidoscope of conflicting symbols. "Two-thirds of my sisters were killed. I understand there are always two sides to every issue, but...."

"Lack of involvement isn't synonymous with approval of the

status quo. I'm not permitted to become involved."

"I could try," said Hornet.

"Having Gaea's Grace will probably deactivate any penta passing through you."

"I'm the logical choice," said Pistachio. "I may not be the most proficient weaver, but I appear to have the only loom."

Chapter 15

SCRIMMAGE

We began moving towards the Death Knights after breakfast. We didn't intend to attack until the sun was at its brightest, but there could be delays. Predicting a specific unexpected event was problematic, but for there to be one, it was nearly guaranteed. The painted-women completed numerous reconnaissance missions. Every ten minutes we received a fresh report. "The Death Knights are preparing to withdraw. All structures have been demolished. All mongrels, killed. They'll attack the cove next. They won't be satisfied until every re-creation becomes extinct except their own."

"Our plans have changed," stated Centaur. "If we wait until the sun is at its brightest the octos won't have enough time to make it to their new destination. Inform them they must attack immediately after the Death Knights begin to move."

The painted-women left.

We moved closer to the ruins of the mongrel village. When the octos engaged the Death Knights we intended to be in a position to give immediate support with our ranged attack. That time could come any minute.

On the perimeter of the village we began seeing bodies. They were grotesquely mutated. Someone who had never seen a mongrel before may have believed this disfigurement occurred while they were being killed. I knew better. The mongrels and Death Knights were connected---some may say related. Both were created from re-creations gone wrong. There was enormous variability in the mutations. What the mongrels had in common with one another were the number of mutations and their variety. Occasionally someone---or thing---was re-created as a combination of two creatures, such as a lion and an eagle. A griffon was a beautiful creature, having the best attributes of both animals. Mongrels didn't have *any* attractive attributes. The *worst of the worst* is what they were sometimes called. The most extreme had dozens of appendages: hoofs and tails, arms and beaks. Attached in places that made movement difficult. Did the Death Knights choose to eliminate the mongrels first because they determined no one would miss them? Was it a dry run? A costumed rehearsal? Or could their obliteration have been done as a---perceived---favor. To some extent they must sympathize with them.

The time had come. The Death Knights left the mongrel village and began heading towards the cove. The octos went into action. They didn't have much hope in being victorious on their own, but they were able to delay them enough for us to begin our attack. The dozens of swords and axes did no damage to the armor, but occasionally they met decaying flesh. The new wounds were an inconvenience, but not devastating. Poking out an eye decreased accuracy, but they were still able to perceive their surroundings. The first octo went down after making the fatal assumption that a Death Knight with such affliction couldn't fight back. The Death Knight's armor wasn't just defensive. When a weapon made contact with it, it became heated. After extended contact, the weapon would become so hot the octo holding it would have to discard it---usually after the arm became so badly burned it wasn't able to hold a replacement weapon. The octos had a special defense of their own. They discharged oil from their abdomens that made the ground slick. The partially dead weren't particularly graceful to begin with. They became less so on the slick surface.

After the Death Knights became fully engaged, Hornet, Centaur, Dinga, Pulp, and General Paint began shooting cold tipped arrows into them. There was a sizzle as the arrows made contact with their armor. Death Knights didn't feel pain, but it still must have been disconcerting. The holes the arrows created began to enlarge. A purplish rind formed around the wounds, like they were infected.

The octos were no longer the Death Knights primary threat. They clumsily charged us. One of them slipped. It fell into another. The octos struck often and substantially as the Death Knights awkwardly picked themselves back up.

Pistachio swallowed two of the vials he stockpiled in his frock's plethora of pockets. It wasn't wise to mix elixirs, even if they contained the same penta. There was a possibility that having two penta in such close proximity might scramble their bonds. There were numerous reconfiguration possibilities, some of them quite deadly. Pistachio was concerned the power generated by one elixir might not be enough to restrain all 13 Death Knights, so he tempted fate. His face became bloated. His eyes appeared like they might pop out of their sockets. He thrust his hands in front of him. They danced in an intricate pattern. He looked like a mime sewing. He snapped his arms. Energy rushed out of him. Air began to attach itself to it, like it was iron shavings and the energy, a magnet. As the last drop of energy fled from his body Pistachio fell backwards. I rushed to his aid. He was still alive, but unconscious.

Air continued to enter the energy beam. A moment later the energy transformed, from being a collector into modifying itself. From its steadfast initiation, the beam crawled closer to the Death Knights, stretching, like a rubber band. It wound around them like a constrictor snake. After all were ensnared, its terminus also became resolutely immobile, held in place by invisible stakes. The Death Knights weren't completely immobile, but they were slowed, substantially.

Arrows continued to be launched. The holes in the blood metal became more numerous and larger. The surviving octos became more successful. With octos becoming more of a threat, the Death Knights oscillated between attacking them and heading towards us. One of the pieces of blood metal had been ruptured so many times it fell from the Death Knight it protected. The octos concentrated on it. Unlike trolls, the half-and-halfs couldn't regenerate, but their residual flesh could re-cluster. A second, and then a third Death Knight lost its protection. Losing its tension, the air cords could no longer restrain the corralled Knights. Instead of assaulting us they turned, then fled, towards the mound of earth. Their brains were partially dead, but not entirely.

"WE NEED TO FINISH THEM OFF BEFORE THEY ESCAPE!" shouted General Paint. "If they are allowed to heal and repair all we have accomplished here is a delay."

We rushed towards the mound of earth. Fighting in close quarters, our effectiveness with bows would be greatly reduced, but we had no other option. The octos were ahead of us, but they traveled so slowly it was likely we would pass them before they reached the mound. We did.

With the octos no longer blocking our view, a tunnel appeared at the base of the mound. It was tall enough for Pulp to enter without hitting his head. It angled down steeply, dropping one meter for every three forward.

If we had any possibility of catching the Death Knights we had to do so now, before they lost themselves in the catacombs of the underworld. General Paint led. Trog senses were finely tuned to deviations in strata, and vibrations, naturally produced, or synthetic. Centaur was next, with Twig, Hornet, Pistachio, and Pulp following. Cats weren't particularly fond of dirty holes. All that washing afterwards didn't balance the curse of curiosity. Not wanting to lose my companions, and the means of escaping this prison, I padded after them, being careful not to rub my coat against the dirt walls.

The Death Knights were very easy to track---at the moment. There was just one tunnel. After a few initial crooks it straightened out. Sounds echoed, limited egress causing them to swirl instead of flow. We heard movement ahead. It was too dark to determine the distance. It was as likely to be a hundred meters away as ten, or a thousand. Fighting in the middle of the day hadn't required torches or lanterns.

"Hold up." Pistachio opened a vial and drank it. He touched each of us. Whatever article of clothing he made contact with, be it a shirt or a piece of armor, began to glow.

Pulp smiled. "There goes us being able to surprise them."

General Paint resumed the chase. We hit bedrock. The tunnel continued to look manmade. Nature was more concerned with aesthetics than uniformity. We heard shouting ahead---human voices.

"Allies or foes?" Hornet questioned.

"Are you suggesting something living allying itself with half-and-halfs?" General Paint enquired.

Sounds of conflict. It took five minutes to add our arrows to the skirmish. Pulp and Hornet, being the most gifted with a bow, stood in front of us, releasing arrows as quickly as they reloaded.

The two Death Knight closest to us---those in back relative to their formation---were caught completely unaware, so focused were they on first escaping, then countering their new threat. Being blocked by their associates, their options were limited. They charged us. Bows were ineffective close range. We were in trouble. A gush of air swooshed past us. It concentrated in front of Pulp and Hornet, forming a wall. We could still see the Death Knights coming, but the view was distorted. They attempted to tear their way through the air barrier. Their blood metal blades ricocheted back at them, creating further damage to themselves and their armor. Not having the sense to recognize the futility, they continued to strike at the barrier. More of their armor and pseudo-flesh was damaged. They began to get frustrated. The attack on the barrier, and consequently on themselves, intensified. They didn't stop until there wasn't enough left of them to raise their swords.

"They definitely need an anger management course," Centaur commented.

"It's amazing what a bit of concentrated air will do," said Pulp.

"I could have sealed the tunnel with rock," Pistachio explained, "but I thought you might want to get past this point eventually."

It was difficult for my companions to just stand there and watch as an unknown ally fought our foe. There were still enough Death Knights standing to block our view. Then we saw a glint, light reflecting off a polished surface. Then another Death Knight fell, revealing an entire metal plate. It was an Octagonal Knight, and not just one of them. It was difficult to distinguish details through the translucent shield.

Hornet verbalized what Centaur and I were thinking. "Is that Stick?"

The elem-infused platinum swords didn't just damage the Death Knights, they annihilated them. The last two to be destroyed where the ones crawling in front of us, on what remained of their tattered flesh and broken bones. They continued to strike at the air shield, their hands no more than nubs. One of the Octagonal Knights thrust his sword through a sternum. He skewered the body then twisted. The Death Knight disintegrated into ashes. The Octagonal Knight withdrew his sword. It retained its gleam, showing no signs of making contact. It was free of any stain or residue. A pinpoint of red light remained within the half-and-half shell. A moment later it vanished. The Octagonal Knight next to him performed the same maneuver with the remaining Death Knight, its light also going out after a few seconds.

An Octagonal Knights looked through the air barrier at us, then smiled through his helmet. It was Stick.

"Can we dismiss the shield now?" asked Hornet.

"We can, but it will take another elixir to do so," Pistachio replied. "I prefer to allow the shield to expire on its own. It shouldn't be too much longer."

Hornet pointed at the barrier, then made a hopeless gesture. Five minutes later the murkiness of the barrier lessened. Slowly, the air became less dense. It took another minute for it to completely disappear.

Chapter 16

TRAINS

Centaur placed his hand on Stick's shoulder. More symbolic than comforting, the platinum armor preventing not only lacerations. "So good of you to finally catch up to us. You missed out on fighting another couple of troupes of trolls. How were you able to find us?"

"We didn't. We found *them*. We've been following them since I was revived in the Octagonal Prism. There's a tunnel below us that looks like that one in that abandoned city."

"If they enter Trogdom it will be the last thing they'll ever do, I promise you," stated General Paint.

"*Enter*, not yet," spoke one of the other three Octagonal

Knights. "But they appear to have at least breached the Platinum Mountains."

"Likely the cause of the immoral vein being breached," Stick added. While visiting Trogdom, it was believed the trogs were behaving erratically. *Blood lust* was inconsistently rampant. Being Positive and Orderly, such altering of morals was unlikely to occur naturally or be indigenous.

Stick made introductions. "This is Meadow. On his right is Tornado. On his left, Sting."

"I'm not going to be able to keep you four straight," Twig voiced. "You all look alike to me."

"Each of the Octagonal Knights has a number designation," Sting enlightened. "I believe at one time those were the only names members of our order went by. Our predecessors wished to appear mysterious. I believe our actions alone are strong enough to intimidate anyone who needs to be intimidated. You see those three marks on my breast plate across from the infinite eight? I'm the Third Knight." The other Knights were also examined. Meadow had four slash marks. Tornado, six. Stick, two.

"Does the number represent a hierarchy?" asked General Paint. "Are you the third highest ranking Knight?"

"More like serial numbers. We retain our designation until we choose to leave the order. Octagonal Knights make group decisions."

"Isn't that inefficient?"

"Those of us who were chosen for the profession are of similar mindset. Disagreements arise, but they are few, and are promptly resolved, or omitted. All eight Octagonals must agree before a policy can be modified."

"When did you first begin to track the Death Knights?" asked Centaur. "Did you just go down into a hole and begin looking for them?"

"The Death Knights became careless," Tornado answered. "The Octagonal Prism has morality radar. Within a certain radius we can sense aberrations in morals, those entities who are extremely Negative, Positive, Chaotic, or Ordered. Occasionally, intermittent blips appear. We believed them to be just irregularities in instrumentation---a person can't just suddenly appear, then disappear. Years later someone had an epiphany. Morality is scanned on a horizontal plane. It was possible for something--- morally extreme---to fly *over* Gulag unnoticed. Or burrow *below*."

"That's when we discovered the tunnels," said Meadow.

"And confirmed the existence of moral extremes using a portable device," added Sting. "We eventually built an improved morality radar that scanned in *all* directions."

"The dots were dark blue," stated Tornado. "Dark designates Negativity. Light, Positivity. Blue, Order. Red, Chaos. When only Neutrals are present nothing shows up at all."

"So, what you scanned were not the Death Knights?" Pulp conjectured. "They weren't Chaotically Negative?"

"They weren't Death Knights, but anything with Negative morals that clandestinely rambles beneath the Octagonal Prism we must take seriously," said Meadow.

"So, you just dug a hole beneath the Octagonal Prism to enhance your investigation?" asked Twig.

"We didn't have to," said Tornado. "There was access from Gulag already."

"It was beneath one of the Wizards' penta shops," added Meadow.

"We had discovered something similar in Jasper," said Centaur.

Tornado continued. "After dropping 50 meters, we arrived at a narrow gallery. Extending in both directions were a pair of metal rails."

"Train tracks?" asked Hornet.

"Apparently. We followed them in the direction of the moral anomaly. Five-hundred or so meters later we found a train. It didn't look that exotic. What you would expect a mining operation to have used before automated processing became prevalent. Each compartment was three meters long. There were ten of them. Half were full of rubble---primarily stone, varying in size from ten sims to a meter. At the far end of the train was a passenger car. There were three benches. The furthest one faced outward. The two closest faced each other. There was a single lever beside the far seat. We wished to experiment with it, but the risk of those operating the train becoming aware of us was too great---we had additional reconnaissance to do. Perpendicular to the train was another gallery. It appeared to be of a newer construction than the one the train was in. The moral compass pointed in that direction, as did a source of illumination. We distinguished our own light source and moved stealthily closer to the other. Hobs hauled rubble from the far wall. One of them approached. Unless we wished to confront all of them we had to back away. Before we did so we saw something that shocked us as potently as the appearance of hobs: a flash of light, then energy discharging from the hands of a human. It coated the far wall. As it dissipated, the wall in front of him crumbled."

"Wasn't that wasteful, using elem to bore a tunnel?" asked Pulp.

"We thought so too," said Sting. "Searching the library in the prism, we located a report mentioning people being able to store excess elemental energy in their bodies for short periods of time. The energy released had been minor. If the full brunt of the penta had hit that wall the entire tunnel may have collapsed."

"So, a single penta might be rationed into a dozen charges if the person manipulating it was gifted enough in its use?"

"Precisely."

"What would it be like for someone to retain that much energy? I'm noxious after releasing a single burst."

"Did you remain hidden?" General Paint interrogated. "You didn't attempt to capture the hob, or kill it?"

Tornado answered. "It turned around before we had to

make that decision. You're probably right about the consequences of an encounter. If the hob was discovered missing, it was unlikely we would be able return to the tracks without an armed escort. We needed to discover a few more things before we countered the Wizards, and their servants."

"When did the Death Knights come into the picture?" asked Hornet.

"Many years later. We allowed the Wizards to continue building their tracks. The inequitable exchange of knowledge was an invaluable advantage."

"Did you know about these tracks, Stick?" Centaur questioned. "You never mentioned them when we were beneath the Sabre Desert. This must be the transportation system the Lich spoke of."

"I didn't learn of them until my second revival a week ago. The urgency of returning to you---the first time---prevented an extensive dialogue."

"Once we became aware of the Death Knights we had to force the issue," said Meadow. "Thirteen blood drops appeared beneath the city---briefly. Gulag was a signpost, not a destination. The dots sometimes varied in size. We hadn't designed that into the system. We came to the conclusion that there was a relationship between the size of the dots and the magnitude, the intensity, of the moral anomalies. Those dark red dots were gigantic. Something major had arrived from Chaneg."

"So, we gathered all the Octagonal Knights present," Tornado continued. "Stick had just been revived. We convinced him that following the Death Knights, and possibly countering them, was more crucial to the survival of humanity than reuniting with you. After briefing him on the situation, we dropped down to the tunnels and confiscated one of their trains."

"So, the Wizards are probably aware of you now?" Pulp commented.

"Likely," said Sting. "There weren't any witnesses when we

confiscated the train, but a train doesn't just wander off by itself. An investigation will be made. After they discover one of their own didn't go for a joyride, they'll assume the worse."

"There's something that has been bothering me," said Hornet. "How were you able to get past that Wizard that managed that penta shop?"

"There were times the Wizard wasn't in his shop. We chose one of those. Stealth, no matter how well executed, doesn't guarantee anonymity. We determined the rewards outweighed the risks. After discovering the train tunnels, we bore our own access."

"That must have also had its risks," Twig commented.

"Not as risky as going through the penta shop every time we chose to do a little snooping. The tunnels occasionally passed through a natural cavern. We chose one of them to become our insertion. We had to dig further, but in exchange for mitigating potential undesirable interactions."

"What are we going to do now?" asked Pistachio. "We may not have the luxury of preparing for war at a leisurely pace."

"It may not come to that," said Meadow. "There will certainly be animosity between Wizards and Octagonal Knights now, but I don't think a physical confrontation is eminent." We shared with the Knights what we could without mentioning collecting pieces of the portal. "I stand corrected."

"We must return to the Octagonal Prism immediately," said Sting. "Our preparation is three-fold: designing a battle plan, protecting the Prism, and notifying the remaining Knights."

"Our part in this is to continue to gather allies," said Centaur. "The Sumopotts have the largest, best-trained fighting force. We hired two of their battalions to assist us in the Twin Hills. What might their entire army be capable of?"

"Mercenaries might be useful in a pinch, for a specific battle," stated General Paint, "but we can't rely on their loyalty for a sustained war. We must also procure funds if we wish to hire them."

"Who else has an army that well-trained?"

"Trogs can hold our own in any brawl."

"Can you convince your king?"

"Those moral fumes have wounded my kind. They'll be itching for a fight. My race has never been too fond of elem. Wizards are the epitome of it. We wouldn't mind proving heart and brawn can overcome their brand of trickery."

"The odds of success improve, significantly, with the Sumopotts assisting you," I stated.

"What are the odds without the Sumopotts?" asked Centaur.

"You wouldn't want to know. A supplemental parameter is included with their exclusion. Unemployed mercenaries will look for work."

"So, if we don't hire them, the Wizards might? So, we're going to have to come up with the money somehow? It's going to be a long walk to the Mercenary Hills."

"Not if you take the train," Sting suggested.

The Knight vs. Knight battle occurred relatively close to the tracks. A couple of minutes of walking brought us to a pair of parallel tracks within an infinite gallery. "That way to Gulag," Meadow informed us. "The other to Jasper."

"Think of the time we would have saved if we used a train to travel to the Sabre Desert," Pulp proposed.

"But think of what we would have missed," Hornet countered. "We would never have met Jasmine or Crystal. Sometimes the journey is as significant as the destination."

General Paint looked extremely agitated. He was able to contain his anger, but just barely. His brow furled. His body shook. If the immoral influence hadn't dissipated, the blood rage would have consumed him. Through clenched teeth he uttered, "How dare they. When I return to Trogdom there will be a reckoning."

"Which would assist our foes," said Centaur. "*Death* and

Disorder would reign if trogs engage in a holy war."

"What's wrong?" Hornet asked the trog.

"This tunnel leads to the Platinum Mountains." He was referring to the passage in the direction he was facing.

"I thought it went to Gulag."

"Apparently in a roundabout manner," Sting suggested.

Hornet attempted to console the trog. "Maybe it just goes to Kenwood."

After General Paint had calmed down---a bit---Centaur said, "It surprises me, a little, the Wizards being involved. I thought they were as Neutral as Octagonal Knights."

"There are two ways of looking at Neutrality," Tornado explained. "The absence of Negativity, Positivity, Order, and Chaos---or a balance. If moral extremes run rampant, but balance, Neutrality is still achieved."

"And if the extremes cancel each other out, eliminating each other, all the better for the Wizards."

"Exactly."

The Octagonal Knights, including Stick, boarded the train heading to Kenwood.

"Aren't you coming with us?" asked Centaur.

"When I joined the Order, I made a vow to protect by becoming a proponent of Neutrality. I can do so more efficiently by assisting the other Knights." We wished him well.

Before the Knights left us, they showed us how to operate the controller. It was quite simple, actually. If a hob was required to operate it, it had better be. The single lever controlled movement, direction, and magnitude. A neutral position stopped the train. Forward or back moved the train in that direction, the distance proportional to the velocity.

"HOLD UP!" General Paint barked as the Octagonal Knights' train was pulling away. "I need to head to Trogdom---now. You shouldn't have any trouble in the Northern Spine. There are only Neutrals there." General Paint climbed out of our train, into the other. "You don't mind a traveling companion for couple of hundred kays, do you?"

"CAREFUL YOU DON'T START THAT HOLY WAR!" Centaur yelled at him as the Octagonal Knights' train began moving away from us slowly.

"TROGS DON'T START WARS. WE END THEM!" General Paint shouted back at him. Once the train merged onto the single track it began to accelerate. Whatever powered the vehicle's movement must have also powered its lights. It took many minutes for the diminishing illumination to completely disappear.

Depression set in. Our two greatest warriors had abandoned us. "I believe General Paint overlooked us having to travel to the Northern Spine first," said Centaur. "You don't think there will be anything dangerous in the Underworld, do you?"

"The train will frighten off most of the things that may cause us trouble," said Pulp. "I don't believe anything will attack us while we're moving. What would you do if something charged you at 100 kays per hour with its bright eyes shining on you?"

"How long will it take us?" asked Hornet.

"That's to be determined," Pistachio answered. "But quicker than walking---assuming there's access to the Northern Spine. If not, our next stop is Jasper. If that happens we would have been almost as well off climbing back up to the surface."

"Then let's hope there is."

Centaur looked at his map. "Assuming the route to Jasper doesn't deviate we're still going to have to travel a couple of hundred kays, by foot, to reach the Mercenary Hills."

"That's better than four-hundred."

Chapter 17

FACES AND ARMS AND LEGS

Pistachio having---by far---the most experience with elem was chosen to operate the train. It was much smaller than the one the Octagonal Knights left on. It had just two cars: the controller, and a passenger wagon. We put our packs in the back car and sat together in the front. Our comfort of spreading out between the two compartments outweighing our concern that the cars might separate.

As Pistachio pushed a lever forward, the train began to move slowly in that direction. The dual headlights provided ample illumination. Once the train merged onto a single track, Pistachio progressively lowered the lever. The train sped up. By the time the lever was horizontal the train was going as fast as a horse gallops.

"What's the train's power source?" asked Hornet. "It's too quiet for a combustion engine. Fusion power? Batteries?"

"Fusion power on this backwoods planet?" questioned Twig. "Possibly batteries, but something has to charge the batteries."

"Elem," Pistachio declared. "There's a gage in front of me. The arrow is in the middle."

"So, the batteries have lost about half their charge."

"How long until they are totally drained?" asked Centaur.

"Unless those Death Knights had elem with them I would guess at least as long as it took to drain them."

"Which means what? Enough left to reach the Dreadful Mountains? Gulag?"

"Assuming the Death Knights didn't recharge in route."

"So, we might suddenly stop moving, hundreds of kays from the surface? Great."

"Less than one if we wish to dig our own tunnel," Hornet remarked.

"Is it possible for us to recharge the batteries?" asked Twig. "Could we inject elem into them?"

"It's probably not a good idea," Pistachio replied. "I don't know how they operate. If we randomly discharge a penta we might overload the battery. It could explode."

"We definitely don't want that to happen." Pulp smiled.

Pistachio began searching below his seat. He pulled out a metal cylinder. It looked similar to a pental rod, but was shorter, and wider. "I believe this is our spare fuel." Pistachio continued to look around. He located an indentation the same shape as the cylinder. "And is inserted here."

"Should we top off the batteries?" suggested Hornet.

"I wouldn't recommend it. Batteries recharge better after they are completely drained."

"Are we that worried about efficiency?" asked Centaur.

"I'm also concerned about being able to regulate how much energy we add. The Wizards are known to package penta in a very user-friendly manner. The rod's energy will likely be completely discharged. That excess energy has to go somewhere."

"Maybe we should wait until the batteries get a little lower."

"Good decision," stated Twig.

A train station appeared about where we wished it to be. When I speak of a train station, I mean a parallel set of tracks, and an alcove beside it, providing room for unloading. After unloading our gear, we began the climb back up to the surface. The batteries were still about 40% full when we stopped. All that time wasted worrying, for nothing.

Centaur led. Twig followed, as SCOUT'S SECOND. Hornet was ART. Pistachio and I were next, trying to stay out of the way.

Pulp was PROC. We needed someone strong to guard our rear. With us being limited on *he-men*, our choice was restricted--- between Centaur and Pulp. If Pulp led, we wouldn't have been able to see past him. Twig held our lantern. With General Paint no longer in our party, my nocturnal vision would be required to lead us out. I preferred not to lead. It was less stressful making *suggestions*. I was also limited in how I could help. Gaea had to remain neutral. I had more flexibility, but if I assisted my companions too much Gaea would be compelled to assist our enemies. All lived within her, not just those that swayed Positive.

Centaur stopped abruptly. "We have a problem." We had come to a dead end. "It looks like the Wizards didn't quite make it to the surface. Either they changed their minds about creating access to the Northern Spine, or they got pulled to a more important project."

"So, our choices are returning to the Right Eye or continuing east and getting off at Jasper?" asked Hornet.

"Or finding our own route to the surface," Pistachio suggested. "A natural gallery bisected this tunnel about a hundred meters back."

"What do you think, Lynn?" asked Centaur. "Will we be able to find our way to the surface on our own?"

"The probability is high. The probability of all of you surviving while doing so is lower. We won't be the only ones using this subterranean highway."

"We don't have much choice, do we? The odds of us being successful in this war diminish the longer it takes to reach the sumopotts, substantially less if the Wizards hire them before we do."

"True."

Traveling through the natural caverns and galleries was much slower than following a passageway specifically created for movement. Not only did we have to make decisions on which prong of the next fork to take, we had to do so in as quiet a manner as possible to not attract attention. From what, we preferred not to know. When walking through the woods it was easier to follow an animal path than to create one's own. Underworld paths weren't as easy to follow as those on the surface, but they were there. Following such paths, however, increased our peril. Slowly, we were getting closer to the surface. Occasionally, a passage dropped a few meters, but accumulatively the passages rose.

We began to hear moans. We preferred it to be the wind, attempting, as *we* were, to navigate through the catacombs. But occasionally, we heard words. Could the wind create words? Elementals might be able to. They were intelligent clusters of air, and water and earth and fire. The sounds became louder as we got closer to the surface.

"FREE ME!"

"I DON'T WANT TO LIVE HERE FOREVER!"

"WHY!"

"WHAT HAVE WE DONE TO DESERVE THIS, GAEA?!"

I would have been able to prevent the screams from invading my thoughts if it wasn't for that last comment. I couldn't allow someone to condemn my mistress. Gaea would never torture someone.

We saw what was making those cries upon entering a large cavern. Faces and arms and legs stuck out from the stone walls, like taxidermy trophies.

"FREE US!"

"PULL US OUT!"

"SHATTER THE STONE!"

"GAEA HAS TRAPPED US!"

Defiantly, I walked up to the head that spoke those defiant words. "Twice you have spoken harshly of Gaea. She has not trapped you here. The way you lived your life has caused this condition."

"Nothing we have done compensates for Gaea's cruelty."

"Who placed you here?" asked Hornet.

"Gaea. She re-created us within solid stone."

"FREE US!"

"We must do something," Twig insisted. She held onto a woman's hand, attempting to add comfort.

Pistachio studied the situation. "If we chisel them out, it will likely harm them, possibly fatally. I may be able to soften the stone around them. Then we might be able to pull them out. If they are part stone, which I fear they are, the modification may kill them."

"You must try."

"Yes, please try."

"Dying would be better."

"Gaea, allow us die so we may be re-created in a better place."

"I can't kill them, even for their own good," stated Twig.

"It would be a mercy killing, an assisted suicide," said Centaur.

"Could you do it?"

"If I thought it was the only way to save them."

"Gaea will not permit it," I said. "Directly, she didn't have a hand in this, but indirectly, she's involved with everything. We don't have permission to choose the time or method of someone's death."

"What if this was the reason we passed through here?" Pulp conjectured. "If we don't put these people out of their misery we may be rejecting Gaea's wishes."

"If we don't know which course of action to take, it's best to do nothing."

"Taking no action is an action," stated Pistachio.

"True. Gaea permits freewill."

"Gaea has given us permission to kill these people?" asked Pulp.

"But we aren't required to do so. Uncertainty remains. The status quo is retained."

"We can't remain here forever deciding what to do," said

Centaur. "The racket we're making will attract something. Time is a variable not yet added to the conundrum. Can we agree we don't have enough of it to commit this mass murder even if we determine we should do it?"

"Let's go," said Pulp.

"DON'T GO!"

"FREE US FIRST!"

"IT MIGHT BE WEEKS...MONTHS...YEARS...BEFORE SOMEONE ELSE COMES BY!"

"BORE YOURSELF, GAEA!"

The voices echoed out to us many minutes after we left the cavern. Did those people really do something so extreme to cause them to be re-created within stone? Or were they just randomly placed there?

What we hoped to prevent by leaving the cavern occurred anyway. Zombies attacked us: corpses animated by elemental means. Had the Wizards finally caught up with us? Zombies had certain strengths, but also weaknesses. Damaging one didn't discourage it from fighting. But because it didn't act through its own decisions, it was limited in its actions. For many of the zombies, this re-creation wasn't their first. In addition to unchanged walking dead, there were hobs and gobs. Each of the three breeds fought slightly differently. Hobs relied on their brawn. Gobs, on their agility. The unchanged, on their intelligence, but since it was non-existent at the moment, it manifested as relying on their weapons.

The conflict was gruesome. It took the complete hacking apart of a corpse before the zombie stopped attacking. The rotting flesh was nauseating, much more than a Death Knights', which was partially alive. The zombies continued to rot, dark, sticky blood caramelizing them. Not caring if they were injured, they took considerable risks. Not being mentally prepared for such an onslaught, members of our party were struck more often than they normally would be. The metallic odor of fresh wounds merged with the rotten ones.

"Can't you counter them somehow, Pistachio?" Centaur asked between gasps. In addition to tearing apart as many zombies as he could, while protecting himself, he also protected the druid. "They are animated by penta, aren't they?"

The druid swallowed an elixir. Flames shrouded him. He moved away from Centaur, to prevent him from receiving an accidental, peripheral burn. The zombies not having sense enough to not attack him, saw him as only a new target. Three of them assaulted him. Not only did the flame shield prevent them from making contact with him, it also set them ablaze. Rotting flesh being burned didn't smell much worse healthy flesh cooking. The difference was the smoke. Not only were my companions gasping for breath due to their exertion, they were now coughing from the smoke particulates in the air.

"Let's see what I can do," Pistachio muttered.

"Don't take too long," Centaur choked out. "There are more of them than us."

I chose, again, not to participate. This time I couldn't just remain on the perimeter. I made myself invisible. Not just invisible, but ethereal. If someone accidentally struck me the appendage and/or weapon would pass through me.

The druid removed another vial. He looked inquisitively at it before he swallowed it. The ring of fire around him was in a meter radius. His movements didn't affect the integrity or shape of the shield. He raised his arms. Energy erupted from his fingertips. It arced over his shield, landing among the combatants, friend and foe alike. As it hit the ground it slowly deflected upward, billowing. The zombies it had encapsulated became sluggish, like they were stepping through molasses. Then their legs fell out beneath them. Their upper torsos continued to attack. Seconds later they too became immobile.

Pistachio's fire shield dissipated. "I wasn't sure if that counter would work. I never experimented on zombies before."

"Apparently it does." Twig applied pressure to her shoulder laceration. Other than Pistachio, and myself, our party was in bad shape.

"Let's see what we can do about that." Pistachio handed Twig one of his elixirs. He also gave Centaur, Pulp, and Hornet one. The one thing the druid knew he would need was healing potions, so he brought plenty of them.

"So, you aren't completed invulnerable?" said Centaur to Hornet.

"I did most of that myself---from my sword recoiling. The zombies kept missing me. It diverted my strikes. Did you think the Wizards sent them after us?"

"Look at their skulls."

Twig gasped as she looked down at one of the zombies. Horror filled her, but she was transfixed. The sight was terrifying but fascinating.

"Something had punctured them." Hornet examined a different zombie. He bent down to look inside the cavity. "It's hollow, like something had sucked out its brain."

"Some people believe brains are a delicacy," Centaur commented.

"What I find most interesting is it appears only the brain has been assailed," said Pistachio. "Why waste all this meat?"

"So, the Wizards probably aren't involved with this," stated Hornet.

"Whatever did this must have a very specialized palate. There is a species of panda that only eats eucalyptus leaves. Maybe this creature only eats brains. Maybe it can't digest anything else."

"But why brains?" asked Twig. "Why not toes, or eyes?"

"Brains contain knowledge," I said. "You've heard the expression *hungry for knowledge.*"

"You don't actually believe these creatures read their victims memories when they consume their brains?" questioned Pulp.

"Why not? Computer files are shared. Why not biological files?"

"But a person can't subsist on knowledge alone."

"A brain is highly nutritious. The tissue is meat and potatoes. The thought patterns, the memories, herbs and spices."

"So, these creatures may also attempt to eat *our* brains?" asked Twig. Worry etched her countenance.

"Let's hope the knowledge they have consumed taught them the possible gains from attacking a party as formidable as us doesn't always offset their potential losses."

After healing, we resumed our journey to the surface. We never saw the brain-eaters. We did our best to ensure that. We kept to major galleries. After a couple of more hours of spelunking we finally saw daylight. It was just a single ray through a single break in the stone above us, but it encouraged us. Somewhere nearby was a way out.

After a frustrating quarter of searching, Centaur had an epiphany. "Maybe we should just break our way out. We see the light. There can't be that much rock between us and the surface." Centaur began banging away at the pinpoint of light with his hammer.   First chips of stone fell away, then a boulder half his size. If it landed 50 sims to the left it would have killed him."

Twig said, "Maybe this isn't the safest method, dear."

I added, "The longer you pound away the more likely you'll create an avalanche. Togetherness is a wonderful thing, but I prefer not to die at the same time as the rest of you."

"I'm almost there." Centaur continued to pound away at the rocks above him. Apparently, togetherness was more important to some people than others. The boulder that had nearly killed him created more sunlight. Another large rock was dislodged. Centaur moved out of the way this time. It landed more than a meter from him. "Enough room for Lynn and Twig to squeeze through. A couple of more boulders for the rest of us."

"I appreciate the compliment, but it won't get my butt

through that small gap," Twig responded. "With you being so close to being done, I hesitantly give you permission to continue. If you get squished by a boulder I won't make any promises of waiting for your re-creation to return to me. I'm going to choose a less careless, more intelligent man for my next mate."

"With such encouragement it should take me just minutes to complete this task." Another large chunk of the ceiling fell. It was round enough that when it hit the ground it rolled down the pathway we had followed to reach this elevation. The slope was steep enough that the boulder kept on rolling, beyond what we could see. "I believe that's now wide enough for *all* body parts to pass through."

Chapter 18

GOLEMS

The Northern Spine was more sparsely populated than the Southern. Its two largest settlements were villages. Spinecrest was near the range's northern tip. Phibton was west of the mountains, in the Phib Marsh. We left the underworld in the northern reaches, near Spinecrest. We could see the lights of the village below us. It was becoming dark. Where might we have come out if the sun hadn't shined through that crack? Would we have left the underworld at all? Would we have wandered aimlessly for days through the subterranean catacombs?

"Shall we?" Centaur looked down at the village.

"It feels like I haven't taken a bath in weeks," said Twig.

"Days."

"Do I smell?"

"Do you prefer a kind mate, or an honest one?"

"I smell that bad?"

"No worse than the rest of us."

"That bad?"

"I'm not sure, but I think I've been insulted," said Pulp.

"I know I have," said Hornet.

"People mock cats for licking themselves," I commented, "but I am able to bath at my convenience."

Gazing at the grime on her arm and frowning, Twig said, "I believe I'll wait for a proper bath."

Spinecrest was poorly protected. It was a good sign. If there was significant danger in the area it would have been forced to protect itself. Smaller settlements couldn't afford to build a wall. The next best thing was persistent perimeter surveillance. When problems were too large for the village guard to handle, the militia was activated. Most able men were members of their local militia. There was no duty more important than protected one's community from a mutant invasion.

The patrolman who greeted us wore a green tunic over mid-grade armor. Spinecrest's tabard---a silhouette of a city above a mountain---was centered on it.

"You're entering the city from an odd direction."

"We're an odd group," stated Pulp.

"Indeed, you are. A gent doesn't often travel with human companions. Does your pet hunt for you?" My response was opening my mouth wide widely, revealing two rows of flesh rending teeth. I believed it best not to reveal my ability to communicate. Most Limboans were aware of mutations. All were fearful of them. One couldn't be frightened of something they weren't aware of. "There's a gent that lives 50 kays down the Spine. He is supposedly as gray and bald as stone. He never enters the city, but sometimes he trades with people who come to him. Do you know him?"

"His name is Granite."

"Seems appropriate."

"Gents have a working relationship with one another."

"That must be why no one in their right mind attacks one of them. Attacking one means attacking all."

"That or they're much larger," Centaur commented.

"Enjoy your stay."

"No protection tax?"

"There are so few of us out here, we don't wish to discourage emigrants, even temporary ones. Be warned: most things in Spinecrest cost more than you're accustomed to, but the prices are derived fairly. Our remoteness has burdened us with more than beauty and a scarcity of residents."

Spinecrest had cobblestone streets and wooden houses. Both were narrow, but well-constructed. The residents of the village strived for a high quality of life. Quality was more important to them than quantity. The village flowed down the mountains like a landslide. From the park-like town square we could see both spires and forest. Sun and rain alternated, creating a pleasant temperate environment. Spinecrest never became too hot or too cold, too wet or too dry.

We stayed at *Crest Home*, a large inn on the top terrace of the village. It was four stories high. Its common area was open to the ceiling. Stairs climbed from the cavernous room to its three levels of guest suites. Ours consisted of two rooms on the top level. Substituting as a bathhouse was a small pool chiseled out of a rocky shelf. The steaming water smelled of minerals. Privacy was lacking, the four men and one woman in the pool---all nude---evidence of that.

"The pool is complimentary for our guests. The water comes from hot springs."

Twig began to disrobe. Centaur hustled to block the view of her. She shooed him away. "This is one of those places it is acceptable to be naked. It feels very innocent here, like we're all children." Twig stepped into the water. She sighed as she dropped down to her neck. The men looked relieved once the areas of her that looked different than them became covered. "Aren't you guys coming in?"

They didn't respond. "I think they might be a bit more old fashioned than you," stated Centaur. "Why don't you guys come back after Twig gets out?"

"That's making the assumption that I'll ever get out," Twig cooed.

"I'll also be leaving," I said. "Being around all this water is making me nervous."

Twig eventually forced herself to leave the embracing water. It was now Hornet, Pulp, and Pistachio's time to bathe. They didn't stay as long. Women preferred to soak longer than men.

After dinner, Centaur indicated that he and Twig were going to spend the evening as wolves. It had been awhile since they had transformed. If they didn't soon their bodies would do it for them. It was better they picked the place and time. They enjoyed being in wolf form. The problem was having to eventually abandon it. Toxicity accrues that will, if given enough time, kill them. They climbed above the village, wearing as little as possible. Disrobing before they changed not only protected clothing, it prevented the most excruciating wedgies.

"You think they'll be safe?" asked Hornet.

"Safer as wolves than humans," Pulp replied. "Their senses are so highly tuned they'll become aware of danger before it approaches. I don't expect them to encounter anything too disconcerting. We're in Neutrality, and the residents of Spinecrest appear to be at peace."

We turned in early. Hornet and Pistachio shared a bed. Pulp, being larger, had a bed to himself---before I joined him. I leapt up at the foot of his bed, then nuzzled my way into the crevice between his legs. I sensed he wished to turn over in the middle of the night, but chose not to so he wouldn't disturb me. I could have abandoned his legs on my own, but that would have diminished the sacrifice he was making. Cats don't deny nobility.

We were woken half-an-hour before dawn. Someone was at the door. He, or she---or it---turned the doorknob. The door was pushed inward a sim before the lock caught.

"Let us in," someone whispered harshly. It was Centaur.

"Close the door." Pulp unfastened the latch after the door was snapped shut. He reopened the door. Centaur and Twig were dressed in what they wore last night---but poorly. Twig's shirt wasn't buttoned all the way, and Centaur's was buttoned wrong. It bunched out in the middle.

"We need to leave immediately." Centaur rushed off to his room.

"What happened?" asked Hornet.

"No time to explain." Twig followed her mate.

We left the inn as quietly as possible. The less the innkeeper and his patrons could share about us, the better. Being at the top of the village, we had to traverse most of it to reach the road to the north that would lead us to the Northwoods. The Mercenary Hills were northeast of it.

"Should we be following this road if we're being followed?" asked Hornet.

"It won't matter," said Pulp. "You'll see."

Half-an-hour later we broke through the Floral Fringe, the forest at the base of Northern Spine. There was a 20-kay gap between it and the Northwoods. No matter where we walked we would be out in the open.

We moved quickly through the prairie, half-walking, half-jogging. My companions did. Four legs were better equipped to move swiftly. I easily kept up with them, even without galloping. The only problem I had was if I was moving I wasn't napping. Paradise to a woman may have meant taking a hot bath. To a cat, it was taking many naps. I was a good sport and only complained about the lack of napping every 10 minutes. It took us just an hour to reach the Northwoods. The stress drained from Centaur and Twig's countenances once we became concealed in the trees again.

"Now might be a good time to go off-road," Pulp suggested. Having spent so much time in the Copper Forest, he was the logical choice to lead us through this forest. He left the road at a tangent, following a game trail. A few minutes later he left the trail for another, this one being roughly parallel to the road. "That will make it more difficult for whatever follows us."

"What exactly is following us?" asked Hornet. Centaur and Twig hadn't yet shared what they saw. So focused were we on crossing that break between the two forests, we hadn't broached the subject.

"Golems," stated Twig. "Not just one or two, but hundreds, in every shape and size. Golems of stone and iron. Golems of flesh and clay. Golems of bone and wood. Many of them were constructed of more than one medium. Most of them walked on approximations of legs, but some rolled on wheels, huge goliaths that looked like they could roll over or through anything."

After Twig got out what she could, Centaur took over. "What was most disturbing was---what appeared to be---golems giving orders to other golems."

"Intelligent golems?" Pistachio was shocked.

"We met someone who had their essence relocated into a golem against his will," said Pulp. "Being given a powerful golem body is a potent aphrodisiac for those wanting power."

"Nimbus wasn't too pleased with becoming a golem," said Hornet.

"It wasn't his choice, and he was a drak at the time. For an average man, becoming a thing of stone weighing thousands of kilos would be intoxicating."

"So, you just happened to run into this army of golems?" I questioned. "There was a near certainty we would run into the Wizards' minions, but for it to happen today the probability was low. The probability rises considerably until the war begins."

Twig had recovered enough to reply. "Centaur and I were running freely. Stretching your legs as a human is different than stretching them as a wolf. After being away from running for a few days our legs begin to ache for it. Every stretch, every strike of your paws against the ground massages. We heard voices ahead, human ones. We ran towards them to investigate. We climbed a rise. Below it, on the other side, were these uninhibited, feral exaggerations of men and women. They numbered between a dozen and a score. Their bodies were too intermingled to get a more accurate count. They took pleasure in each other, as men and women do. It was sensual, but also innocent. They laughed gleefully like they were playing nursery games. It was intoxicating. If we weren't in wolf form, we may have joined them. The longer we lingered, the more tempting it became, even transformed."

"We knew we shouldn't be watching, but we couldn't' take our eyes off them," Centaur explained. "They were insatiable."

"Then the golems came," Twig added before losing it again.

"I don't believe the nymphs were even a target, not something the golems had planned to attack. Target practice, perhaps. Like how the mongrels were used by the Death Knights. It took the nymphs a moment for it to register. Either they didn't realize the golems were there until it was too late, or they assumed it was some elaborate game. They weren't just massacred, they were pulverized. I don't believe we were noticed, but we didn't wish to risk it, so we fled."

"What do you think, Lynn?" asked Hornet. "Are they pursuing us, or were Centaur and Twig innocent bystanders?"

"It's likely they were just in the wrong place at the wrong time, but the probability that we were the ultimate target is greater than it was at the Right Eye. The nymphs weren't much of a challenge for golems."

"But that doesn't mean we were the target," insisted Pulp.

"No, it's more likely that Spinecrest was."

"We must return," Twig insisted. "WE NEED TO WARN

THEM!"

"It's too late," Centaur responded, distantly. "If Spinecrest is their intended target it will be under attack before we can reach it."

Chapter 19

THORNIES AND SHROOMERS

Norwood was the largest settlement in the Northwoods. For the same reasons we chose a clandestine retreat from Spinecrest, we bypassed it. We remained off-road. Whatever time we might lose by walking around trees and fallen logs was ample compensation for not being detected. We were determined to not stop again until we reached the Mercenary Hills. That meant hiking in the dark, an acceptable inconvenience. Crossing the Northern Plains was best done at that time of day. If our visibility was limited, so was the visibility of those seeking us.

We kept our thoughts to ourselves. Not only might extended conversations become a beacon, we had too many things on our minds to be able to share them. After a saturation point is reached thoughts tend to clog, preventing any from escaping. With trepidation I pondered, first, the calculated specifics of the war, then me leaving Limbo. Why were there always obstacles in front of something you wanted? It was never easy, was it? There were still so many things that must happen before I could step through that reconstructed portal. Preparing for war would delay us from finding that last piece of the portal. Occasionally, my thoughts drifted from escaping, when I heard a branch fall or an animal scurry across the forest floor. A moment later my thoughts would rebound, to escape again. The anticipation was making me ill. It wasn't like I was just waiting a week or a month for my freedom. It's been more than a century.

We heard barking ahead of us.

"They don't sound too pleased," commented Hornet.

"We better investigate." Twig began removing her clothes. "Aren't you going to turn around?"

"You weren't too concerned with that in Spinecrest," Pulp protested.

"That was under different circumstances."

"Naked is naked."

"So, you're saying that having a doctor examine you is the same as skinny dipping?"

"Well...."

"The thoughts of impropriety have already entered your mind. You're beginning to blush. Turn around."

The men did what they were told. How much easier it was being an animal and always clothed in fur.

Centaur also undressed. He and Twig rushed off after transforming into wolves. They weren't gone long. They gestured for us to follow them.

Pulp, Hornet, and Pistachio picked up their gear. Pulp stared at the two wolves. "This is just an excuse for us to carry your stuff?" The wolves smiled, then ran back towards the barking.

The barking came from a score of creatures, as large as medium-sized dogs. They may have behaved like dogs, but didn't look like them. The small tree stumps looked like they had been partially consumed by insects. Instead of fur they had spiky bark. Their eyes, nose, mouth, and ears looked very dog-like. Spines extended from their lower torso to the top of their heads. The same schema that associated equine mutants with *centaurs*, made me think of these creatures as *topiaries*.

The topiaries weren't paying any attention to us. They

weren't even looking in our direction when we approached. They were facing south. We had come from the southwest, the most direct route to the Mercenary Hills.

"They don't seem too happy," Pulp commented.

"Something is heading this way, isn't it?" asked Hornet.

"Do you think the golems bypassed Spinecrest and are heading directly towards us?" Pistachio looked at me.

Each attempt at replying was circumvented. My thoughts were muddled. The calculations, inconsistent. I gave up. "I don't know."

Centaur and Twig could understand what was said while in canine form, but they couldn't communicate very well. They transformed back into humans.

"You didn't wrinkle my clothes, did you?" Centaur examined them before putting them on.

"Maybe we could construct saddlebags for you," Pulp suggested, "so you can carry your own gear when you change into a dog. Or tie a rope to you, so you can pull your pack behind you."

"Twig, remind me to bite Pulp really hard the next time I change into a wolf. I can usually understand what humans say, if not all the words, at least the intent. Did I really hear something about Lynn not being able to predict the future?"

"The variables are in flux, and many of them don't have parameters. Making a prediction involving the golems is like taking a shot in the dark, but I usually see well in the dark. It's more like taking a shot blindfolded behind a wall. The probabilities change so often, and they vary by so much, predictions become a coin flip. When it comes to the golems, I'm foresight blind."

We heard a whistle. The spiny-dogs' ears perked up. They darted towards the whistle. We followed them. We couldn't keep up, eventually losing contact with them. We continued to travel in the direction they headed. A few minutes later we spotted them again. They surrounded a dozen or more humanoids---their size. They ran circles around them, constantly barking. The sounds they emitted were less intense than before, but still emotional. They were lively, happy sounds, not derived from fear.

The humanoids intermittently monitored our approach as they petted the spiny-dogs. Our sudden appearance didn't appear to disturb them. Their skin was gray, with the texture of a mushroom: smooth, firm and spongy. Dark tendrils, looking like corn silk, hung from their bodies in certain areas, leaving others bare. Their midsection was covered with the stuff, giving them the illusion of wearing loincloths. They also had the stuff hanging from their shins, making that part of them look like a Shetland pony. They had patches of the silk on their forearms, in the middle of their chest, and on their shoulders. The cluster on the top of their heads was long, tied back in a ponytail.

"Noble midday," spoke one of them.

"You don't appear too concerned about us," Centaur commented.

"The thornies perceive intention. Their lack of fear assures our safety."

"They *were* concerned about something before you summoned them," said Twig.

"Those things they fear are still 20 kays away."

"How do you know this?" asked Pulp. "There is no way you can see that far, even if the trees weren't in the way. Do you have a tower?"

"The thornies told us. We can't hold an extended conversation with them, but they are able to relay basic information. The range of their perception is slightly greater than the 20...." A brief, succinct barking interrupted the conversation. "The range of their perception is slightly greater than the 19 kays that separate us. There are at least twenty of them. The thornies aren't confident in that estimation. At times greater numbers flash at them. The uncertainty disturbs them. They have never experienced it to this degree."

"The twenty they persistently perceive must be the

autonomous golems," spoke Pistachio, "the ones with souls. The animatrons, the others. Being nearly alive they must emote a resemblance to the living."

"You must flee this area if those the thornies sense come," insisted Twig. "They'll destroy you just because you are in the direction they travel. They don't understand the concept of *walking around*."

One of the thornies broke away from the pack and rubbed itself against Twig. The sharp spines ripped through her leg like it was made of paper. Blood began to drip from the deep scratches.

"Get back here." The thorny ran back to its master. He struck it on the nose. "Bad thorny." It whimpered, then backed away. It lay down, with its head lying flat on the forest floor. It stared mournfully at the shroomer---what would you call it?---who struck, firmly, but without malice. "Sorry about that. She didn't intend to harm you. She has a tendency to become overly enthusiastic, especially when we have visitors, which doesn't occur very often." The shroomer tore a patch of silk from his chest and placed it on Twig's wound. It was sticky enough for it to stay in place.

"That feels wonderful. Warm and soothing."

"You'll be completely healed by tomorrow."

"Thank you for sacrificing a bit of yourself to help me."

"It's the least I can do. Do not be concerned for my wellbeing. The silk will grow back. It actually feels good to get a bit pulled out now and then. It doesn't fall out on its own. To remove the stale silk, we must prune ourselves. We make our beds with it."

"Could you make clothes out of it?"

"We never tried. If we could weave the strands, do you think we could trade with it?"

"You'd become rich. Who wouldn't want to wear clothing with that sheen? And there's also the medicinal benefits."

"The silk loses its effectiveness once it dries."

"The clothes created specifically for healing could be kept

moist, until needed."

"Please spend the remainder of the day with us. We wish to celebrate our new business venture."

"We believe those things the thornies sense might be following us," said Centaur. "We don't wish for them to catch up."

The shroomer we have been having a conversation with barked once at the thornies. They rushed off into the forest, returning a couple of minutes later. They barked at their master. "They made a detour. To Norwood. They've stopped moving, for the moment."

We shuddered. Were they destroying the village, like---we feared---they had destroyed Spinecrest?

"The thornies will notify us if they begin heading in our direction again."

"We could at least stay for a meal," Centaur suggested. "We left Spinecrest rather precipitously this morning."

The shroomers' diet consisted of mushrooms, exclusively, but there was quite a variety of them. We ate raw ones as a salad, and cooked ones as an entrée. For desert we ate some that were caramelized. I expected there to be mushroom juice. Instead, we drank crystal clear spring water. The simple liquid cleansed our palates between courses.

I never needed an excuse to take a nap, but that food did encourage me a bit. Before I drifted off I heard Centaur say, "Sleeping until dark might be a good idea. It will be easier to walk through the night if we're revitalized."

The shroomers escorted us into their lodge. It had been carved out of the brambles, dozens of corridors and rooms nestled in the prickly vegetation. The vines and leaves were so dense there was barely enough room for light to trickle its way into our rooms. Each alcove contained a bed. More like a nest. A pile of shroomer silk. Soft and malleable. Like sleeping on someone, but not as lumpy.

"It's time for you to leave." A soft, rubbery hand gently woke me. I opened one eye, not wanting to completely commit myself to waking unless we were truly getting up. I heard the others also being wakened by shroomers. The sun was dimming, transitioning the already dim interior of the briar lodge to full-blown darkness. I opened my other eye. I stretched while still prone. Then I stretched again after I stood. "You wanted to be woken when it got dark."

"Can't we have a few more minutes of sleep?" I heard Twig utter.

"Those that follow are on the move again. They are heading this direction."

That got Twig up, and added a spark to the rest of us. Outside the brambles it was also dark. Being in a forest, surrounded by vegetation, it got dark sooner here than if we were in the open.

"Don't wait too long to evacuate," Centaur advised. "Once they see you they won't stop until you're all dead and your lodge is leveled."

"When we close the door to the lodge they won't know we're here."

"I wouldn't count on that," said Pulp. "If they're on the move again that probably means they have destroyed Norwood already. How long do you think it will take them to destroy the brambles?"

"Before you go, we have something to give you." The shroomers handed each of my companions a silk cloak.

"Did you just make these?" asked Hornet.

"While you were asleep. How do you like them?"

"They are beautiful." Twig already had hers on. "At night I might wear this and nothing else. It must feel fantastic on bare skin."

"You sure you want to give us these?" asked Pistachio. "Selling just one of these would make you a bundle."

"It is a gift. Gifts should be valuable, shouldn't they? You can do one thing for us. Tell those you see on your journey who made them. We can't sell any if people don't know about us or our silk cloth."

"We'll be happy to." Twig studied the shroomers. Something looked different. More of their skin showed. "You made them from freshly plucked silk, didn't you?"

"Virgin silk is the best. If it lays around too long, it's only good for bedding."

"Well, that bedding was plenty comfortable," said Pulp.

"The silk will grow back in a month. If we are going to make clothes on a regular basis, we'll have to become comfortable with various stages of bushiness."

The Mercenary Hills were north-northwest of us. We still had a couple more hours in the Northwoods before the forest transitioned to prairie. It was more difficult for my companions to maneuver through the forest than it was for me. If there was any illumination at all it was enough for me to see by. After a couple of brushes with the brush, it was determined that something had to be done to improve the ease of our journey. Lighting a torch was suggested, but was quickly rejected. It was unlikely it could be seen from such a distance in the middle of a forest, but the risk couldn't be taken. It was decided I was to lead. To prevent us becoming separated, we were tied together by a rope. Humanoids may have enjoyed having a rope tied to them. Cats weren't too keen on the idea. Whenever someone wandered off course my chest got squeezed. That's where the rope was tied to me. They wanted to tie the rope to my tail, but I refused. One thing a person should never do is pull a cat's tail. There haven't actually been any known incidents of tail-pulling, because those who had committed such a heinous act were rumored to be dead.

When we finally saw the moonlight through the trees in front of us I nearly wept with joy. I squirmed my way out of the rope harness before Centaur could untie it. It would still be dark for another couple of hours, but without trees to block the moon-rays it was light enough for even the blindest of humanoids to tread confidently.

We returned to the walk-jog gait we used in crossing the gap between the Northern Spine and the Northwoods. The Mercenary Hills were still 30 kays away. It was unlikely we would reach them by moonbrighten, but it will be close. At most, an hour of amplified exposure.

Chapter 20

MERCENARIES

So focused were we on our arrival to our destination, we didn't look behind us until moonbrighten. There was no sign of the golems. Every few minutes after that we glanced behind us until we reached the Mercenary Hills.

It became drier. Not just the stunted grass beneath our feet, but also the air. Gaea didn't mess around with transitions, not if she wished for all environmental conditions to be exhibited on less than one-percent of the planet's surface.

The low-lying hills in front of us looked like a pile of dirt clods. Or feces---as a random voice declared in less elegant terms.

There were 17 hills in all, each being home to one of the Sumopott's mercenary battalions. Each battalion had its own traditions, its own history, its own crest. Each had a number designation, but also a moniker, like the *Sand Panthers*, or the *Dust Devils*. The leader of the sumopotts was Captain Cottonwood. All sumopotts belonged to a Battalion, even the Captain. His Battalion was the 17th, the *Prickly Wolverines*. Leaving your home didn't mean renouncing your family.

Visitors were perpetual, but revolving. To hire a mercenary, one had to come to the Mercenary Hills. Impartiality had to be retained. To make their guests more comfortable, the sumopotts created an oasis in the center of the hills, and an inn constructed in its center, beside an emerald pool garnished with palms. The sumopotts kept their distance, only entering the oasis when a business contact was requested. Pampered luxury was a detriment. Softness wasn't the characteristic one was looking for when hiring a mercenary.

It was mid-morning when we arrived. It was already becoming warm, hot a brief transition before becoming unbearable.

"What's it going to be like by mid-afternoon?" Pulp wiped away a bead of sweat from his forehead. Gents preferred cooler weather. That's why most of them lived in the mountains. I wasn't complaining. What cat turned away a morsel of heat?

The inn's staff was exclusively human, neutrality the most welcoming to diverse clientele. The building had an open concept, designed for breezes to pass through the structure. We ate an early lunch beside a fountain. A windmill turned gears that carried the water back to the top in wooden buckets. Most restaurants on Limbo employed women, usually scantily clad. The Mercenary Inn had men. The sumopotts weren't in the entertainment business. Those hired were the most willing to work in desolate locations. Women were more social, and not fond of dust.

We had to wait until the afternoon to talk to someone about hiring an army. It was not customary for guests to arrive so early in the day. We attempted to catch up on sleep as we waited, my companions on beds, I on a warm stone beside the pool---next to a lizard. It wasn't a real reptile. The rumor that cats slept anywhere with anyone was an exaggeration. We preferred warmth, which excluded snuggling up to cold-blooded animals. Comfort was a close second. Why weren't there more cat statues in the world? Would their beauty be too much of a distraction?

Captain Cottonwood greeted us. "Your stay has been pleasant." A statement, not a question. Bold and confident. This venture will still likely be unsuccessful, but to a lesser degree. The three-meter tall humanoid shook my companions' hands. His pasty gray hands were meaty, over-sized and muscular. His head looked like a hippopotamus. Sticking out from both sides of his duck-billed cap were hemispherical ears. His eyes were set back in pronounced sockets. His mouth and nostrils blended together in a single wide jutting protrusion. When he spoke his large, square molars were displayed. His hair, on his head, and body, was sparse. His khaki uniform looked like it was constructed of heavy canvas. It was covered by ribbons and medals. Four stripes were embossed on his left sleeve. Attached to his belt was a well-polished wooden club, and a pistol.

"A friend of ours carried a pistol like that," said Centaur. "Does it also shoot darts?"

"Energy bursts from elem."

"One penta per charge?" asked Pistachio.

"It depends on the setting. I can shoot one large burst, three medium, or ten small. The small bursts don't do that much damage. They can kill jack rabbits at twenty paces, or stun a man for a couple of minutes."

"That weapon must have cost you a fortune," Centaur commented.

"I made it myself. I modified a Wizard's rod. I'm a bit of a renaissance sumopott. My kind usually prefers to use brute force. It gives us a better workout, and it's more predictable."

"How do you acquire elem for your pistol? Do you deal with the Wizards, directly?"

"You ask a lot questions. That's welcoming. The typical benefactor just wants the job done. They don't care who does it or how it's done. After we complete our mission they're not always pleased with the results. The elem I power this pistol with is part of the compensation we receive. If someone can afford our services, they can afford to buy penta."

"We would like to hire as many of your battalions as available."

"That might be a problem. We have already checked your references. Sergeants Leaf and Needle, who you worked with a few weeks ago, feel you are worthy of using our services again. The problem: it's unlikely you'll be able to pay for it."

"It's true we don't have much money with us," said Twig, "but in time we'll be able to more than adequately compensate you."

"I sense you are sincere in what you say, but sometimes things occur that prevent us from doing what we wish to do, like being re-created into a form that either can't or won't pay us what we are owed. Being paid on credit on Limbo is highly speculative."

"We have partial ownership in a very lucrative mine," said Pulp. "It's highly unlikely all of us will be so badly mutated we won't be able to repay you."

"Do you know how expensive it is to hire twelve battalions?"

"We have an idea," said Hornet. "We have hired you before."

"Unlike merchandise, leasing mercenaries is more expensive in bulk. Taking that many sumopotts out of commission means we can't provide our services to all that require them. We will lose some repeat business over your monopoly on our troops. This is the amount of gold I need before I can loan you the twelve battalions." He handed a slate to Centaur with a number written on it in chalk.

Centaur would have fallen out of his seat if his reflexes weren't so finely tuned. "That's outrageous. We can support a permanent army for five years for that amount."

"You are free to do so."

"Our need is dire. What if I told you the survival of Limbo as we know is dependent on you helping us."

"Limbo could use some changes."

"Not these," I insisted. "The Wizards are plotting to control the world. If there was just one faction on Limbo instead of many, how might that effect business?"

"I imagine we would become even more desired. There are always those who oppose the status quo. If the Wizards become as omnificent as you predict, we might be one of the few groups who could still counter them. We'll have more business than we can manage."

"Assuming you are not also destroyed." I had to be careful I didn't interfere too much. I was on the verge of forcing Gaea to step in and give the opposing side advice.

"Sumopotts are neutral. The Wizards know that. Who we fight for, or against, is strictly business. If the Wizards wish to hire us, even after attacking us, they may do so after a one-year waiting period. Our ethics forbids us from immediately harming the hand that once fed us. We will speak again once you acquire the appropriate funds. If you change your mind and wish to hire fewer battalions, it might be easier to come to an agreement." Captain Cottonwood shook our hands and left.

"Now what?" asked Pulp.

"We find alternate troops, I guess," Centaur replied. "Do you think any of the gents might be willing to fight for a good cause?"

"The Brotherhood was established for the mutual benefit of gents, so a consensus could be reached. Grouped together we are much stronger than we are as individuals."

"Where is the closest gent?"

"Granite lives in the Northern Spine. And there's Lord Hide, in the Twin Hills. Considering the altercation we had with him, it's unlikely he'll want to ally with us."

"Or we with him."

"So, to the Northern Spine we return," said Pistachio. "A

shortcut would be preferred."

"Or at least a detour around those golems," Twig added.

"I wish there was a train station here. It's not very likely though, is it?"

"The Mercenary Hills wouldn't be a good staging area for troops," I said.

"But it might be a good area to spy upon," Hornet conjectured. "Wouldn't the Wizards want to know who was hiring troops and where they were being sent?"

"I believe it's time we collected that last piece of the portal," said Centaur. "If we can't gather enough troops to counter the Wizards we'll need to leave Limbo as soon as possible."

We placed the five metallic spheres on the floor of one of the rooms we rented. Each was a different color: green, blue, purple, yellow, and orange. The give and take of electromagnetic forces that forced them together, kept them about a meter apart.

Pistachio's mouth dropped. "That looks like a...."

"It is," said Hornet. "A portable portal. Didn't we mention something about a portal?"

"Well, there are portals, and *portals*. I was assuming something like what the gents used, but that wouldn't get us off the planet, would it?"

Hornet lifted the middle sphere---the green one. Centaur and Twig held the ends---the orange and purple spheres. The contraption began to move. It stopped, pointing in a southeastern direction.

Pulp sighed. "It's back to the Dreadful Mountains."

"From where we are that would be south-southeast of us," I corrected. "It's more likely in the Grim Mountains."

"Aren't they on the Neuneg-Orneg border?" asked Hornet.

"Some of the deadliest monsters live there," Twig stated.

"The difficulty escalates as the rewards become greater."

"Like our worthiness of receiving this ultimate reward is being tested," said Centaur.

"We have more walking to do, don't we?" asked Pistachio, rhetorically. "One of the reasons I became a druid was to circumvent doing so much physical labor."

"Aren't you on your feet the entire time you are collecting herbs?" asked Pulp.

"That's different. When I'm collecting herbs, it feels more like I'm playing than working. Like I'm participating in some elaborate scavenger hunt."

I leapt onto the bed in the room. For some people this conversation might appear to be enlightening. To me it was just a delay in taking my next nap. I walked around in a circle then curled up and closed my eyes.

I must have been an inspiration to my companions, because when I awoke Hornet was lying beside me on the bed. The others were gone, but likely similarly reclined.

I leapt down from the bed and stuck my nose in Hornet's pack. There had to be something still edible in it. As my head squeezed inside, the drawstring loosened. I found a piece of stale dried fish and an even more stale piece of cheese. I still ate them, but that didn't forbid me from complaining about them.

GONG!

I leapt straight up. When I landed my hair was sticking up, doubling my size. I dashed under the bed.

Hornet stepped down---onto my tail. I squealed, leaping straight up again. I hit my head on one of the wooden slats that supported the mattress. The day had been blissful up to that point. Any day I was able to take two naps, one in the sun, and the other on a bed, was a good day.

Hornet rushed into the hallway. He stopped 50 sims short of running into other members of our party. I was last to arrive, still sore and confused. The humans and the gent rushed outside. I waited until the hallway was clear before I made my escape.

DONG!

The inn's staff had also rushed outdoors, to ascertain the motive for the alert, looking similarly oblivious.

DONG!

Sumopott battalions could be seen in the distance, marching down hills, and through the clefts between them. They formed up in an open area south of the oasis. It took many minutes for, what had to be the entirety of the mercenaries---less those in the field---to arrive. Thirteen ordered clusters stood at attention in front of Captain Cottonwood and two sumopotts with three stripes on their sleeves. A round piece of metal hung on a wooden post beside the mercenary leader. One of the officers beside him struck it one last time with a heavy wooden mallet.

DONG!

As Captain Cottonwood began to speak, his troops became mesmerized. They greatly respected their commander. An opportunity to receive his wisdom was rare. They were determined to not miss a single word. "To hear the Call is both glorious and tragic. It is so rare when we all come together like this. It is even rarer when we fight together, brothers united. Never before have we had to fight for ourselves instead of for others. Today you have been given the Call. An army arrives from the south. We haven't yet ascertained its objective, but an army does not hire another army. We must assume its mission includes our demise. Who wishes to rid Limbo of its sumopott mercenaries? Lieutenant Piranha will brief you on our opponent."

One of the officers beside Captain Cottonwood began to speak. "The one-hundred eighty you will target are unlike anything you have gone to battle with. Your opponents consist of creatures constructed of wood, stone, and metal. Such materials aren't intimidated by taunts, superior numbers or tactics. Due to the durability of the materials they are constructed with, normal fighting tactics will prove ineffective. Club strikes and belly flops must be replaced with attacks from pulverizing metallic hammers. We can't break bones and crush-in lungs if our opponents don't have any."

The Captain spoke again. "I expect there to be casualties, but dying on the battlefield is just part of our job. If you fight nobly, never giving in, never giving up, you're guaranteed to be re-created as a sumopott. May Gaea not modify your mutations."

The officer who hadn't spoken relayed specific battle tactics, including how the hammers were to be used to maximize their destructive power. The weapons were distributed after he finished speaking.

Once properly equipped, the thirteen battalions marched out of the Mercenary Hills, heading towards their opponents who were nearly upon them.

"Another coincidence?" Pulp questioned.

"At least something good comes from this," said Centaur. "The sumopotts are apparently going to do the work we intended to hire them for, for free."

Pistachio looked concerned. "How shall we proceed? What support can we give the sumopotts?"

"A perfect time to continue our flight," Hornet advised. "With the golems preoccupied for a couple of hours we'll be able to put some significant kays behind us."

"But in which direction?" I questioned.

"In as opposite a direction as the golems as possible," Twig suggested.

"Why not go in the direction they came from?"

"You haven't woken from your nap yet, have you?" said Centaur.

"I don't mean walking through the battlefield. We'll make a wide detour. The one place they wouldn't expect us to go is the direction they just came. They're probably haven't even noticed us with all the commotion."

"Logical," stated Pistachio.

"And a very high probability of success." Centaur looked at me.

"Not that high, but it does provide a much higher probability of surviving than either staying here or fleeing in the opposite direction."

"And it gives me an opportunity to speak with Granite," said Pulp.

The fighting was intense. The sumopotts attempted to stay in their respective battalions, but after a few minutes chaos reigned. The golems didn't fight with precision, or with honor. The only benefit the mercenaries received from their opponents' fighting style was the golems sometimes getting confused in the complexity of battle and striking at one another instead of the sumopotts. The powerful hammers were effective against stone, wood, flesh, and bone, but almost useless against metal. Dozens of golems already lay broken in the battlefield, but just as many sumopotts were crushed, stabbed, and beaten to death. The mercenaries initially did well. They were energized and highly motivated. After the easier to destroy golems became obliterated, the kill to casualty ratio dropped drastically. Insecurity began to set in. Success, or the lack there of, didn't faze the golems. Most of them weren't alive, so they couldn't be driven by emotions. The contraptions of metal and stone and wood persisted. The tide was turning. We accelerated our pace around the battlefield, jogging more than walking. One of the last things we saw was Captain Cottonwood pulling out his pistol and firing it at the rolling monstrosity charging him. The weapon must have been set to a full charge, because the stone tank shattered, flinging stones at golems and mercenaries indiscriminately.

Chapter 21

GRANITE

We travelled in a manner most compatible to us putting the most distance between ourselves and the golems. Concealment was imperative, but not as crucial as pace. We marched expeditiously through sparse prairie until crossing the headwaters of the Serpent River. Along its far bank was a road that returned us to the Northwoods. We risked lighting a lantern. It had been dark for the past hour, but under a perpetual full moon.

Every quarter or so we passed a small group of individuals who said they had come from Norwood. The golems had destroyed the village. I don't know what surprised me more, the number of groups we saw from Norwood, or that they were so few.

We saw the smoke before we saw the village. It was unlikely the golems used fire. Lanterns must have been knocked over as people fled and homes and businesses were destroyed. Not a single building was left untouched.

Twig was particularly devastated. "We should look for survivors."

"Anyone who survived has probably already fled." Centaur held her as she began to sob.

"Maybe someone is trapped under the rubble. As wolves...."

"We won't be able to smell anything through the ashes." Centaur had to practically drag his mate through the streets of Norwood. She wasn't forcibly trying to stay. She was just too numb to move.

We headed south across the gap between the two forests.

142

The passage of the golems was prominent. A 50-meter-wide isthmus connected the two continents of trees. The ten-score animated chunks of stone and iron gouged the earth, scraping away the grass and shrubs.

The devastation continued into Spinecrest. That beautiful inn was demolished. The steaming hot springs fed bathing pool had been ruptured. The remnants of its soothing drizzled down the hillside, like the last drops of blood from something already dead.

We continued to follow the *Golem Trail*---what we called the remnants of their passing. It provided the quickest route into the Northern Spine. Half-an-hour after leaving the ruins of Spinecrest we passed through the nymph camp. Scavengers had already begun to harvest the carrion. Some of the plastered bodies had already been pried up and partially consumed. All we could stomach was a passing glance, curiosity briefly overriding our disdain for the abomination.

At the nymph camp, the Golem Trail took a hard jog into the mountains. It led us to where we entered the surface from the underworld. The opening had been widened since we passed through. There were pieces of stone, wood, and metal scattered near it, possibly scraps from those who squeezed through the opening too closely to its rim.

Twig lost it again. "We brought this devastation. If we didn't disembark here the nymphs would still be alive, and Spinecrest and Norwood not destroyed."

Centaur held his mate as she sobbed into his chest. "We weren't the ones who did the killing. If we had come out at Jasper the same thing may have happened there."

"The nymphs must have distracted the golems," Pistachio hypothesized. "Instead of heading directly to Spinecrest they were attacked first. That knowledge could prove useful."

"If we wished to use living decoys," said Hornet.

"It was just an observation."

"It's going to get dark soon," said Pulp.

"How long will it take to reach Granite?"

"At least another day."

"Then I propose we create as much distance between ourselves and this opening as we can until sundim," said Centaur.

A sloped forest, laced with sporadic boulders and rocky protrusions made movement difficult. We barely trudged five kays before it got dark. A hundred meters short of the crest, we made camp beside a lake fed by snowmelt. We didn't risk lighting a campfire. We turned in early, immediately after consuming most of what remained of our food. We intended to break camp at the hint of dawn. Our hasty escape from the Mercenary Hills prevented us from restocking our supplies.

Nothing bothered us during the night. We left before it became completely light, eager to make it to the relative safety of a gent's lair. It had been many days since we had been at ease in our surroundings.

An animal trail connected the lake to the crest of the range. On top we were able to see to both the east and west--- intermittent mist and blue sky above descending granite and green. The interior of the Northern Spine was one of the most remote areas on Limbo. There were no settlements up there, not even any trails or roads. The only roads at all in the area where at the base of the mountains, deep in the foothill forests, one on each side of the range.

The crest was curvy. Occasionally we walked a flat stretch, but more often we were walking either up or down. In the higher elevations there were patches of snow, particularly in the crevices that were shadowed from the stationery Limboan sun. Intermittently, we passed a peak, either within our path or adjacent to it. Those on the crest we had to skirt around. Occasionally, we saw an animal---a bighorn sheep or a mountain goat---but most chose to remain within the lowland forest.

We spotted a castle atop one of the central crest peaks. A

trail spiraled around the mountain, terminating at the structure. Statues were carved into the castle's walls, which had been chiseled out of the mountain.

"That's Granite's keep," stated Pulp. "Like many of the Neutral gents, he likes his privacy."

At the stone bridge connecting the trail to the castle, we were greeted by Granite. At six-meters, he was one of the taller gents. His gray skin was completely hairless. The only clothes he wore were stone shorts. Thin slabs of stone had been connected together like chain mail. His expression was indifferent. He didn't appear particularly happy with our appearance, nor did he appear particularly disturbed.

"Pulp."

"Granite."

"Is your transport platform broken?"

"It wasn't nearby."

"You brought an entourage?"

"It's more enjoyable traveling with friends."

"I prefer traveling alone. There's no questions about where we're going or what we're going to do. Or how much longer until we get there. I don't prefer to travel at all, but sometimes it's necessary. The farther I am from my keep the more likely I will meet someone. They'll feel obligated to communicate with me."

"Are you painfully shy?" asked Twig.

"Let's just say I prefer my own company over someone else's. Most people behave like insects: hovering around you, buzzing, biting. What do you need? You didn't come all this way just to interrupt my schedule."

"What are we keeping you from?" Twig couldn't believe someone actually wished to have no social contact. She wasn't going to quit prodding Granite until his way of life made sense to her.

"A short walk, supper, then bed."

"And you are upset we jarred that routine?"

"I enjoy it. It's predictable. If I don't take that walk, I may not become hungry at the usual time, which may affect when I go to bed and fall to sleep. Changing one task disrupts the entire day. If my sleeping is affected, it may also modify the next day."

"This is Twig, by the way," said Pulp. "Her mate there, is Centaur."

"My condolences."

"Are you trying to be rude or does it come to you naturally?" asked Twig.

"Some of each I believe. Being re-created in this form permits me to do what I want. I don't try to be rude, I just don't care if I am. It's so empowering, so invigorating being who you are, not having to put up a false front so everyone around you won't despise you."

"Haven't you heard the expression: You can make more friends with sugar than with vinegar?"

"I don't care if I make friends, and vinegar isn't that bad. It adds zest, to food, and to life."

Pulp continued his introductions. "This is Hornet, and the lynx is Lynn."

"If I don't care to know the name of a person, why would I want to know the name of a cat?"

"Because this cat is more intelligent than you."

"A talking cat isn't an improvement. It makes it seem more human. Pulp, I'd appreciate if you don't introduce anyone else to me. If I don't know their names, it's easier for me to ignore them."

"May we stay the night?" asked Pulp. Granite's face convulsed. "There is something that needs to be brought to the attention of the Brotherhood. My companions need to stay somewhere safe while I'm gone. If they camp out in the open and wander aimlessly, how many things might they attract to your mountain?"

"What are you going to tell the Brotherhood?"

"It would be best if I waited to speak to all of the

146

Brotherhood, so I wouldn't have to repeat myself."

"Are you going to invite us in?" asked Twig. "It's starting to get breezy. Maybe you could also offer us something to drink."

"I'm not thirsty."

"You didn't just climb 500 meters."

"You'll get something to drink in a few minutes. Now, Pulp, I will allow you and this group of bullies to stay in my keep for one day on the condition you tell me beforehand what you will say to the Brotherhood. You don't have to give me all the details, just the crux of this emergency that can't wait until our next, scheduled, meeting."

"The Wizards have finally shown their true intent. They have begun their assault. An army of golems has ravished the countryside north of you. Some of the half-and-halfs may also be involved, but why they would wish to is beyond me."

"To torment others, I imagine, like I'm being constantly tormented by taking in strangers. This offensive by the Wizards satisfies their cravings. Come on in. If I'm to give you something to drink I might as well feed you."

Granite walked beneath the raised portcullis into his lair. He raised a lever. The gate dropped. I nearly got crushed by it. It didn't register with him that others might still be beneath it if he wasn't.

Scones lit the interior of the castle. The walls were as well-adorned with carvings as the keep walls. They were intricately detailed. "You're very talented," I told him.

"The images of them in my mind aren't complete until they extend through my hands."

"You shouldn't be hiding your sculptures," said Twig. "They should be shown to the world."

"Sometimes I wish others could receive as much enjoyment from seeing them as I do making them. If I only I didn't despise people so much."

The food was simple. Why would one create an elaborate

multi-course meal when one usually ate alone?

"You may sleep where you wish," spoke Granite.

"Where might the bedrooms be?" asked Twig. "Dumb question. If you didn't want guests why would you provide a place for them to sleep?"

"Granite and I are heading to Toe's castle," said Pulp. "He's the one who announces meetings of the Brotherhood. I don't know how long I will be. It could take a day or two for all of us to gather."

Granite said, "Feel free to examine the sculptures."

Pulp and Granite returned late the second day. The latter didn't say anything to us as he headed towards his bedroom.

"He's had his fill of social interaction for another year, or two," said Pulp. "Gents aren't shy about expressing their opinions, even if it means talking over two or three others. It's amazing Granite was able to stay as long as he did. Halfway into the first day he walked away from the table. I wasn't sure if he was going to transport home or throw himself off the cloud. He did neither. Spending a quarter by himself was enough of a break to get him through that day. The second day he just pushed himself until he could take it no more."

"So, nothing was resolved?" asked Centaur.

"Nothing resolved *was* the resolution. The Neutrals don't want to get involved. The Positives are all for a fight. The Negatives too, but on the other side. To prevent gent from fighting gent the Brotherhood has decided to not get involved."

"But you said they were still discussing the issue?"

"Arguing is more like it. None of the three factions are likely to be swayed. Some of them will continue to argue their point until they pass out. When only one of them remains awake the discussion is over. Depending on who that is, sometimes that last person even argues with himself until he passes out."

"So, we had come all this way for nothing?" Hornet questioned.

"We are now certain we have one less ally," said Twig.

"Actually, two," said Pistachio. "We weren't able to hire the sumopotts, and for all we know they may no longer exist."

"We really need to find that last sphere then, don't we?" said Hornet.

"Do you think Granite will allow us to borrow his transport platform?" asked Centaur.

"Even if he would, there would be nowhere for us to go," stated Pulp. "What Negative gent will want to receive us---on a full stomach?"

"So, we're going to have to walk to the Grim Mountains or...."

"Or hike back down to the train station."

Chapter 22

ACORN

We left in the morning. Granite remained in his room. Goodbyes were often unbearable even when everyone was sociable. We restocked our supplies. There was a downside to hiding. If a person wasn't present, he couldn't prevent others from borrowing from him.

No sign of the golems---yet. Maybe---for once---we lucked out.

We cautiously passed through the opening into the underworld. If we were to make contact with the golems, or one of the Wizards other minions, it was most likely to occur there.

Nothing.

The trip to the tracks took a fraction of the time it took to rise to the surface. The Golem Trail was prominent, even in the underworld. Scattered, near the zombies, were the smashed remains of humanoids with tentacles on their heads. They were so badly damaged it was difficult to distinguish details.

Something moved.

"Let me borrow that lantern." Pistachio handed the illumination to Centaur. "Back there somewhere." Centaur walked cautiously towards the movement. The lantern's range was about ten meters. The thing that had moved was a couple of meters beyond that. An old man hobbled out of the crevice he was hiding in. His clothes were in tatters. His face and arms were badly scraped and bruised. From the way his left arm hung it appeared to be broken. He looked so delicate. If anyone touched him he might crumble.

Pistachio removed a vial from his smock. "Drink this. It will revive you." He handed it to the decrepit man. He uncapped the vial and swallowed its contents. His color improved. He no longer appeared like he was going to pass out. "I believe you've recovered enough for your body to be rejuvenated." Pistachio pulled another vial from a pocket and handed it to the man. He swallowed it without comment. A moment later the bruises and scratches became less pronounced. "I'm going to have to physically set that shoulder. Centaur, hold him." There was a dull popping sound as the bone returned to the socket. The man flinched, but remained silent. The druid felt the lower part of his arm. "The ulna is broken. I'm going to have to set it before I give you another elixir. How did you receive so much damage?" The elderly man smiled sadly. Pistachio pulled back the man's sleeve. A bone could be seen pushing through the skin. He bent the man's arm in a precise manner, forcing the bone to rebury itself. "Centaur, hold his arm for me, in exactly the same spot, and manner." He did so, exchanging places with the druid. Pistachio removed another vial from his smock. He handed it to the elderly man. He downed it as un-hesitantly as he did the first two. "Centaur, keep pressure on it until I tell you to stop." Five minutes later Centaur was given permission to let go. The man twisted his arm. "Almost good as new."

"Now tell us how you came to be here," Centaur demanded.

"I don't think I've ever seen someone appear as old as you," Twig commented. "Have you ever been re-created?"

Pulp cocked his bow. "Either you are extremely unlucky to find yourself here, or you're a Wizard. Which one is it?"

"The first." The decrepit old man's voice was surprisingly vibrant. "Thank you for healing me. In another hour I may have expired. My intent was simply to investigate, but the golems didn't view me as an innocent bystander. Dead voyeurs tell no tales."

"Why were you down here in the first place?" asked Hornet. "Did you follow the golems from where they came?"

"Gaea, no. I live down here."

"We've known some people who like their privacy, but isn't this taking it to the extreme?" asked Centaur.

"You are making that assumption based on my present form. Do not be alarmed by what I transform into. Stand back." The elderly human morphed into a very large red drak. "As you see, living in the underworld is not so odd for me." My companions went into a defensive stance, their weapons and reflexes made ready. "Dismiss your concern. I'm not going to attack, unless you provoke me."

"But aren't you...."

"Thorn? The queen of Negative drak. We have a similar appearance. That's one reason I spend so much time in the underworld. She has this *reputation* that puts people in a bad mood, quite deservingly so. She is larger than I and more vivid, a truer red. She also smells like sulfur. My breath is more astringent. You may call me Acorn, originally from the Breezewoods."

"Golems were able to do this much damage, to a drak?"

ERIC CARLTON NEPERUD

asked Pulp.

"You must not have met them then, gent. In the numbers they were in they are extremely deadly. I don't even think Sands, the most powerful of our kind, could survive a prolonged battle with them."

"We have had the displeasure of meeting them, from a distance. They've already destroyed two towns. I just thought...."

"That drak are omnipotent? Many have the same assumption about gents. I imagine you might disagree, at least internally. I did put up a good fight. My astringent breath is from the corrosive gas I expel. It's as devastating to metal as it is to flesh and bone. Its weakness is it does very little damage to stone. The golems constructed from that medium are the ones that injured my left arm and shoulder---after I dissolved many of their less protected cohorts. An advantage of a gaseous attack is the corrosion persisting until the cloud dissipates. Cognizant of my demise if I didn't flee, I transformed into a serpent. My more slender form was able to slither into areas the golems were too bulky to travel. They attempted to tear down the underworld to get to me, but some of golems appeared to have their own sovereignty, and they directed the others to back away."

"The Wizards have perfected the art of black elem manipulation," stated Pistachio, glumly.

"Why transform yourself into a human?" asked Twig. "Weren't you better protected in one of your other forms? Did you choose a human form to influence us? To make it more likely we would help you?"

"Partially. People *are* more likely to help those that look like themselves. No, the main reason was energy conservation. I was dying. It takes less energy to subsist as a human than in one of my larger forms."

"So, you truly were dying?"

"Yes. And for a drak that is a horrific fate. You see, one is mutated into a drak just once. Once that one life expires he will never be mutated into that form again. We believe our species is the grandest form of life on Limbo."

"Definitely the most feared," said Centaur.

"I greatly appreciate you saving me. In return I will do for you whatever is in my means to do."

Centaur's immediately responded. "You could help us fight the Wizards. They have more than an army of golems in their arsenal. They're attempting to conquer the world."

"To fight the Wizards is foolhardy. Great might recognizes great might. The elite are often targeted in war. I will not fight for you, but there are other things I can provide…. Reconnaissance. I can see more from the sky than you can see from the ground."

"Any help would be appreciated," said Hornet.

We pondered for a moment, to formulate a plan. Centaur asked, "Can you rendezvous with us in…?" He turned towards us. "When?"

"Three weeks," I responded.

Centaur faced Acorn again. "Can you rendezvous with us in three weeks? North of Zephyr, along the Sparkling River. Do you know where that is?"

"Yes. About 100 kays west of Gulag."

"If we don't have our armies in place by then to counter the Wizards it will probably be too late."

"I will meet you there at dawn in this form."

After so much disappointment, the news of a drak helping us added a bit of pep to our steps. If felt like it took just minutes to return to the train station. Two multi-car trains, plus our own, waited for us on the pair of parallel tracks. "Would you do us the honor again, Pistachio?" said Centaur. The druid gently pushed the lever forward after we and our provisions were loaded. The train's headlights lit up as it began to move. After it merged onto the single-track, Pistachio slowly added more pressure to the lever.

"Should I stop in Jasper, or continue to the Grim

Mountains?"

"We must determine if Cone has returned," said Pulp. "We should make at least one attempt to reunite with him."

"It will be dangerous coming up through that Wizard's shop," said Centaur.

"A druid is more than a match for any Wizard," stated Twig confidently.

"There may not be a Wizard there at all," said Hornet. "We did kill the proprietor of the penta shop?"

"And it's very likely his replacement will be more prepared for us than he was," said Centaur.

"We must make the attempt," Pulp insisted.

Twig had never met the sheriff of Jasper, but being part wolf, it was instinctive to assist with reuniting her pack. She seconded the gent's decree.

Centaur relented. "All right. I like Cone too. If we all get mutated in the attempt I promise you I'll return bigger than...all of you, so I can beat the *I told you* out of you."

"I know how close we are to finishing this," said Hornet. "But there are some things more important."

What are you doing to me, Gaea? I'm so close to freeing myself from this prison, after 141 years, and you continue to create ways to delay me.

Chapter 23

WORLD GUARD

It had to happen, eventually. A train was heading towards us, from the other direction. "Well?" Pistachio was a scientist, not a leader. He was content to allow Dinga to lead the druids. His lack of decision making had become habitual. He could no longer make a decision---even if his life depended upon it.

Centaur was a natural leader. His size forced people take notice, and he took advantage of it. He honed his people skills enough where he was able to direct people without thinking about it. "I suggest we stop and allow them make the next move. We may need to back up suddenly, so let's be prepared."

As our train slowed, the train heading towards us wasn't getting appreciably closer. "I believe they have formulated an identical strategy," Pulp speculated. The train then abruptly turned. Seconds later it had completely disappeared. "Not entirely identical."

Pistachio pushed the lever forward delicately. We slowly moved closer to where the train appeared to vanish. The track split, veering off to the southwest.

"To Gulag?" Hornet conjectured.

"Likely," said Pulp. "Anyone else notice the train's cargo?" No one answered. "Hobs *and* gobs."

"I didn't think they got along very well," Hornet commented. "Our adventure in the Twin Hills evidence of that."

"They don't," I assured them.

"Why would they agree to work for the Wizards?" asked

Twig. "And together."

"Spoils of war, perhaps," Centaur speculated. "Think of all the cities they could plunder. They have never been organized enough to attack a large settlement. The Wizards have provided that organization."

"I thought demons didn't leave their homeland for extended periods of time. Don't they have a psychological, possibly even a physical, addiction to it?"

Pulp answered. "Our desire to return grows with time. But if there is something equally as desirable beyond the homeland we can stay away longer."

"Let's start moving again," said Centaur. "That fork must mean we're close to Jasper. The sooner we leave this train the better. That was too close a call."

The tracks forked again, this time as parallel rails. There was an alcove to the left.

"FEEK!" And another train was coming.

"Don't stop until we're back to a single rail," Centaur directed. No one questioned him---verbally. There were a lot of concerned looks, tempered with trust. Centaur wouldn't let us down. Or was the kind or person to commit murder-suicide. As Pistachio slowed down, barely overshooting the double rails, Centaur shouted, "Grab your gear and RUN!"

We vaulted into the alcove, then scrambled up the tunnel we believed would lead us to the surface, as the approaching train hit our train head on. Initially we heard groans, then squeaks, grunts, growls, and multiple footsteps.

The occupants of the other train were very determined to share their displeasure with us. The disbursed hobs and gobs were gaining on us. They ran towards their prey as individuals, but we had to flee from them as a group. Pistachio was very capable of estimating our escape velocity. But achieving it? Scientists weren't renowned for their athletic prowess. "You have anything in those pockets of yours to aid us?" asked Centaur.

Pistachio paused to consider. Twig grabbed him by the arm and pulled him along. "You can contemplate while you run. I guarantee you, the hobs and gobs won't be standing around *thinking*."

"Should I create an air barrier again, or a solid one?" Pistachio spoke to himself, but loud enough for us to hear.

"Either or both," Hornet replied through staccato breaths, as much induced by anxiety as exertion. "I recommend you do so quickly. I think I can smell them."

"Do we plan to remain in Jasper for days or hours? It makes a difference in what barrier I create."

The footsteps behind us was getting louder. "Just do something---anything," Pulp demanded. "Delaying them even a couple of minutes might make the difference between us escaping and being captured or killed."

Pistachio stopped. He retrieved a vial, pulled the stopper, then drank the liquid within it. A very enthusiastic gob caught up with us. At the precipice of assaulting the druid, the person closest to him, Twig, swung her sword at his legs, nearly amputating one of them. He toppled. She finished him off by stabbing him in the back.

"I'm glad you're on our side," said Centaur.

"Remember that if you ever consider straying."

Pistachio raised his arms, midway between horizontal and vertical. The air shimmered before and above him. The ceiling began to drip large muddy drops.

Another eager gob caught up with us. A handful of others were just steps behind. There was still no sign of the bulkier, more heavily armored hobs. The second gob to reach us slipped on the pile of mud that was now a meter high. After he pulled himself up, Pulp shot an arrow at him. He fell backwards onto his companions who had finally caught up with him. The ceiling in front of us couldn't be seen at all now. It was one continuous wall of mud. Pistachio swallowed a second vial. Another wave erupted from his hands. The mud no longer dripped. Moments later it solidified into stone.

"That ought to keep them away from us for a while," said Hornet.

"When they finally bore their way through they'll have an unsettling surprise," said Pulp.

Twig shuddered. "What would it be like being encased in solid rock? Would claustrophobia kill a person before they suffocate?"

"It looks like we aren't going back this way," said Centaur. "The cost of riding the train has risen considerably."

We hastily rose to the surface. There weren't any forks or spurs to contemplate, until....

"We have been here before," Hornet announced. "How could we have overlooked this tunnel?"

"Look behind you," said Pulp.

The tunnel we had traveled through appeared to vanish. Hornet felt the wall behind him. He moved down it with his hands until they abruptly slipped into air. He walked forward. He should have bumped into stone, but he kept walking. He turned and rejoined us. "It's an optical illusion. The rock is so similar here and back there that is looks like one continuous slab."

"Why not just put a pental illusion here instead, instead of visual one?" asked Twig. "The Wizards have penta to spare."

"Pental illusions don't last forever," I enlightened. "A natural one might. Also, there are means of detecting elemental energy. There is nothing about this illusion that will draw someone to it."

"Do we go through the penta shop or the cheese factory?" asked Hornet.

"The threats will be more numerous in the cheese factory," said Pulp. "But they'll be stronger in the penta shop. Multiple Wizards, possibly, or traps we may not be able to detect."

"Then it's to the cheese factory we go," said Centaur.

I hadn't been with Hornet and his companions when they had come to Jasper. They appeared to know their way beneath the city, quite well. I had to drastically reduce the probability of us making a negative contact with the locals, at least until we reached this *Cheese Factory*.

A door blocked the end of a narrow spur tunnel. "I believe using stealth might be a better strategy than just barging in," Twig suggested. She turned the knob as she put pressure against the door. It wouldn't bulge. "It was worth a try."

Centaur sighed. "If Pebble was here...."

"What if the door wasn't here at all?" Pistachio removed a vial, drank its contents, then placed the palm of his left hand in front of him. He swirled it. The heavy wooden door dissolved into a pile of sawdust. Twig had the awareness, and reflexes, to catch the metal doorknob before it hit the ground.

Centaur led the charge up from the cellar into the building. Instead of confronting the rat men my companions had described we met....

"CONE!" Centaur gave the former Sheriff of Jasper a bear hug. As did Hornet and Pulp. "You don't look like you mutated into a rat?"

Cone was not alone. The room was full of men dressed similarly to him: brown trousers and shirts, blue belts, and an image of Limbo, a brown globe with the four seas in blue, over their hearts. Attached to their belts was a sword in a tabard and a dart pistol in a holster. The only distinguishing difference between their attire and his were their collars. Cone had three silver diamonds attached. No one else had more than two.

"Why don't you set your gear down and stay awhile. We're perfectly safe here. As safe as anywhere on Limbo, which isn't saying much." Cone escorted us to a lounge. "Have a seat. You look as exhausted as I feel, but I haven't been to the boundaries of Limbo and back again." I curled up on a couch. I closed my eyes, but was too curious of Cone's tale to sleep. "You have new companions, but lost a couple of old ones. Are Stick and General Paint...?"

Centaur answered. "Stick died not long after you, but we've seen him since he was restored in the Octagonal Prism. He has chosen to become a more active member of the Knights."

"A loss for you, but a satisfactory decision for him, I imagine. Sometimes it works out for the best being with one's own."

"It shouldn't surprise you then that General Paint has returned to the trogs. This is Twig. She's my mate." Twig held Centaur's hand and squeezed it for emphasis.

"I see that."

"And this is Pistachio," said Hornet. "He is a druid, a member of that scientific order my wife created in the Raspberry Mountains."

"And I'm Lynn. They forget about me until they need my assistance."

"That's because you keep to yourself most of the time," said Pulp. "You don't participate, particularly when we're fighting for our lives."

"Let me tell you my story, then you can tell me yours. Would you like something to eat or drink?"

"Well...."

Cone stood back up. He stuck his head out the doorway, signaling one of his men. He spoke quietly to him. He immediately left. Cone sat back down. "It will take a few minutes. I was initially shocked when I was re-created in Jasper. The city is barely in the Negative Frontier, but it is still in it. What had I done to deserve being re-created here? After some soul searching I realized I've had done some immoral things in order to provide a stronger moral foundation for Jasper. I don't regret doing what I did, but doing those things did change me. Instead of allowing my Negative re-creation to depress me for the remainder of my days, I was determined to exploit my moral sacrifice. My morality was already damaged, so why not take advantage of it. One of the reasons I left

Jasper with you was my dissatisfaction of being isolated in one city. I mentioned to you establishing a world police force one day. Well, that time has come. The Octagonal Knights are devoted to defending the people, as long as doing so brings the moralities in balance. But they number just eight. The *World Guard* will have a similar mission, but in a grander scale. There were enough people of like mind that recruiting wasn't difficult. We've chosen to retain Jasper as our headquarters---instead of moving it to Gulag---due to it being on the fringes of the Negative Frontier. In the short time we have been in operation we have already established a second precinct, in Port Moor."

"And it appears you have also taken over the cheese factory," said Pulp.

"We couldn't have rats and Wizards running wild within the World Guard's capital, could we? As we did more snooping we discovered a previously unknown tunnel. It led down to some train tracks."

"That's how we got here so quickly," said Twig.

"Which I surmised. If anyone could use them to their advantage it would be you."

"They run all over...under...Limbo. The Wizards appear to manage the enterprise."

"We didn't know that, not with certainty. We had seen hobs and gobs pass through, but not yet Wizards. With the penta shop having that subterranean access it doesn't surprise me."

"Has there been a replacement for the Wizard we killed?" asked Hornet.

"I don't know. It has been very quiet in there. No one comes or goes, but that doesn't mean someone isn't there."

Food and water was brought in: bread, fish, and a shredded kelp salad.

After the meal we shared our adventures.

"So, the Wizards are really planning to conquer the world? But why? The trouble doesn't appear to warrant the gain. They have a substantial financial hold on Limbo already. Why would they want to become administrators?"

"I don't think there will be much to administer after they finish," spoke Pulp. "We've seen two towns completely demolished."

"It doesn't make much sense, does it?" spoke Hornet.

"Forced emigration will provide the Wizards with all the men and women they need to repopulate," said Pistachio. "Once they establish their world order the new arrivals will fit nicely into whatever role they feel fit."

"You've said you've seen hobs and gobs pass through," said Centaur. "How many?"

"At least one train full every day. We have someone stationed near the tracks."

"I think we may have trapped him down there. We sealed the tunnel leading down to the tracks. There were some hobs and gobs chasing us."

Cone appeared saddened, but he forced a smile. "He'll be all right. He was one of my deputies while I was sheriff. He's been on numerous stakeouts. This one will just take longer. You're concerned for Gulag?"

"We believe that's where the first major battle will occur. Once the central city is subjugated it will be easier for other cities to fall."

"Then that is where the World Guard needs to be. I will send envoys to all the major cities. I'm sure there's enough people itching for a fight for us to gallantly counter the Wizards and their minion. The only thing that has made Limbo livable has been the Human Pact. If the Wizards are going to abandon it, to essentially become traitors to humanity, that's all the motivation we'll need for recruitment. You want to help me?"

"We're still piecing together the portal," said Hornet. "We found the fifth sphere and are searching for the last."

"You don't want to stick around and see how this war turns

out?"

"We have already recruited trogs, arbols, and druids, and attempted to hire all available sumopotts," Centaur responded. "We plan to be there for at least the beginning of the war. That said, it would be foolish not to have an escape plan if things go badly."

"I'll do my part in keeping you around, so you can congratulate the victors. Where is the sixth sphere by the way?"

"The Grim Mountains."

"That's where the Wizards are getting most of their troops."

Chapter 24

SWAMP

"I guess waiting until the hobs and gobs dig their way through that cave-in, and then slipping past them, is out of the question?" asked Hornet.

"We walk," said Centaur.

Hornet sighed.

"Our legs were starting to atrophy. About time we provided our own locomotion."

Hornet sighed again.

"What can we expect in the Grim Mountains?" Twig asked. "I've never been that far north. What made Chaneg exciting was the unexpected. Orneg ought to be more predictable."

"Predictability isn't necessarily beneficial, not in the Negative Frontier," Cone commented. "Chaos permits goodwill.

You won't have any pleasant surprises in Orneg."

"We had just one army chasing us in Neutrality," said Centaur. "We might have dozens of interactions in the Grim Mountains."

"It's dangerous enough during peaceful times," Cone added. "On the cusp of war, with troops being immobilized…. You sure you don't want to join the World Guard?"

"Great," said Pulp. "And I just took a bath." Twig had insisted the men wash themselves thoroughly before we left Jasper. It might be weeks before they would have the luxury of a prolonged hot, soapy soak. Twig felt her bath would be wasted if she had to surround herself with individuals less enthusiastic in their hygiene.

Jasper was a walled city atop a stone-crested hill in the center of the swamp formed by the Naga River emptying into the Eastern Sea. A rampart led down from the city's southern gate to a boardwalk until terminating on more solid ground. The air was saturated, with moisture, and insects. They flocked to us like we were celebrities. Some were many times their traditional size. They were annoying, but caused modest physical harm. The route to the sea was a dreadful one-and-a-half hour trek through jungle and marsh, which mercifully terminated at a sandbar that separated the murky astringent water of the swamp from the brine of the sea. Without vegetation blocking it, the breeze became more noticeable. Not only did it expel most of the swamp's stench of decay, it banished most of the insects. There wasn't a distinct track on top of the sand----wind and the tide perpetually modified the terrain---but enough people had traveled this route earlier in the day to leave ample footprints to follow. The swamp began to be left behind. As it did, the beach was devoured by a bluff. The grass on top of it, although sparse, provided a better opportunity for a trail to develop.

We hoped the sky might clear once we vacated the swamp.

It never did. The murkiness was called *negative haze*. Did the clustering of wayward souls prevent the sun from shining brightly? Or did the dimness attract them, like a magnet? Our collective mood, although not overly enthusiastic, was at least resolute. The lack of sunlight began to take its toll. Our expressions became blank, our pace diminished.

At midday we passed through Wave, a hamlet well protected in a cove. A spur road dipped below the bluff to the wharf and wooden buildings shoreward of the diminutive rocky bay. At the end of the road, a wooden wall and gate protected the hamlet's inhabitants from unwanted intrusion. The other sides of the hamlet were naturally defended by stone and surf. The settlement looked nearly abandoned. Its small fishing fleet was still out. We bypassed the hamlet, but just seeing it disrupted the monotony, improving our mood.

An hour later, water began to pool in the lowlands. The sole welcomed feature in the area was a sandy isthmus that kept us dry between the jungle and the sea.

"Where do you think we should cut across to the Grim Mountains?" asked Centaur. "Port Moor?"

"There isn't a direct route from there," said Pulp. "We're going to have to go to Cedar View."

"That's another 200 kays."

"We could bushwhack, but I wouldn't recommend it. The Moorwoods might be drier than the Muck Moors, but they're just as deadly."

"I believe we need to direct our thoughts to something more urgent," said Twig. "I can't be certain with it being so gloomy here, but I believe the sun is dimming."

"It is," Pulp confirmed. "My internal clock tells me we got about ten more minutes before it gets dark." To compensate for the sun never setting or rising, Limboans have developed a very keen sense of time. The longer they spend on Limbo the more finely tuned it becomes.

Pistachio said, "It looks like we have three options: we make camp up here, we make camp down there, or we hike through the night."

"I say we continue hiking," said Hornet. "I don't think I'll be able to get much sleep tonight. I'll either keep myself awake by thinking about finding that last sphere, or listening to the sounds of the swamp, imagining the things making those sounds visiting us in the middle of the night."

"I've got my second wind," said Twig.

"Well, let's take an extended break now, while we still have light," said Centaur. "We'll eat a good meal. After fueling and resting we ought to be rejuvenated enough to hike another couple of hours."

We had re-supplied in Jasper. The types of food we brought were those that were lightweight and wouldn't spoil. There were a few exceptions. We also brought cheese and bread. They would keep for a while, but not indefinitely. Our dinner consisted of the bread and cheese and some dehydrated vegetables we reconstituted in boiling water. When spices were added it created a tasty soup.

An unexpected benefit of the isthmus being exposed was the moon providing enough light to travel safely. Our one significant encounter occurred an hour after it got dark. A handful of bipedal lizards, knee-high to a human, investigated us. They climbed up from the swamp and spit at us. Every time one of them did that it would dart back towards the swamp. Once confident no one followed, it would turn around and start the process all over again. Whatever it was they ate, left a rankness to their saliva.

Centaur was the first to have had enough. He chased after one of little buggers, down the banks of the isthmus, into the murky shadows below. The visibility wasn't the only thing murky. The soil gave away under him. The quicksand he had stepped into pulled him further down with every panicked motion he made. His thrashing was like waving a flag. Additional lizards appeared, dozens of them popping out of the syrupy pools.

Twig was first to react. Death may be temporary on Limbo, but the emotional, intellectual, and physical changes that resulted, where devastating for a relationship. The individual still existed, but the modified bond often became too complicated to continue. Twig reacted more with emotion than common sense. Her intention was to pull her mate out, but she came too close to the unstable ground. She also became caught in the debilitating sludge.

Pulp and Hornet prepared to pounce. Before I could warn them to use extreme caution, Pistachio said, "Hold up. There's a better way." Recognizing that no additional prey was going to leave the safety of the isthmus, the remaining lizards joined in on attacking Centaur and Twig. Pistachio pulled a vial from one of his pockets and swallowed its contents. How many of them did he have? He must have removed a dozen already and his pockets still looked full. The druid raised his hands in front of him, with his palms facing down. Slowly he raised them. In concert, Centaur and Twig began to rise from the water. Their chests emerged first, then their legs and feet. It looked like they were standing on the water. Each was covered in lizards. The lizards weren't attacking anymore. They clutched protectively to prevent their prey from escaping. Centaur and Twig continued to rise. They were now completely out of the water. Lizards began to fall off, on their own, and with assistance from those they hung from. Centaur and Twig were now level with the isthmus. The last lizards fell with a plop into the swamp. Pistachio pulled his hands back in, towards his body. Centaur and Twig moved towards him. The druid backed up to allow enough space for them to land. He raised them up a bit more, to insure they had enough clearance. The final few meters were excruciatingly slow, like he was reeling in a fish he didn't want to get away. After dropping to the ground, they embraced each other, then Pistachio.

The druid reddened. "Just glad to be of assistance. With you mighty warriors doing most of the work, I try to chip in where I can."

"You do more than that," said Centaur. "Your contribution is crucial. How many times have your elixirs saved us? Not only by supplying them, but knowing what to use, and when."

The bi-pedal lizards looked up at us: distress---and desire. But they kept their distance. They had enough intelligence to connect their prey's escape with potentially more unpleasant interactions if they made too much a nuisance of themselves.

Pistachio studied the muddy pair in front of him. Underneath the goo there was an indication of injuries. He pulled out another vial.

Centaur shook a hand in front of him. "No. We're not that hurt. Save the healing for when we really need it."

I interjected. "We still have many kays to go before we sleep. Curing a cold might prevent pneumonia. There is no benefit to saving medication if we're all dead."

"I agree," said Pulp. "Hiking will only aggravate those scrapes and bites. If we get attacked again I prefer you to be at full strength."

"Go ahead," said Twig. "Men want to prove they're infallible by not going to the doctor. It proves the contrary, exposing their mental fallibility."

"Well, woman sometimes take too many medications. They are hypochondriacs, going to the doctor when they have a hang nail."

"Sometimes hangnails get infected."

"I'm going to try something slightly different this time," Pistachio announced. "If it doesn't work it won't hurt you, just be less effective." He stood in front of Twig. He swallowed an elixir and extended his arms. With fingers parted he slowly lowered them.

Twig began to squirm. "That tickles."

Pistachio turned to face Centaur. The same procedure was done with him. He chose not to respond to the uneasiness he felt.

"Well?" asked the druid. "Through all that grime I can't tell if your injuries have healed or not."

"Feel free to examine me," Centaur suggested.

"Your mate was quite insistent I bathe in Jasper. I don't believe I wish to be forced to do so again until I feel it's necessary."

Twig first checked herself, then Centaur. "There appears to be some scarring, a small scab here or there, but for the most part we are healed."

"What did you do differently?" asked Pulp.

"Didn't you notice? I used one healing elixir on both of them. If the Wizards, and sumopotts, can allocate the discharge of a penta, I thought I might be able to. I first transferred the energy into a mental urn, then disbursed it."

"That could really save elem," said Hornet. "An advantage like that could make the difference in the war against the Wizards."

"Or eliminate a disadvantage," I added. "If the Wizards are able to ration a penta's discharge in the operation of their trains, it's likely they'll also be able to do so in battle?"

Our dim environment became slightly less dim when the moon brightened. Day-*light* was an exaggeration. We had been on the move now for a full day, less the delay for breaks, and the altercation with the lizards. The dawning of the pseudo day provided a burst of energy and enthusiasm, but after the novelty of it wore off we began to slog again, both physically and emotionally.

Midday, the water below us began to recede. The dark, drowned trees of the swamp began to be replaced by lush oaks and maples. The abundance of vegetation and negative haze perpetuated the darkness, but instead of there being a gray hue, everything appeared to be green. At the terminus of the isthmus, the trail fell into the Moorwoods. The trees went to the brink of the Eastern Sea, their waters lapping at their feet. It was a cheerier environment, but simultaneously more frightening. Visibility was reduced. Before, we could see kays into the moors, now, as far as the next tree.

"I'm going to change into a wolf to better catch the scent of something approaching," stated Twig.

"Me too," Centaur blurted.

Pulp response, "We'll, I'm not going to carry both of your packs and gear. Even if I was somehow able, I still wouldn't want to do it."

"You could trade off," Hornet suggested.

Being a gentleman, Centaur suggested his mate go first, after she promised a few things that weren't appropriate to repeat. There were some pauses, and minor detours, but we never made contact with anything.

Port Moor was reached midafternoon. Villages were normally not walled, not having the tax base to afford such accruements, but considering it was located in what was considered to be the most dangerous forest in the Negative Frontier, it was money well spent. Being in the Ordered portion of the Frontier, the streets were precisely spaced and met at right angles. A wooden bridge spanned the Tea River, connecting Port Moor to the coastal road. The waters of the Tea were shallow and slow moving. It looked more like a narrow lake than it did a river. We looked down at the fish and lily pads as we crossed the structure. My feline instincts took over. My heart began to race. I wasn't even that fond of fish. Bones got in the way. As soon as I saw the creatures swimming I did all I could not to leap into the river. For a cat to contemplate getting wet proved how lustful my drive for fresh food was. An extended breath was released when I leapt down from those wooden slats. Entertainment and lunch all rolled into one was almost too much for me.

As expected, in a Negative Frontier settlement, the villagers were rude. Not only to us, but to each other, especially to women. I was thankful I was now a cat. I felt sorry for Twig until I saw how she handled such interactions. She did not back down. She did not drop her eyes. She did not ignore what was said---or done---to her. The first man who touched her backed up with a broken hand. It wasn't only the damage she delivered that modified their behavior towards her. It was also her demeanor. Some of her canine behaviors carried over into her human persona. She was a wild animal that held a prominent position in her pack.

Being a port city, Port Moor had many visitors who stayed a single night. Those who hadn't spent much time in the Negative Frontier stood out. They looked uncomfortable, like they expected to be mugged. They were much more docile than the locals. They didn't want to be noticed, but in behaving so they stood out.

There was one particularly meek man who sat by himself at a small table against one of the walls of the pub we ate in, the *Merry Piranha*. He was hansom, but he would have appeared even more so if he smiled. He looked grim, grim and scared. What had brought him to the Negative Frontier? Most likely he came from one of the fishing boats moored in the harbor. The most successful fishermen migrated with the fish. If the fish moved on, they moved on. Fishermen often stayed on their boats at night, but it wasn't uncommon for some of them to go into town for a meal, or entertainment, usually in the form of paid female companionship. The meek man was likely forced to spend the night away from the fishing boat, for his own good, to toughen him.

A well-dressed older man was watching him. He wasn't elderly, but he was middle-aged. For him to look like that, he must have been on Limbo a long time, without mutating. Or possibly, the reverse. On rare occasions mutations caused people to age at an accelerated rate. There have been rumors of people actually dying of old age. They are re-created of course, and sometimes into the same terminal form.

The meek man finally left. Either he had enough excitement away from the fishing boat, or he was just tired and wanted to turn in. A moment later the older man left. I was confident he intended to harm the meek man, in one manner or another.

"I need to leave for a while," I informed my companions.

Pulp smiled. "No sand box here?"

"I use your clothes for that while you're sleeping. I'll meet you upstairs." We had rented two rooms in the inn above the tavern.

That *old man* moved with remarkable stealth. If I wasn't as experienced with such movement myself I would have lost him. He was indeed following the meek man. I didn't see or sense anyone else in the vicinity. The old man pounced, with an unnatural burst of speed. I intended to save the meek man, but after becoming aware I was too late, I remained low in the shadows. The old man squeezed the meek man from behind with one arm while covering his mouth and nose with the other. The meek man struggled for a moment, then appeared to pass out. The older man carried him over his shoulder with the strength of a man his age shouldn't possess. I followed him into an alley. He set the man down gently, then cupped his hands over his head. A subdued burst of energy passed from the older man to the meek one through his hands. If I hadn't been studying them so closely I would have missed it. The old man fell backward. The meek man opened his eyes. He smiled, which would have made him appear more hansom if the wickedness behind it hadn't shone through. The once meek man stood up. He stripped off his clothes and exchanged them with the stationary older man. He stealthily sauntered away.

I returned to the Merry Piranha to inform my companions what I saw.

"That reminds me of what happened to Nimbus," said Hornet. "He was forced out of his drak body into a golem's by a Wizard. Do you think that man you saw was a Wizard?"

"If he was, he didn't behave like any Wizard I have ever met. Everyone has a morality signature. It's an aura that surrounds them. It's not visible, but it is something some people can sense, including myself. Wizards are *True Neutrals*. They don't assist, but they don't act out of malice either."

"Are you telling me the Wizards striving to brutally conquer Limbo aren't *evil*?" Twig was shocked.

"The Wizards choose to rule because they feel it is necessary to do so. Doing so makes them selfish, but it doesn't necessarily make them evil. True Neutrals are apathetic."

"But some of those they use are from the Negative Frontier."

"Implementing evil doesn't necessarily make one evil. The reason they use hobs and gobs might be that they can't kill wantonly."

"The man was too evil to be a Wizard?" Hornet questioned.

"Probably. The Wizards may have gotten the idea of essence transfusion from someone like him, though. Many engineering designs are influenced by nature."

Chapter 25

FEEDING TUBE

We continued down the coast in the morning. Cedar View was 200 kays away. With no settlements in between, that meant another three nights in the wild---two if we pushed. No matter the scenery---and no, we hadn't yet escaped the dreary monotony of the swamp---camping in the Negative Frontier was more basic training than vacation. Fortunately, the day, and evening, passed without major incident.

We passed into Neuneg---the Neutral-Negative Frontier--- the following morning. The terrain appeared less wild. The differences between it and Chaneg were subtle. The major similarity was the perpetual negative haze. All days began dreary, and ended in a similar manner. There were no bright colors. There was no warmth from stray sunrays. In exchange, there was a muggy pervasiveness. It constantly weighed down upon us, zapping our strength: physical, mental, and emotional.

Cedar View wasn't a particularly attractive town, but it was at least something different, a change of scenery from the monotony of the homogenous Moorwoods. Even hell had some variety: flames *and* wind, swamps *and* ice. A wooden wall surrounded it, like Port Moor, but its was much taller, and because it enclosed 4000 inhabitants instead of 2000, much longer. The cedars the town had been named for were used in the wall's construction. Apparently, the entire forest was consumed, because none of the trees could be seen. In an attempt to be as secure as possible, the town had one point of entry---and egress. Traffic flowed poorly because of this limitation. A road circled the wall. From it, three highways branched off, to the north, south and east. The wharf was directly across from the town gate---due west. Substituting for a proper road between it and the town was an exposed strip of earth defined by heavy travel.

Cedar View was considered to be the crossroads of Negativity. Being such, many unwholesome mutants passed through the area. The town's solution: barring anyone visibly modified from entering the walled settlement---inconveniencing us.

"I'm from the *Positive* Frontier," Pulp pleaded.

"Rules are rules," a gate guard insisted. "We don't have the luxury, or ability, to make conjectures on morality. By forbidding all mutants from entering, we avoid making a potentially fatal mistake."

"Do I look like I'm dangerous to you?"

The guard looked up at the three-meter tall gent, then at his proportionately prominent bow. "Mutants aren't allowed within the gates. No exceptions."

"Where...."

"There are a couple of inns in Demon Town."

"Where's that?"

"You can't miss it. It's about a kay down the Grim Pike. The buildings all look like they're about to fall down."

The guard wasn't exaggerating. The buildings were poorly constructed, to begin with, and not taken very good care of. Whatever scraps of wood Cedar View didn't want, the architects of Demon Town apparently snatched. Both sides of the highway were littered with these haphazard shacks. They varied in size from one room hovels to three story mansions---if size alone designated a residence a mansion. There were businesses too, some trying to make an honest living. Most not. One of the busiest districts of Demon Town was the Pharmacy. Mood altering herbs and elixirs were abundantly displayed on tops of crates. Many of the Pharmacy's patrons came from the west, from Cedar View, or from the ships docked in the harbor. Prostitution and gambling were also rampant in Demon Town, but not as popular as the distribution of pharmaceuticals.

After a heated debate, we finally agreed upon spending the night in one of Demon Town's inns. In most circumstances it would have been prudent to *camp out*, but there were some things in the Moorwoods that were more dangerous than anything found in Demon Town.

We shared a room---all five of us. We locked the door---a token gesture. If someone wished to attack us, they could do so easily by knocking down one of the walls. The inn was in that bad of shape. We kept a vigilant night watch, two people on at all times. There were numerous venues providing sustenance, of one form or another, at all hours. We ate as soon as we arrived, then turned in early. With forty-percent of our company up at a time we reserved plenty of time for sleep. Sleeping was a challenge, with half of the shanty town partying all night. Peace finally settled in about the time we got up. We weren't intentionally loud, but didn't try too hard not to be. Paybacks were best at the crack of dawn.

Before renting the room, we made inquires, of *strange*

happenings, specifically hinting of hobs and gobs. After buying a couple of rounds of drinks, tongues loosened. There had been substantial activity in the Grim Mountains, but nothing this far west. The individuals we talked to were more concerned with a green drak terrorizing people in the Deep Wilds. That area of the Moorwoods was so dense, the Grim Pike had to be bored through in some places. At times the passage looked more like a tunnel than a highway.

With dread we headed west. The day was going to be stressful and boring. Monotonous, because one kay of jungle looked much like the next. Traumatic, because what was behind some of those trees and bushes might be 30 meters long, and hungry.

"I met my first drak in the Bluewoods," Hornet shared. "It mentioned a green drak it wasn't particularly fond of. Do you think it was referring to the Moorwoods' drak?"

"Not necessarily," Pulp replied. "Each drak is unique, but as we discovered with the one below the Northern Spine, some share characteristics, including physical features."

"It spoke of the green drak's cruelty."

"For a drak to say that about another of its kind is significant," said Twig. "That's like one murderer chastising another because he killed an entire family instead of just one person."

The floral tunnels were intermittent. Sometimes they were only 10 to 20 meters long. Other times they went on for nearly a kay. The first time we entered one of the longer variety, I panicked. We were partially trapped if something attacked us, being forced to flee in only the direction we were heading or the direction we came. A domestic cat may have been small enough to fit through the interlocking branches and leaves. But I was substantially larger than that. Cats don't like to feel trapped. A closed door makes any room a prison. I constantly turned and re-turned, to confirm nothing was following. My hearing was as good of a detector as my sight, but both was better. My senses became so focused I began hearing things kays away. There were creatures moving around everywhere. I became more rattled.

"Something's coming," I blurted out. To prevent us from being trapped in the tunnel, we rushed towards the nearest exit. Just a few meters more and we would be out.

As we abandoned the tunnel we were met by eight bi-pedal rodents. They were dressed, indicating they had once been human. They appeared to be intimidated, but also belligerent. They carried a javelin in each hand. They thrust them at us as they grunted loudly. Instinctively, we backed up. Pleased with our reaction, they thrust their javelins out again, making an even louder sound.

Centaur didn't like to be bullied, especially by someone half his size. He made his own aggressive statement. He jumped towards the creatures with his battle axe raised. "BOO!" The rodents scattered, fleeing a few paces in the direction they came.

"Let them go." Twig grabbed a hold of the arm that held the weapon.

It took a couple of minutes for the creatures to regain their courage. They thrust their javelins at us one more time, then rushed passed us down the tunnel in the direction we came.

Although unharmed, we were still shaken by the encounter. It took us a moment to recover. About the time we were ready to resume our journey, we heard grunting, then squealing. I ran down the tunnel to investigate.

"Lynn," called Hornet from the opening of the tunnel. I knew it was a stupid thing to do, but there was a reason cats needed nine lives. I was compelled to investigate.

At the far opening of the tunnel most of the rats lay dead. One of those still alive scurried towards me. Before it reached me, it was caught by a talon. The green drak connected to it was 40 meters long. It completely concealed the view of the forest beyond it. It was camouflage green, a mottled kaleidoscope of both dark and bright patches. The talon dragged the rat back towards it. Then it released it. A moment later it was caught again. This went on for many minutes. It reminded me of the games I played with my prey. I was momentarily disgusted with myself. I reminded myself that I only ate animals. The rats were intelligent, moderately so perhaps, but still intelligent. The green drak finally got careless. The rat went too far into the tunnel for it to be captured. It ran past me. The forest could now be seen. I followed the rat, but at a more leisurely pace. It walked into the drak, who had now blocked that end of the tunnel. The drak was done playing. It blew out a cloud of green gas. The rat fell to its knees retching. The drak slurped it into its mouth with its tongue. I was either too far away for it to notice me, or I wasn't on its menu, because it flew off immediately after swallowing.

I exited the tunnel, being concerned for my friends. That may have been the first time I acknowledged they were more than my companions. I was forced to stop when I entered the green cloud that hadn't entirely dissipated. I returned what I had eaten for breakfast. So intense was the regurgitation, I recoiled, involuntarily, to balance the forward thrust. I backed up into the tunnel, took a couple of exaggerated breaths, then rushed out. I leapt at the precipice of the cloud. I rolled as I landed, gasping for fresh air.

My friends rushed towards me from where they had been hiding in the forest, to access my condition. "Nothing some lunch won't cure," was my reply in response to their concern.

Pulp looked back at the tunnel. "An accidental encounter? Or taking advantage of the environment to create a feeding tube?"

"Or a straw," Twig added.

The Moorwoods may have been vast, but not in the direction we traveled. By lunch the forest thinned. Foothills could be seen. The Grim Pike paralleled them, slowly getting closer.

"The Moorwoods weren't that bad," commented Hornet.

"Because we passed through them cautiously," Centaur responded. "Unlike those rats."

"And having that drak in the vicinity likely scared away most of the monsters," said Pulp. "There are thousands of hectares of forest. Why congregate in the area most likely to being consumed?"

The scrub between the Moorwoods and the Grim Mountains was surprisingly sparse---a void between two massive vegetative clusters. It was the safest we felt since entering the Negative Frontier. We camped in a copse of dogwoods beside a meandering stream, crickets crooning us to sleep.

Chapter 26

AN EXPENSIVE SLICE OF HEAVEN

We woke refreshed. We were almost there. The final piece of the puzzle. The solution to all the riddles. We connected the pieces of the portal we already had to confirm the location of the piece that would make it whole.

"It looks like it's in the middle of the mountains," said Pulp.

"No, further to the east," Hornet corrected. "I've had enough practice with the spheres to approximate the distance within...a dozen kays."

"How far east?" Twig's elation of being so close deflated.

"We'll lie low in the scrub until we're close to the sphere," said Centaur. "We'll be able to bypass most of the mountains."

Twig began to cheer up again. "You guys wouldn't mind carrying my stuff for a while, so I could run?"

Turning to Centaur, Pulp said, "Don't even think about it. I'm willing to put up with carrying *one* extra bag for a couple of kays. And Twig's *gear* is much prettier than yours."

"That's sexist. Why couldn't I be traveling with a group of women?"

"I don't think that would have made that much of a difference," said Hornet. "You're not that pretty."

"I think you're very pretty." Twig handled her mate her gear as she began to disrobe.

"Couldn't you do this thing instantaneously?" asked Pulp. "I like both the before and after. The middle part is what makes me uncomfortable."

"Maybe it's time for you to find yourself a wife," Hornet suggested.

"And abandon the arbols? After you romance them a bit they forget your name, and you can move onto someone else."

Twig was now a wolf, but was able to understand enough of what was said. She snarled at Pulp before she began running in the direction we intended to travel.

The vegetation became sparser the further east we went. The copses became single trees, then not even that. Shrubs remained, but most were stunted. The Grim Pike crossed the Murky River---via a pontoon bridge---near the end of the second day. Wanting to retain the relative safety of the plains for as long as we could, we diverged from the road as it entered the foothills.

Being too dry for crickets, our thoughts serenaded us to sleep---expectations of subsequent days, equal doses of excitement and dread.

Vegetation became more abundant our fourth day. Shrubs grew and clustered. Trees began to appear, singularly, then as groves. A forest began to form, but with plenty of space between the trees to walk between---more orchard than wild woodlands.

Five kays into the forest we intersected the Reed River. Being more creek than river, we easily crossed it via a ford. The waters were shallow and surprisingly warm for being mountain fed.

My companions removed their boots. After safely depositing their gear on the other side, they returned to the water. Not being content with just their feet getting wet, they stripped down to their underwear. The river not being deep enough to cover their bodies, they had to sit in the water for it to reach their chests. I washed myself in my way, then took a nap.

Underwear was changed, and dry clothes put back on. We had stayed too long. It would be dark soon and we hadn't reached Appleton yet, a village upstream. We quickened our pace to compensate for the time we lost. It was completely dark when we reached the village. Following the river had guaranteed we would reach it, but the longer we spent in the forest after dark the more likely we would be attacked, by animal, man, or monster.

A wooden fence surrounded Appleton. More picket than wall, it didn't look strong enough to keep more than rabbits and deer out. The guard who interrogated us at the western gate acted more like he worked for the chamber of commerce than a defender of the village. We were informed of a nice place to stay and the best restaurants. And where to re-provision our supplies.

We hadn't seen any apple trees in the forest, but the village was full of them, and most were blossoming, blanketing it in white.

We stayed in *A Slice Of Heaven*. It was primarily a restaurant, but there were a few rooms above the kitchen. The dining room was open to the ceiling. A fire burned within the hearth. It was small, creating more ambiance than heat. Windows were open to freshen the air. The dining room consisted of twelve butcher block tables, each accommodating six people. Dinner was served family style. Pork loin and grilled chicken were served with a bounty of vegetables and bread, after an initial course of soup and salad. Apple strudel was the dessert. Everything was delicious. Hornet prepared a plate for me and set it on the ground. I would have been content to eat off the table, but some people were shockingly prudish of cats being that independent.

The first night in the plains was reclaimed and bettered. Not only did the sheets and blankets appear to be clean, they smelled nice. The furniture was dust free and the windows clean. For once the men didn't complain about taking a bath. Scented oils were added to the warm water. Afterwards, they were given massages. The downside to this decadence was the price. Even accounting for all the extras, it was higher than it should have been.

Centaur, as he had a tendency to do, complained. It wasn't in his nature to allow an opportunity to express his displeasure to be ignored. "We could have bought this inn for the price of spending one night here."

The innkeeper, a man named Firefly, was characteristic of those successful in his profession: he was obese, bordering on rotund. No one wished to eat in a restaurant that had only skinny people working in it. "The protection tax does increase the price a bit."

"By how much?"

"Double."

"Are you saying your tax rate is 100%?"

"Just the protection tax. There is also the city tax of 50%."

"That's insane, paying more in taxes than for products and services."

"Are you enjoying your stay?"

"Yes, but…."

"Did you feel threatened by anyone or anything?"

"No."

"Then I guess it was money well spent."

"The city doesn't appear to have much of a police prescience," said Pulp. "How is the protection money spent?"

"It doesn't go to the city guard. That's funded from the city budget. It goes to Lord Nettle. He keeps the Apple Woods safe. There hasn't been a demon in these woods for 10 years."

Before leaving Appleton, we confirmed the location of the final piece of the portal. Using triangulation, we were able to pinpoint it more precisely. I had a very good idea where it would be. The probability was quite high.

Centaur drew two lines on the map he carried. They intersected about two-thirds of the way from Appleton to Grimboro, the largest settlement in the Grim Mountains. It was just south of the Neuneg/Orneg border.

Pulp's eyes opened wide. "That's the location of Nettle's Lair."

Twig looked puzzled. "I thought Thorn was supposed to have the last sphere?"

"You don't think they are in cahoots, do you?" asked Hornet.

"Gaea protect us if the Negative gents and draks have formed an alliance," said Centaur.

"I don't think that would ever happen," said Pulp. "Not only is there an animosity between the two species, gents involved in such an alliance would we ostracized from the Brotherhood."

"What if they felt their new alliance was stronger? Maybe it wouldn't matter too much if they were forced out of the Brotherhood."

"The alliance may just consist of Thorn and Lord Nettle," Pistachio suggested.

"Either suggest we must investigate the situation," said Pulp.

"And retrieve the final piece of the portal," I insisted.

Chapter 27

GRIM

The road through the Grim Mountains followed the Reed River, snugly. When the river was wide and slow, the road was directly beside its banks. When it became narrow white-water, the road climbed higher up, often looking down at the silvery ribbon from atop a canyon. The setting remained peaceful. No dangerous animals or demons were spotted. Sun shined through the pines. The scent of needles and resin permeated.

The amiability abruptly ended at the top of a pass. *Do Not Enter* was painted in what we believed to be blood, on a rock to the left of the road. *Entering a Non-Protection Area* was written on a similar rock on the right side.

"Someone could have warned us," said Centaur.

"Would it have made any difference?" asked Pulp.

"No."

Twig looked up. "The sun is becoming obscured again."

"It was cheerier in the Orchard Woods, wasn't it?" Centaur commented.

"No Negative Haze," Hornet announced.

"Now that you mention it, there wasn't any, was there? Like there was a hole in the clouds, allowing some sunlight through. Or fog clearing. Could the two be connected? The Orchard Woods being protected, and it not having any Negative Haze?"

"It might be worth it, paying that exorbitant tax if someone could guarantee safety *and* charm," Twig commented.

"No, it wouldn't," Centaur immediately responded.

"How long until we reach Lord Nettle's Lair?" asked Hornet.

"We're about halfway," Pulp answered.

"I recommend we devise a specific plan before we do so," suggested Pistachio.

"The Lich suggested Thorn was greedy," said Hornet, "hinting that she could be bribed."

"As good a reason as any for her to form an alliance with Lord Nettle," said Twig. "Thorn was once a woman, and women have a reputation for liking nice things."

"Even you?" Centaur questioned. Twig returned an icy glare. "I have never seen you wear an expensive dress or flashy jewelry," he attempted to explain. Another look from his mate, this one more ambiguous. "You are nearly flawless. To wear too much would conceal your beauty, denying the world of your loveliness."

"*Nearly* flawless?"

The terrain became more severe on the other side of the pass. The vegetation was almost non-existent. Stone and earth, earth and stone. That's all we saw, except for the trickle of water that the Reed River had become. It flowed through a chiseled-out trough that looked more like a sewer than a streambed. Light wasn't the only thing that became murky. Sounds and odors dimmed. Our surroundings became stale. There was nothing worth living for here. Emotions became non-existent. We continued walking, to sustain the monotony. Our contentment had been so high in Appleton, and now so low in the Grim Mountains. As if one was somehow able to siphon from the other.

We were relieved when we heard fighting. It shattered our dispassionate cocoon, freeing us from our stupor. The Negative Haze sustained, dimming our senses. We saw sluggish movement in the shadows, and heard muted echoes of metal upon metal and distant screams of exultant triumph and agonizing defeat. Odors began to attach themselves to the sticky air: musk, sweat, blood, urine, feces, and other scents that couldn't be described, that couldn't have come from humans. Our sinuses and clothing became permeated with the odors. By the time we could distinguish details we had become acclimated to them, a psychological restraint to prevent us from going insane.

Our focus now was on us not getting killed. We found ourselves on a battlefield when we had gotten close enough for the shadows to take form. Once there had been a hamlet. Two armies fought over what remained of the broken buildings.

Closest to us were these grey creatures, bipedal, with black greasy hair, and white sightless eyes. Their skin and eyes strongly suggested they were primarily a subterranean race. They wore pale leather tunics that appeared to be made from skin, possibly human. They carried large two-handed stone axes. The razor-sharp blades were chiseled from stone. *Grim* they were called, named after the mountains, or was it the other way?

Their opponent, on the far side of the hamlet, looked like hobs, but they were larger and better equipped. When we first entered the battlefield, one of these *superior*-hobs launched a boulder from a catapult. It smashed the two grim closest to us. We backed up.

"We were warned, weren't we," commented Pulp.

"Lord Nettle was negligent in protecting this hamlet," Hornet commented.

"Its citizens should demand a refund," added Centaur. He looked at his map. "This place is...was...called Zipper. It looks like the sphere is still about five kays north of here."

"So, we must pass through this?" Twig questioned.

"I would suggest passing around it," said Pistachio.

"Better said than done," said Pulp. "There's a reason the road was built where it was. The river created a path through the mountains. If we detour from it the terrain gets much more rugged."

"I don't think we have a choice," said Hornet.

"You may wish to look over there," I advised.

"GET DOWN!" shouted Centaur.

Flames spread out over the half of Zipper we were in. A significant number of grim had been caught in the conflagration. Being warriors until the end, those in flames ran towards their adversaries, attempting to take out as many as they could before they expired. The hobs, being highly disciplined, did not panic. They patiently shot crossbow bolts at them as the flames came closer. Most of the grim dropped before they reached the vanguard. The few that made it that far were cut down and stomped upon, to prevent their flames from spreading.

"Thorn still has that ruby pearl dangling from her neck," Twig observed.

"Lord Nettle's bribe?" asked Hornet.

"Could be," said Pulp. "I wonder how long it will sustain her. Eventually we all get tired of our beautiful things."

Centaur looked at Twig. "It depends on the gem."

Twig became solemn. "There may come a time when you do become tired of me. Relationships are dynamic. When our relationship runs its course, I will only look back on the good times. Remember, I left a long-term relationship for you. Beak made peace with the decision."

"He committed suicide. You can't become more at peace than that."

"I will always love you. As confident as I am that Beak still loves me."

The pillow talk was interrupted when Thorn returned and attacked the hobs, causing nearly as much devastation as she did to the grim. The hobs countered by throwing boulders at her. The catapults weren't constructed to attack aerial targets. They landed harmlessly on the grim who hadn't recovered enough from their own incineration to counterattack. The unintentional strike was a strong enough catalyst to return them to action. Dozens of grim had been killed by the flames and the boulders, but their numbers never appeared to diminish. If you overload a septic tank, its contents will eventually ooze back up to the surface.

"That's a novel way of announcing a divorce," said Pulp. "If I ever get divorced, that's the way I want to do it."

"But doesn't that mean you have to get married first?" Centaur questioned.

"Technicalities. Do you always have to put a damper on everything?"

"She's flying southwest," said Hornet.

"To Gulag or the Wizard's Tower," said Pistachio.

"Everything appears to be coming together there, doesn't it," said Pulp.

"It's where life began on Limbo," I stated.

Centaur sighed. "So, we're going to have to travel another thousand kays if we want that last sphere."

"Yes, but we may not have to walk," said Pulp. "I don't think Lord Nettle will be too happy when he learns of his partner leaving him in such a despicable manner. I believe he will be amenable to us borrowing his transport platform if doing so assists in defeating his new arch enemy."

We still had to get past the battlefield, which had intensified. As we examined Centaur's map, hoping it might provide some assistance in circumventing the hamlet, excitement erupted on the hob's side of the battlefield. The ugliest gent I have ever seen charged up to the front and began knocking down grim with his two-meter long mace. Razor-sharp shards of metal stuck out of it. Whatever he hit was sliced open and pulverized. Lord Nettle was more lightly armored than his army. Whatever protection he lost in having his arms, legs, and face exposed he gained from the nausea he caused his opponents. Lord Nettle was covered in welts and warts and boles and pimples. Many of them oozed in a variety of milky and translucent colors. He stood twice as tall as the tallest grim. He went through their troops like a one-man battering ram. Some people got out their frustrations by jogging, he got out his by butchering by the dozen.

Pulp attempted to get his attention---a challenging task.

Lord Nettle was completely absorbed in his work. Pulp may not have been as large as Lord Nettle, but he was significantly larger than the grim, resulting in him ultimately becoming noticed. The grotesque gent lost his concentration for a moment, allowing one of the grim to get in a good strike. The axe slightly scratched his leg, breaking open more boils and pimples. Lord Nettle made him pay for his insolence. He was knocked to the ground as his intestines where ripped out of him. Lord Nettle pounded him a few more times, coating the ground with a gooey paste.

He began to clear a path towards us. Maybe this wasn't too great of an idea. Seeing that they weren't going to be victorious this day, the grim finally retreated, sinking back into the underworld. "Pulp, did you see what I did to that grim?"

"If the condition of one's body was related to how long it takes to be re-created, it will be weeks before he returns."

"I apologize for not being very presentable. I wasn't expecting company."

"When have you ever been presentable?"

"Be kind. My hobs haven't had their fill of fighting. Your friends may not be as worthy of their proficiency as the grim, but as the saying goes, *if you can't strike the one you want, strike the one you're with*."

"You'll be surprised what they can accomplish. They have received a few scrapes and mutations, but they have survived."

"You haven't mutated substantially, have you?"

"A little webbing between my fingers and some gills. The same surface features get stale after a while, don't they?"

Lord Nettle wiped off fresh puss from his most recent injury onto his skin tunic. "I wouldn't mind a bit of change myself. Most people think it's my fault how I look. This mutation could have just been bad luck. Even if my lifestyle encouraged it, do I deserve it? Does the punishment balance the crime? I constantly itch. I try to fight it, but eventually I give in, causing my skin to ooze even more."

"I feel bad for you," Twig responded, sincerely.

"See, there are still some people whose compassion hasn't been mutated out of them. I would invite you back to my keep, but I'm not in a particularly good mood right now. That flying bitch just stabbed me in the back, with a searing poker."

"That's why we're here. We'll provide retribution, in exchange for transportation."

Pulp shared with Lord Nettle as much as he needed to hear. The grotesque gent was more than willing to send us to wherever we wished for the possibility of us being able to harm Thorn in some manner. The gobs eyed us as we made our way to his keep, but they kept their hands to themselves. They were too disciplined to harm their master's guests. We were given accommodations in a barracks. The food wasn't particular tasty, but it was hearty. The beds were similarly austere. Fatigue was a magical condition. It made a cinderblock a mansion. A stone slab, a pillow-top mattress. We fell asleep instantly, sleeping soundly until the hobs in the adjacent building rose at the precursor to dawn.

We were provided breakfast and our supplies re-provisioned.

"How many protection contracts do you currently have?" asked Pulp. The rest of us were careful not to speak directly to Lord Nettle. Most gents were xenophobic, and arrogant. Speaking out of turn could create significant difficulties. We didn't have the time to reform our party after being re-created.

"Feather and Appleton are the only two settlements of any size. There are hamlets like Zipper we are also attempting to maintain, but we are running them at a loss. I'm considering dropping those contracts. I'm working on an agreement with Grimboro. It would more than double my business, even with giving them a considerable discount. If we get the contract I could use some help. Even if I don't get it I could still use the help now that Thorn left me."

"I will think about. I have pressing business at the moment."

"Don't we all. I must keep a close watch on the grim. If we

hit them too hard at Zipper they may move more south. It would be devastating if they invaded Appleton. It was our first success--- my first child. The operation there is running smoothly, like clockwork. The nastiest things left years ago and haven't dared return. You've probably noticed the halo over the village. That's what some of its residents call it. I think of it as more of a moral bubble. If the grim invade, the bubble will pop."

"Then let's not have that happen," Twig spoke out. Catching herself, she bowed. "My pardon."

"No apologies. I'm pleased you admire my work. So where do you wish to be transported to?"

"To Scree, if you wouldn't mind. Thorn is apparently heading to the Southern Spine. Maybe Gulag after that."

"Then let me not delay you any longer. Some people believe revenge is more satisfying if one allows it to simmer. Stew that sits too long becomes rank. I have found if I eat an appetizer I don't have room for desert."

A gent's transport portal was large enough for one gent. Most of us not being gents, small groups of us could be transported together. Pulp went first, to announce our prescience. A moment later Centaur and Twig went together, followed by Hornet, Pistachio, and myself.

Chapter 28

PREPARATIONS

Scree was a very formal gent: reserved and dignified, graceful and polite. A green toga draped flawlessly over perfect posture, the color coinciding with predetermined daily coding. His proximity to Gulag predisposed him to become a historian. It never became a vocation, but it was more than a hobby. He was invited to dine with the most prominent people of the city, which he reciprocated. A road had been constructed specifically for his guests. It was maintained 1000 days a year, sun, rain, sleet, snow, or high winds. Scree's Castle was constructed of stone, but inside, it felt homey. It was filled with exquisite furniture, tapestries, and pieces of art. The greatest honor bestowed upon an artist was having his or her painting or sculpture displayed within the mountaintop edifice overlooking the city.

"It's a mistake starting a war with the Wizards." Scree was the ultimate Neutral. He believed following a cause, informally or tactilely, was being unfair to those who didn't believe in it. He lives his life in balance. He doesn't hinder or help. To promote change is to disrespect *Gaea's Will*.

Pulp replied, "We aren't the ones starting it. The Wizards already have golem and demon armies on the move. We're just trying to balance things out. Wasn't that why the Brotherhood was formed, to prevent one faction from controlling Limbo?"

"And the Brotherhood agreed not to participate in this war. The issues associated are like a polyhedron: multi-dimensional with many sides."

"We do not ask you personally to assist us, just to borrow your castle, for reconnaissance and logistics."

"If I was to support you, in any manner, it will likely force others in the Brotherhood to support your opponents. Please leave, immediately. When this altercation is over you are permitted to return."

The journey to Gulag was an arduous one. The road was well constructed, providing a gentle decline into the Springwoods. The problem was having to do the 30-kay hike unprepared. Fortunately, we had a decent sleep the night before. Physically we were capable. We struggled emotionally---one more obstacle put before us.

Gulag wasn't walled, the only major city on Limbo not provided that protection. There have always been people living in it, beginning with the first inmate to step through a transport portal onto reformed soil. Dozens of people followed, then hundreds, and finally thousands, accumulating to over two-hundred-thousand souls in the surrounding area. Most of the city's growth had occurred to the north and west, into the Arrival Plains. Land was cheap there and easy to build upon. The more expensive homes were in the Springwoods and the foothills of the Southern Spine. Most of Gulag's organizational issues resulted from it always being there. Buildings were built randomly on whatever exposed piece of earth that could be found. To balance the chaos, lot standards were established. There was a certain radius around one's home or business that no one else could build upon. Agreements could be made to circumvent the provision, typically involving some form of monetary compensation. The only *true* roads in Gulag after 144 years were the five leading away from it. Finding a specific person was difficult. Addresses were a series of landmarks. Most of them were manmade. Modifications, including demolitions, required addresses to be changed. Lots adjacent to the five roads sell for a premium, and extend for many kays beyond the developed borders of the city. The value of a lot decreased the further it was from a road. It wasn't economically feasible to enclose a city so dispersed. The benefit of a city being so scattered was the time it would take an invading army to reach its center. Many alarms would be sounded, and many battles fought, before the core was breached.

As we passed through the city, memories of what it looked like more than a century ago returned to me. It had been so small. And rural. There were people everywhere now. I looked for the Mounds and Trunks, the inn I had worked in when I was still human. An apartment building had replaced it. How many buildings had been torn down and rebuilt there? The only two to remain steadfast were the Third Time Church and the Protectorate Keep. The first sold Church paraphernalia, and the latter was now a museum, honoring those who have defended Limbo from demons.

We walked into the one place in Gulag we still felt safe---the Octagonal Prism. The eight-sided platinum---plated---building glistening in the late afternoon sun. Few people outside of the order ever set foot in the building. Security was tight. The best method of securing a building was limiting who entered it. We had met half of the Knights, so it was likely at least one person within recognized us. No worries. Seven of the eight were inside, including Stick.

"It looks like you haven't recovered the last sphere yet?"

"It moved," said Centaur. "Likely into the Wizards Keep."

"Do they...."

"I don't think they are aware of its significance," said Pulp. "A drak---Thorn---wear's it around her neck. We believe she has joined their cause."

"Great. Now we also have to battle dozens of drak."

"Unlikely. Drak are independent. Thorn probably goes it alone. I don't think she would agree to assist the Wizards for any treasure if she had to share it with others of her kind."

"So, to counter, we need our own drak," Twig suggested. "If not for the firepower, at least for the reconnaissance."

"There's Acorn," Hornet reminded us.

"Can we trust him?" Centaur questioned.

"He's Neutral," Twig responded.

"But still a drak. Can any of them be trusted? Perhaps not intentionally deceitful, but predisposed to less altruistic pursuits, when tempted, or distracted."

"There's also Nimbus," Hornet suggested.

"Do you think he would agree to it?" asked Centaur.

"It was a Wizard who transferred his essence into a golem. I think he'll be quite motivated to enact his revenge. Our problem will be tearing him away from tearing into the Wizards. He probably won't want to just observe."

"I'll accompany you to the Raspberry Mountains," said Pistachio. "I need to check in on the druids, to see how they're coming along on harvesting the herbs and turning them into elixirs."

"I'm going to head back to the Copper Forest," said Pulp. "I want to check in on how the recruiting is going. I might have some influence. I know many of the arbols by name...mostly the females."

Twig smiled. "You actually spent enough time with an individual arbol to learn her name?"

"We multitasked. And who says I was ever alone with just one arbol? They group date. Two can be fun, but not as fun as four. You might think that eight was superfluous, but...."

"That leaves Twig and me to confirm the trogs will fight with us," said Centaur. "Or should we stay here to round up local support?"

"We've already begun to do that," Stick responded. "Octagonal Knights have been regarded as celebrities since our inception. To fight alongside one is all the motivation most of them will need. To assist, is to become."

"How do we provision them, with weapons and armor? You don't have 100,000 of those suits, do you?"

"Gulag has a militia. It hasn't done much more than drill, until now. Its duties include acquiring and storing weapons, to be dispersed if Gulag is ever attacked. The militia volunteers are called *centurions*, in reference to them supervising 100 civilians, in times of crisis. We've already briefed the militia. The centurions are preparing to distribute arms."

"Are there still troops arriving?" I asked. To make the best prediction I required the most current data.

"Yes. There appears to be a subterranean holding area between Gulag and the Wizard's Keep."

"How much longer do we have?"

"That's a bit unpredictable. They'll probably begin attacking smaller communities immediately. The armies are being concentrated here more for their proximity to the Wizard's Tower than to Gulag. They'll wish to blood their troops before they attack their main target."

"Then we still have time?" Twig questioned.

"Gulag does. We need to warn the outlying hamlets and villages."

"We all have something to do now, don't we," said Centaur. "Shall we meet back here in two weeks?"

Chapter 29

BALANCE

Once we split up I had to step away from contributing to their cause. I could not help them in even the most subtle of ways anymore. Being so near to the start of the war, even minor assistance could turn the tide. Gaea already had to assist the

Wizards a couple of times to counter the slight imbalance I created.

"I'm sorry."

"You pushed the boundary too far, poking a hole through. The wound is patched. It's human nature to help your friends, and yourself. You may physically resemble something else, but you are still essentially human, as are all mutants. I will miss you all, your triumphs, and your defeats."

"Are you going someplace? How is that possible? You're the planet."

"I have chosen to expire after the war. If the Wizards win they will soon develop the technology to enslave me. If they don't, those off world, who already have the means, will likely do so."

"Nothing dies on Limbo. How is it possible for you to die?"

"I was never born, not in the manner others are born. It will be simple, a willing of myself to not exist. Much easier than sustaining. Balance will be restored."

"How will Limboans function without you guiding them?"

"Once the walls of their prison are torn down they will have to take care of themselves."

"Most of them have spent the bulk of their lives on Limbo. How will they survive once they are thrown out?"

"All must leave the womb eventually. The instant it happens we are startled, but eventually we adjust."

Chapter 30

WAR

Smaller communities *were* attacked first. The Wizard locomotives were active. Every day dozens of them passed beneath Gulag, redistributing troops. As more settlements fell, Coalition forces, as the anti-Wizard alliance began to be called, became antsy. There was an extensive debate when they should attack.

"Every day we delay another town falls."

"And another hundred re-created."

"If we attack the Wizards before we have all of our troops in place we will be massacred. We have one opportunity to defeat them, and that can't happen until arbols, trogs, druids, and militias from other cities combine forces with us."

So many lives have been lost already. How many of those who have been re-created have died in a second battle? In a third? If the two sides become balanced the war could continue indefinitely. How long would it take for everyone to become a mutant? Would the only true humans be those who have just arrived?

Pulp was first to return, with 200 arbols. They wore vests with pockets, bulging with vials, reminiscent of ammo pouches laden with grenades. They constructed a tent city southwest of Gulag, on the outskirts of the Springwoods, far enough from the city center to not displace indigenous residents.

Cone arrived a day later. He had 1000 individuals with him. The hodgepodge of humanity had a single article of clothing in common: a metal cap with the People's Militia logo on it.

Apparently, hobs and gobs and golems liked to hit their opponents on top of their heads. The weapons they carried varied from swords to pitchforks. Some of them also carried bows, but more didn't. *Some* wore armor. Of those who did, it mainly consisted of leather jerkins, most of them unpadded. The People's Militia camped northwest of Gulag, 15 kays into the Arrival Plains, just beyond the fringe shanties.

Hornet arrived a couple of days after that. He and Dinga and Hope flew in on Nimbus. The drak landed many kays west of the city in the middle of night, to not frighten anyone. Most people were incapable of considering the advantages of having a drak as an ally. Once on the ground, Nimbus changed into his other form: a four-meter tall gent. Gents were less exotic than draks. It didn't hurt that most Gulagians either knew Scree personally, or knew someone who did. They were in awe of gents, but not frightened into impotence. Nimbus was the only known mutant able to appear as either of the two most powerful races on Limbo. This ability prevented him from being accepted in either society. Preferring isolation, it was more irritating to him than depression inducing. He enjoyed both forms equally. He loved flying, but he also liked being able to commune with Jasmine, as a peer. Traveling between his home in the Raspberry Mountains, and hers in the jungle named for her, 1200 kays away, took him less than half a day.

"We spoke to Acorn," Hornet announced.

Nimbus frowned.

"Draks having this aversion to others of their kind, Nimbus was able to sense his prescience."

Nimbus frowned again. "Like ants crawling over a poison ivy rash."

"He's still coming?" Pulp asked.

Hornet nodded. "An understanding was reached---between Acorn and Nimbus. Acorn will monitor the perimeter of the battlefield. Nimbus, the interior."

Nimbus smiled for the first time since his arrival. "More

treasure for me."

"You do realize you won't be permitted to forage Gulag," said Dinga.

"Hobs sometimes leave things behind."

"Scrap iron at best," said Pulp.

"But I'll be able to collect more of it than Acorn."

The druids arrived later in the day.

The leaders of the arbols, the People's Army, and Gulag's Militia met in the Octagonal Prism. Hornet and Dinga were also present, as was Nimbus, and the Octagonal Knights. I was permitted to listen to the discussions, but not participate.

"With their troops being so scattered over Limbo, maybe we should attack the Wizard's Tower," suggested Cone.

"The building's defenses are formidable," said Stick. "It's likely they could counter us unassisted. They'll be able to hold us off long enough for supplemental forces to arrive to finish us off."

Two Octagonal Knights rushed into the war room, excitement more prominent in their features than panic. "A battle has begun below the city."

"Did some of the locals become impatient, or is it the hobs and gobs fighting amongst themselves?" asked Pulp.

"Bright blue dots."

"You think General Paint commandeered a train or two?" asked Hornet.

"The war has finally begun," said Nimbus. "People will see worse things today than draks. Let's see if our troops are responding overland as efficiently as they appear to be in the underworld." Nimbus transformed into a 40-meter long drak in the middle of the Octagonal Prism's courtyard. Shrieks and coos where heard outside as Nimbus rose into the sky.

A moment later he returned. "The trogs must have stopped up the sewer pretty badly. Minion are overflowing near the Wizards Keep. They are marching this way, ignoring prime pillaging opportunities. But hobs will be hobs. You can only dissuade their natural instincts for so long."

"I believe it's time to assemble our own troops," stated Centaur. "I suggest sending a majority of them to the center of the city. There may be entrances into the tunnels we aren't aware of, but we are certain of one."

The Minion armies consisted of hobs, gobs, and golems. Primarily, but not exclusively. Mutant hybrids of reptiles, rodents, and birds were also recruited. Everyone was promised something by the Wizards. Battles meant deaths, and deaths meant many possessions up for grabs. Limboan wills were implied---first come, first serve. Unless you had very loyal friends when you were re-created, your wealth was dispersed.

Gulag's eastern districts were evacuated. Without people to butcher distracting them, the Minion were able to sustain a fleet gait. Their arrival was earlier than anticipated, but not debilitating. Our plan was to put a wedge through their troops, separating them. Those underground would be attacked from behind. It was impossible for the Minion to escape through thousands of trogs. The People's Army and the Gulag Militia, with the assistance of the Octagonal Knights, were first to attack. The arbols, with their elixirs, were held in reserve to counter the Wizards when they arrived.

The Coalition got the upper hand. Low intelligence and a dictatorial command structure delayed the Minion's adjustment to the alteration of strategy. In time their natural instincts took over. Semi-disciplined soldiers became frenzied berserkers, swinging wildly at anyone they believed to be their enemy. Sometimes they got it wrong, resulting in fatal internal battles. The golems had the most trouble reacting to the change of combatants, initially, but after their sentient leaders directed them they became efficient killing machines, as the residents of Spinecrest and Norwood could corroborate.

The Minion now had the advantage, at least above ground.

The longer the battle waged, the stronger the golems got relative to their flesh and blood opposition. They didn't tire physically, mentally, or emotionally. The human troops were being decimated. Two of the Octagonal Knights were also down. They were revived in the Octagonal Prism, but it would take them a few hours before they were at full strength again. The only thing that delayed the golems was the barricade of bodies that began to pile up. Golems were less graceful when there were obstacles in their way. Many of them tripped and stumbled. Some of them ricocheted off the bodies and hit forcibly into others of their kind or other minion. When they hit other golems, they just knocked them over. Within seconds to minutes, depending on the entanglement, they would pick themselves back up. When they hit the living---particularly hobs---the living hit back. Often, the advantages of employing vicious troops---their ferociousness---didn't outweigh the disadvantages---they didn't care who they took their aggression out on.

The wear and tear the golems generated became critical. In was inevitable now that the Coalition couldn't win. Fleeing, or genocide, were the only options.

Before a decision was determined, a rumbling was heard. It was very regular, very rhythmic. Then singing, deep voices in cadence with the thumping. It took a moment for the lyrics to become understandable: ditties about bravery and exploits, and rival's mothers.

Dinga was beside me with her baby. They weren't allowed to participate in the battles either. Why were children so fascinated with an animal's tail? They made up for it when they nuzzled your fur. They loved you unconditionally, except when you moved away, then they forgot that you ever existed.

"It looks like the sumopotts weren't completely destroyed," stated Hornet.

"Sumopotts are renowned for their resistance to mutation," Centaur reminded him. "They retain their form through dozens of re-creations."

The sumopotts learned from their first battle with the golems. They couldn't compete physically, but intellectually they were their superiors. Through specific attack and counter-attacks they were able to guide the golems to where they wanted, their goal being to force them to crash into one another. When one large piece of stone or metal strikes another significant damage is done to both.

Cognizant their minions were losing, the Wizards stepped in. They wore colorful trench coats. It was unknown if they symbolized rank or specialization, or individual tastes in fashion. They entered the perimeter of the battlefield, queued horizontally, in small clusters, reminiscent of gunslingers.

The arbols countered by entering the battlefield from the opposite perimeter. They preferred earthy pastels, predominantly greens and browns. The concern with arbols was their tendency to go off task. They were notorious for becoming distracted. It was assumed being attacked was enough motivation to remain focused. It was easy to recruit them. Providing them penta was like giving them a toy.

The arbols' role was predominantly offensive. The druids', predominantly defensive. If necessary, the latter would create barriers and other temporary defenses, but they were to concentrate on healing. Re-creations diminished the moral significance of saving someone's life, but if someone could be patched up quickly enough to return to battle it would generate an advantage. The Wizards appeared to be solely offense oriented.

The arbols were exceedingly dexterous, the primary reason they were chosen to be trained in pental warfare. It took them seconds to retrieve a vial from their vests, unstop it, swallow it, and release the elemental energy.

The Wizards concentrated their power in rings. They wore one on each finger, including their thumbs. With proper digit manipulation they could achieve the effect they desired. Having spent years practicing, most of them were quite gifted in their use. The rings were believed to have infinite charges. Once a cluster of elem became saturated it acted like a magnet, pulling in free roaming elem. The problem: with so many Wizards discharging so many penta in one location, there was a limited number of free roaming elem available. The Wizards had been so confident in their ability to use penta they had overlooked its limitations. Rods, although having limited charges, would have been more effective under these conditions.

As humans, hobs, gobs, golems, sumopotts, and assorted mutational malcontents fought on the battlefield, elemental energy whizzed above them, sometimes in invisible arcs, sometimes in exceptionally colorful ones, sizzling with potential destruction. Wizards and arbols were taken out one by one, like bottles lined up in an arcade. The druids rushed in where they could to retrieve the fallen. There were so many bodies to choose from they bypassed the ones who were unlikely to survive before they could be healed.

The battle below the city also continued to rage. The Minion fighting their way down to the blockage appeared to be endless, but insignificant compared to the number of trogs denying them. Trogdom must have been emptied. There were hundreds of the burly, diminutive men. They were in full battle gear. Trogs were known for two things---fighting and metallurgy. The only breaches in their armor were slits in their helmets, permitting them to see and breathe. They weren't afraid of getting hurt. That's not why they wore so much armor. The armor permitted them to fight longer. If they got injured that would limit the time they could spend on the battlefield.

The trogs had cleared the tunnel. They debated whether to assist the Coalition forces on the surface or to proceed forward, towards the Wizards' Keep. The decision was made for them when two new adversaries attempted to mow them down, by hurtling trains at them. Most of the trogs got out of the way in time. Some of the less agile ones didn't. Their armor protected them, but being so jarred it was likely they received internal injuries. A couple of trogs who had been hit head on had become pinned under one of the trains. Their armor had been squeezed in. Blood oozed out of their helmet slits to counter the pressure. The involuntary sacrifices derailed the train, not only knocking it from its tracks, but blocking those behind it.

What leaped from the trains reinforced the trogs' motivation to fight. "GAEA! So, it's true," General Paint muttered. "We have our own shadows." He was referring to the subterranean arbols that were discovered below the Dreadful Mountains. So alike in appearance to their tree-dwelling kin, but opposite in demeanor and morality. And the logical extrapolation that if arbols had their counters, so did the trogs.

"NOT SO WELL MET, COUSINS!" shouted one of the dark trogs. "SO, LIKE YOUR KIND, SPENDING HOURS POLISHING YOUR ARMOR. IT DOESN'T LOOK SO CLEAN NOW, DOES IT?!"

Their armor wasn't clean, or in good of repair---or completely cover them. The freedom they had gained in discarding rigid conformity created a major disadvantage.

General Paint shouted back, "YOU HAVE CHOSEN TO LIVE YOUR LIVES AS AN ABOMINATION! PERMIT ME TO PROVIDE YOU A MEANS TO BE RE-CREATED PROPERLY!" He sprinted towards the person who had attempted to insult him. I say attempted, because General Paint hadn't taken offense. He was steadfast in his beliefs. That being said, the attempt alone was worthy of his retribution.

The dark trogs fought to destroy what they had once been. Their cousins fought for a more noble cause. General Paint had convinced a majority of them the erratic way they had been acting was caused by Negativity and Chaos leaking into Trogdom. It had recently been discovered that pockets of morality, like veins of precious minerals, lay hidden beneath the earth. He assumed the trogs were responsible for the rupturing---a byproduct of their tunneling. When he became aware of a tunnel being constructed below Trogdom, he concluded *it* had ruptured the moral pocket.

Someone preparing to invade their homeland provided their motivation. The prescience of the dark trogs ignited their fervor.

What made a trog a trog wasn't within their dark cousins. Without proper armor or organization, they were overrun. The Wizards had one final minion to fall back upon. Trogs weren't the only race to have their dark counter. The sub-arbols were more sinister looking. The trogs looked like less well-groomed versions of their cousins, both in appearance and attire. They were more animated in their expressions, but they were basically trogs. The sub-arbols were similar to forest arbols only in their physiques. Arbols were renowned for their ability to assimilate into their environment. Those on the surface lived in the woods. The sub-arbols lived underground. There were no trees beneath the earth. Woodland arbols were hairy, like the animals that shared their forests. The sub-arbols were completely bald, like the rocks that surrounded them. The woodland arbols wore clothing---most of the time---more as a fashion statement than for modesty. That said, seeing one romping around completely naked in the Copper Forest, particularly during the warm months, wasn't remarkable. The sub-arbols didn't wear clothing at all. Their attire was intricate brands, expressing what their detached demeanors prohibited.

Like the woodland arbols, the sub-arbols specialization was in ranged attacks. Instead of using bows, they used crossbows, their bolts chiseled stone instead of forged metal. They didn't appear to be very effective, shattering upon impact against trog armor, but there was more to them than just a sharp point. They had been coated in chemicals. The pulverization of the stone aided their dispersion. The chemicals possessed two major properties. The first, caused nausea. The second, dissolved armor. It was difficult fighting when one was vomiting. And much less safe when one's armor was falling off.

A trog's armor was just a tool. It wasn't what defined him. That being said, the nausea and fragmenting armor did take its toll. Their cousins' attacks became more effective.

"We must break through to the arbols," General Paint forced out between retches. Trog armor wasn't constructed for eating. Consequently, it wasn't constructed for vomiting. Helmets were filled with bile and breakfast. "Ignore the abominations. Push through them." Being a well-disciplined military machine, the trogs did as they were instructed. Their crossbows being no longer effective, the sub-arbols switched to stone shard daggers. The sub-arbols weren't as deadly up close as they were from a distance, the decrease in effectiveness due to their daggers not being coated with chemicals. Hand-to-hand combat drastically increased the probability of self-infliction. With so many bodies lying dead or damaged, neither side could claim a victory.

As a percent, fewer died on the surface, but the aggregate was greater. Many more troops could fit into the open than in cramped tunnels.

Thorn had done her part in communicating troop movements and in killing strays on the perimeter of the battlefield, but she was getting impatient. Her side wasn't doing well at the moment. The difference was in the greater sanctity the Coalition allocated to life. The combatants the druids saved, who were able to return to battle, made the difference. Thorn didn't like to lose. She was determined for that not to happen. She dove, towards the most highly concentrated Coalition troops. A colossal conflagration was discharged. As intended, dozens of troops were set aflame, burning them alive. What she hadn't realized was how vulnerable she had made herself. Flame could only travel so far. She had to be within a hundred meters for the attack to be effective. It put her within bow range. Elixirs weren't the only thing the druids created. It was discovered that weapons could be fused with elem to enhance them. A dozen enhanced arrows struck Thorn, nearly simultaneously. One injury, a couple, even a handful, the drak may have been able to escape from, but not a dozen. She fell to the ground head first. It couldn't have been planned better for the Coalition. She destroyed what remained of the Wizards.

Without those who had promised them so many things still alive, the Minion fled. They were permitted to flee. If killed, they would be re-created. Living, they would feel their injuries, remembering who gave them to them.

We knew we had won when we saw the trogs emerge from the ground. No combatants remained above or below. The threat had expired, if not forever, for many years.

Hornet removed the ruby pearl from around the neck of what had been Thorn, the most powerful Negative drak. If she hadn't strayed from her abilities---and limitations---she would still be alive. A drak was the most powerful beast on Limbo, but it wasn't infallible.

Chapter 31

LICH

Six tinted metallic spheres where spread out concentrically on the battlefield. The components of the transport portal were spaced far enough apart to not inadvertently connect---or more importantly, activate.

A skeletal form in a violet robe materialized before us. Two red pinpoints of light glowed from its eye sockets. It was the Lich, the half-and-half demon that had attempted to seize the spheres from Hornet and his company beneath the Sabre Desert. "Thank you for bringing the final two spheres to me. I am pleased my suggestions assisted you in finding them."

"Didn't we already kill you?" said Centaur.

"You can't kill what is not alive. I made you think you had to put you more at ease, making it easier for me to observe your activities."

"Metaphorically speaking," said Pulp.

"No, I have actually been with you since you believed you had killed me. Twig, you are quite the dog when you're alone with a man." Twig was embarrassed, upset, angry, but mute. How could a person properly respond to such a statement?

"I didn't sense your prescience at all." The implications unnerved me. I wasn't all-knowing. A faulty conduit implied a less than omnipotent origin.

"Gaea has no claim to the dead."

"What would someone who isn't completely alive do with a transport portal?" asked Hornet. "Without the properties of this planet to sustain you, won't you become completely dead once you step through to the other side?"

"Likely. But I can prevent others from ever using it."

Why wait until all the spheres were retrieved? Wouldn't destroying one permanently prevent the portal's activation? Carelessness or cockiness? Or, perhaps, a cat playing with a mouse? Freedom snatched at the precipice of escape?

"I prefer the status quo," the Lich explained. "My way of life---I love tormenting the living---may be altered if someone leaves Limbo. Leaving may result in others arriving, those who have the power to make substantial changes."

"You can't receive *that* much pleasure from tormenting others?" Dinga questioned. "It can't be that fulfilling of a life."

"You'll be surprised how much pleasure I receive from watching others wither in pain. I've heard that childbirth is one of most excruciating of experiences. From what I saw it appeared to be for you."

"Insubstantial compared to what I got in return."

I stood close enough to Dinga that Hope was able to reach out to me and grab a handful of hair. I was constantly grooming

209

myself, but that didn't necessarily mean I wanted others to assist me. I couldn't fault the child. I was irresistible. And she was so cute. I particularly liked how she smelled, even those odors humans weren't too fond of. Any intense odor was entertaining to a cat.

"To bring a child into this Gaea-forsaken place…. I consume what has already been killed. You are the hunter---and the gun. I would be doing the child a favor by assisting its development, Limboan style. Or perhaps a child born on Limbo can't be re-created. If it dies it may simply cease to exist." The Lich moved closer to Hope. Dinga backed away. The Lich followed her.

There is often a fine line between doing something exhilarating, and hazardous. The Lich took one step too many. Hornet's paternal instincts took over. He darted towards the most powerful of Dead. The Lich stopped abruptly, begrudgingly. It even began to retreat. Hornet's ability to resist was put to the ultimate test---successfully. Hornet was a *True Neutral*, with equal parts Cor, Min, and Fas. The Lich, being the most extreme of its moral persuasion, wasn't able to make contact with him. Not only was Hornet resistant to the Dead's attack, he was repugnant, like garlic to a vampire, or wolfsbane to a werewolf.

The Lich looked rattled. So close it was to its ultimate victory, it was forced to backpedal for its survival. "Oh, Henry, where have we gone wrong?"

"Where have I heard that name before?" Stick stood protectively in front of Dinga. "There was a name written on top of a temple in Golden Sands: Henry O'Toole."

The Lich stood motionless as it contemplated. Hornet delayed his charge. "Yes. Henry O'Toole. That was what I was once called. How did you go from being that man to this….? But you had no choice, did you? This planet changed you. You have become what you were destined to be."

Pulp approached, to stand beside Stick. "Who you become isn't completely determined by fate. I was re-created in Negativity and Chaos, but I chose my moral inclinations to not dictate every aspect of my life. A murderer can choose to no longer kill."

The Lich became more befuddled. His schema shattered, crippling his decision making. He was frozen in place, emotionally comatose until he could rationalize his existence.

The mental freeze became a physical one after a drak swooped down at the Lich and blew out an icy mist. It coated the abomination in a liquid that solidified on contact. It landed on its second pass. It shrunk to a fifth of its size as it morphed into a gent. Using his firsts as clubs, Nimbus pulverized the ice-coated Lich, shattering more than the outer-coating. The creature had been frozen solid. Its tissues, dead and living, had been transformed, into a crystalline structure. Nimbus continued to pummel, the fist-sized shards breaking into even smaller pieces. Some of them were sharp enough to cause his hands to bleed. Accumulated frustrations of him being forcibly displaced, into a golem, and the decade's-long aftermath, were being taken out on what was once the Lich. Having one's soul raped warranted at least one violent release.

"You must go now," Gaea spoke to me. "Alone." I felt guilty. I was stealing the transport portal Hornet and his companions had worked so hard, for so long, to reconstruct.

The moment I've been waiting for, for more than a century, had finally arrived. I hesitated. Once I stepped through the portal it would be over. There were some benefits to living on Limbo. Being a pseudo-avatar of Gaea, I was nearly omnipotent. Within certain limits I was able to roam the planet freely. Freedom didn't exist in the Agency. But it was time, for it to be over. I stepped through the iridescent ring.

Chapter 32

PORTAL

I expected to find myself back on that artificial satellite above the penal colony. I was in the White Room. Those who currently held the positions of The Three weren't present.

"But we are." The word combination was delivered directly to my mind. I became aware of three points of lights in the chamber, each with a slightly different hue. One was yellow. Another blue. The last, red.

"We are The Three to whom who originally spoke." The thought pattern associated with the second cluster of words was slightly different from the first.

"How is that possible? A medical innovation?"

"Metaphysical." The third thought pattern was as unique as the first two.

The thought patterns harmonized---like music, visual effects, and actors messing together to form a dramatic presentation, greater than the sum of their parts. Often, all three components overlapped, but because each was unique, all were understood.

"So, you have become gods, like Gaea?"

"God is a relative term."

"Once a god is understood, he, she, or it, no longer remains a god."

"The one true God will never be completely understood."

"We have evolved."

"Self-mutated like the Lich."

"So, you aren't completely unaware."

"Upon your return to the White Room."

"An instantaneous assimilation of data."

"My mission is over."

"Yes, this mission."

"I continue to serve the Agency? But how can I if I look like...." But I didn't. Not anymore. Presumably since I walked through the portal. I had been so preoccupied with The Three that I hadn't noticed. I looked exactly like I did when I left this room 141 years ago.

"What is to be done with the Wizards? They have been defeated, but for how long? Gaea believed they would attempt a galactic power grab."

"It will take many years for them to recover."

"Decades."

"Wouldn't it be best to do something about them now, while they're weak?"

"We can't destroy someone for something they might do."

"The Three have evolved, as much morally as we have physically, intellectually, and emotionally."

"So, you're going to allow the Wizards to become more powerful, again, until they challenge you?"

"The Wizards' power will be peacefully neutralized."

"Hope is the first, but not the only."

"As Limbo's population increases a cleansing will occur."

"The harshness of the planet will become diluted."

"As will the power of the Wizards."

"How long can Limbo's population increase? The colony will eventually fill, its resources depleted."

"Gaea's gift will help."

"When she dies the re-creations will cease."

"But her daughter will remain."

"Storage for Gaea's memories."

"The boundary will be breached."

"The entire planet will become available for colonization? Is it sustainable with that atmosphere? With all those clouds? Will more suns be placed around the planet?"

"What clouds."

An image of what I assumed was Limbo was revealed. There were no longer ochre clouds concealing it. It was predominantly blue. Oceans? The land formations, occupying about a third of the surface area, were beige and green. A circular area on one of the continents appeared translucent. A more concentrated cluster of hues, but muted. The penal colony?

"Without the boundary, won't the colony be less secure? Will there be unrestricted immigration---and emigration?"

"Not until the Wizards' power is diffused."

"Power? You three must be despised by half the universe for not sharing *your* power? With you becoming immortal there is no hope for one of your positions to become available."

"Eternal, not immortal."

"New individuals join The Three every generation."

"They are merged into us."

"So, you have continuity and new blood. How is it possible to *merge*?"

"When an entity is added to the collective, it is perceived as new experiences. For the new entity, studying history."

"What if the individual doesn't wish to study history?"

"Then that individual won't be chosen to become one with The Three."

"Balance promotes peace. Within oneself, and the universe."

"Balance? A small cluster of...souls...controls the galaxy."

"You make the assumption the strengths of individuals are equal."

"We all have our role to play to achieve balance."

"There are some individuals so balanced their prescience promotes equilibrium."

"Hornet?"

"You weren't the only person sent to Dartmoor."

"Hornet's an agent?"

"His mission was more passive."

"To neutralize the imbalance around him, to delay the inevitable, to create more time for you to complete your mission."

"Hornet wasn't aware he was an agent, was he?"

"Instrument may be more accurate than agent."

"You manipulated him."

"We all manipulate. It only concerns us when the stakes are high."

"His assistance was rewarded."

"The memory of murder was erased."

"Hornet was sentenced for murder? He doesn't seem like the type."

"He became as ill-informed as you."

"Innocent people aren't sent to Dartmoor."

"Why?"

"Murderer's behave differently than those who haven't murdered."

"I was sent to Dartmoor and I didn't...."

"Commit a crime?"

"Galactic agents commit crimes every mission. They are overlooked for the good they achieve."

"I was manipulated. The court system was manipulated. Is there anything you don't have a hand in?"

"We all manipulate. Even Gaea...."

"Everything she does, it to benefit Her children."

"The ultimate manipulation."

"A mother protecting her children will resort to...anything. Even breaking her own laws. The mutational properties of Limbo were circumvented when Will Amette---Stick---died. He was re-created without flaw. It was necessary for him to become an Octagonal Knight. For him to do so he must have never been modified."

"It was necessary."

"We all manipulate."

"What am I to do now? For the first time in more than…141 years…I feel bored."

"Your next mission…."

Chapter 33

BEYOND

As was expected, once Lynn had passed through the transport portal it became inactive. It had just enough power stored to send one person before Limbo neutered it. Those beside the iridescent ring became as tapped out as the piece of machinery. They wilted. They had persevered for so long, forever more demanding, that when the end came, they fell hard. Then Hope began to cry. Hornet rushed to Dinga's side, comforting her and their child.

He was the first---adult---to snap out of it, but not the only one. Stated Centaur, "It's probably for the best. I heard that when people get out of prison they have a hard time adjusting, and are often more miserable on the outside than they were when they were incarcerated."

Stick said, "I need to return to the Octagonal Prism. The Wizards will eventually regroup. They may counter-attack."

Pulp declared, "I'm heading back to the Copper Forest. Be it moral compulsion or lack of arbol companionship, go I must."

Without speaking to anyone Nimbus transformed back into

a drak and flew east.

The Wizards never made their counter-attack. They may have wanted to rule the world, but they weren't foolish. It would be many years before they were strong enough again to act upon their ambitions.

Hope grew into a sweet girl, at the normal rate of development. She was the center of attention wherever Hornet and Dinga took her. It was remarkable she wasn't more spoiled than she was. Shortly after turning two, the second Limboan child was born. Then the floodgates opened. Every week or so after that there was an announcement of another pregnancy, or another birth. Hope was quite fond of all the children, and they of her. She became known as the *big sister*.

Those who had been part of the quests to collect and connect the pieces of the portal were determined to not lose contact with one another. At least once a year they met to share old tales, and to christen new ones.

Hope's *hand-day* was one such occasion. When a person turns five she is considered to be an adult. It was Hope's decision how and where she wanted to spend her hand-day. She chose Pulp's home in the Copper Forest. She loved the playfulness of the arbols, children and adults alike. Many of the twigs, as the children were called, were abnormally large, and had a striking resemblance to Pulp. Crystal, although not technically part of their group, wished to attend. Who was going to deny Gaea's daughter?

With all in attendance, the drak, who continued to be as small as when she first hatched from the geode, blew out a mist of shimmering particles. It enveloped Hope, coating her body with glitter. It took years for the sparkles to finally leave her---most of them. She always retained a few specs here or there, as did her descendants.

The earth began to shake, subtle to begin with---a shudder---then a burst. No flying debris or flashes of light, but enough of an impulse at the end to knock everyone off their feet. The sky began to glow. A moment later it dimmed back, to slightly greater than normal intensity. A wave of energy rushed past. Then the sun exploded.

It became very dark, darker than it had been in more than a century. Pinpoints of lights began to appear, individually, then as clusters. In one part of the sky the illuminations had become so dense it looked like a sea.

No one spoke. It was too frightening, too awe-inspiring, to be shared. Too intense for others to understand.

The temperature dropped, much quicker than it would have if the shield still insulated them. Bodies huddled. "Maybe this wasn't such a good idea."

The Copper Forest was becoming recognizable. The darkness was fading, but not from above---from the east. Colors that had never existed before on Limbo appeared on the horizon. Depression replaced quiet exultation as the colors faded. Was it better to have never experienced, then to have it taken away?

A ball of energy appeared, pulsating with light and heat, rising from the ashes of expired glory. Blue sky---brighter and crisper than had ever been seen on Limbo, complimenting the hues on the distant side of creation.

The group that had been a hand-day party became an exploratory one. So close they had been to the boundary shield, it took them just minutes to travel to where it had always been.

Barren earth lay where the shield should have been. Beyond the ten-meter wide boundary that seemed to stretch into eternity, was an explosion of growth---a time-lapse in real-time.

"Careful now," Crystal cautioned. "Gaea's sacrifice not only deactivated the shield, it drained the colony of elem. Giving life to the planet has taken your immortality from you. Death is now permanent. You will no longer be re-created."

In the distance was a metallic arch, over 200 meters in height.

"What's that?" asked Hornet as he put his arm around his daughter protectively.

"Gateway to the new world?" Dinga questioned as she put her arms around both of them.

Hope broke free from her parents and ran with abandon, a dozen young children a step behind her. "Time to play."

to balance, the end becomes a beginning

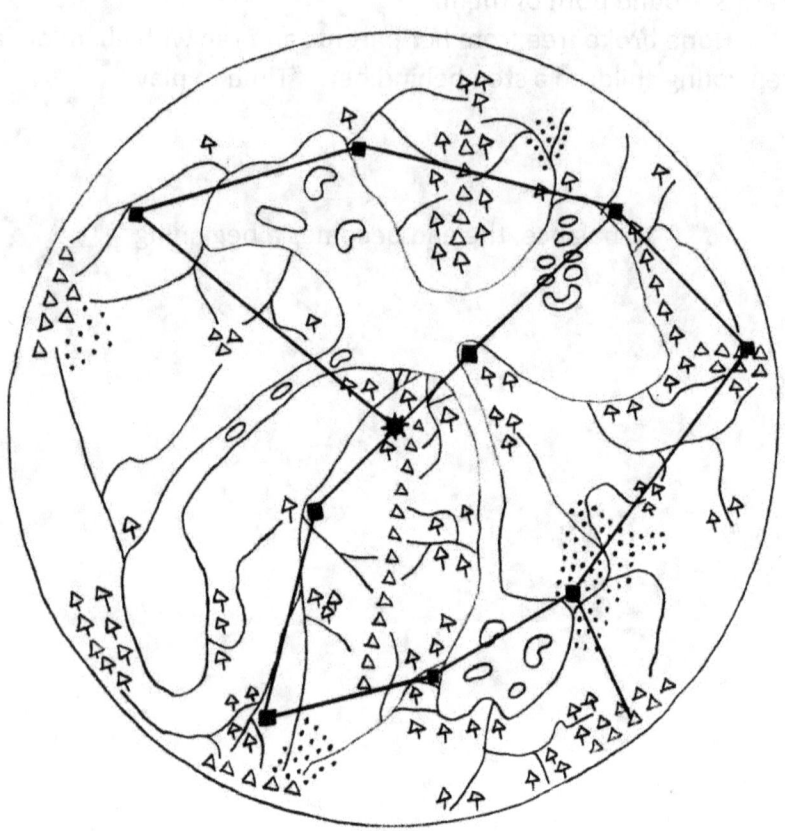